DARK PROPHET

Book Two of the Chronicles of Koa Series

K.N. LEE

www.Kn-Lee.com

The Chronicles of Koa: Dark Prophet/ K.N. Lee. -- 1st Ed.

Titles by K.N. Lee

- **The Chronicles of Koa Series:**

Netherworld

Dark Prophet

Lyrinian Blade (Coming in 2015)

- **Collections:**

Thicker Than Blood

A Gifted Curse

- **Poetry:**

Wicked Webs

Empty Your Heart

- **Anthologies:**

A World of Joy

A World of Worlds

Acknowledgements

I must express my eternal gratitude to my lovely friends, readers, and fans around the world. I write for you, and appreciate your support.

I'd like to thank my incredible editor, Mr. John Davis. He worked tirelessly to make sure that this book was free of typos, errors, and polished to perfection. He is my fairy god-father!

Also, I'd like to thank my beta readers, Kenichi Kamihara, Brett Lister, Nick Foster, Erica Lee, Caridad Chala, Julia Fe Chala, Brittany Paulus, Kristen McKee, Shannon Kendall, and Jacqueline Pfhal.

Once again, Daniel Valverde of Green Valley Photography took stunning author photos of me. Along with his creative director, Andrea Horne, hair and makeup artist, Lisa Aviles-McLain of Lisa Lee Hair, and the beautiful model, Biqi Shi, we created stunning cover art. Special thanks goes to Blu Vector LLC for their graphic design of the cover, and Brandon Jackson for his creative support.

Thank you to Katina for being my hair stylist for my author photos. Also, thanks to all of those that donated to my book tour!

This has been an incredibly fun book to create and I am thrilled to finally share it with the world.

Dedicated to my mother, Brenda Gayle Williams

Part One:

Netherworld Memories

CHAPTER 1

Koa frowned down at her body. A red dress. Koa hated red, but she did not have a choice. Like the blood that Koa had spilled the night before when she had been cut with a glowing dagger, the dress was dark and rich.

Ceremonies such as this were normal in the Netherworld. The wound on her white wrist healed before her eyes. Within minutes, the ceremony was complete, the tests were run, and it was confirmed that she was indeed the daughter of Alsand Vangelis, the vampire king of Elyan.

Only hours ago, Koa was awakened by a team of violet-eyed women tugging at her limbs. They washed her in scalding hot water, scrubbed her raw with oils, and slathered creams onto her snow-white skin. They straightened her thick black hair and painted her face with colors that Koa only thought older women were allowed to wear. Then, she had been dressed.

In a gaudy red wedding gown… at the age of twelve.

Koa wanted to run from the black temple that she and her father had slept in. On the side of a mountain, the temple faced the back of the dark kingdom that was meant to be her prison for an eternity. She wanted to break free from the parade of attendants sent to accompany her and fly home.

The human world seemed so far away.

No one understood just how much she did not want to do this. This wasn't to be a human wedding, but a Netherworld wedding… a vampire wedding.

Koa scrunched up her nose as she looked down at the billowing gown, littered with sparkling crystals and black taffeta. She looked like a gothic spin on a Disney princess.

Vampire Barbie, she thought to herself.

Even at such a young age, Koa knew she did not fit the role of such a character. She was not a doll or a character from the books she read. She closed her eyes and tried to calm her nerves.

Like boiling acid, anxious feelings churned within her stomach, making her feel like she might faint, or worse… vomit at any moment.

How embarrassing that would be, Koa thought as she chewed her lip. She grimaced. Her lips tasted horrible, like tar. She'd almost forgotten that she was covered in makeup like a clown. Her small hands shook and she wanted to cry. It took all of her strength to keep the tears from escaping and causing an even bigger scene. With hot cheeks she held her breath, and prayed for an escape.

Koa was afraid of this dark place, where neither the sun nor moon existed. The entire population was composed of millions of creatures that would have given normal girls nightmares. "Nephilim" is what her father called them. The spawn of fallen angels. King Alsand was a nephilim. Koa was as well.

She was glad that her father was by her side. He never let go of her hand. With her free hand, Koa tugged at the high collar of her gown. She groaned. The black lace made the skin on her throat itch.

Koa looked up at her father. She was small, and her father always looked like such a giant to her. King Alsand walked regally by her side. He commanded such attention. With his head held high, his face depicted an air of authority. Together, they walked at the head of the procession through the wide streets of Lyrinia, while the citizens watched in uneasy silence.

Netherworld vamps, War-Breeders, Jems, Syths, and even ghouls came out of their hiding spots to catch a glimpse of the mysterious half-blood princess.

Koa tried not to stare back at the horrific creatures all around. The sound of metal and robotic buzzing noises caught her attention as a quad of Scayors entered the crowd. Everyone stepped aside to let them through to the front. Like metallic giants, slim, and sleek, the Scayors patrolled the event like silent police. Their eyes cast a dim green glow over what they scanned.

She shuddered when their gaze lingered on her. She feared that they were reading her thoughts and knew that she was afraid of them. That was one thing that Koa hated, the admission of fear. Even the monk-like Syths scared her. They were big, pale, creatures with bald heads and faces covered in tattoos.

Lightning broke out and everyone looked up to the sky. Koa clutched her father's arm and paused.

He smiled down at her. "Don't worry, Koa. It's not a real sky, my love. That is simply the ground of another Netherworld level. I believe they are having a battle up there."

Koa's eyes narrowed as she looked at the dismal black sky. Lightning struck again, but it wasn't the kind of lighting that she was used to. It was green and took the shape of various symbols as it faded into the dark. To think that they were only on one of the many levels of the Netherworld, and that entire civilizations and kingdoms were going about their business with little to no care about what an important day this was for Lyrinia was too much for young Koa to grasp.

When she looked back down, she saw that everyone had returned their attention to her. Vampire women and men stared at her. They were the only creatures that she wasn't fearful of. Father had various vampires over at the manor from time to time, but none of them looked as picturesque as these Netherworld vamps.

Painted faces stared at her. The vampire women were the most beautiful women that Koa had ever seen, and yet none compared to her mother's simple and natural beauty. These women were like painted dolls who she imagined tipping over and watching crack into pieces of porcelain.

Koa noticed how they seemed to be separated into groups. The red lipsticks on the left and the black lipsticks on the right. Koa didn't know if it was simply a fashion trend or something more, but all of the women wore the most elaborate gowns and jeweled arrangements on their perfectly sculptured hairdos.

They watched her, unblinking, unsmiling. She could see the judgment in their eyes.

"Father," Koa breathed. She looked away from their violet eyes and clutched her father's arm.

King Alsand looked down at her. His green eyes were serious today. "What is it, darling?"

Koa looked ahead at the sparkling golden palace before them. The golden plates along the palaces walls shimmered and reflected all of the light from the Disc Moon, the artificial moon of the Netherworld. Her voice was caught in her throat. Something felt odd and yet she felt drawn to the palace. It stood out like a candle in the dark and pulled her in, as if by magic, like a moth to a porch light.

Koa's face paled. This was the place that would be her new home. King Greggan's teenage son, Prince Jax, would be her new husband.

Koa stopped. The guards that were leading them looked back and seemed ready to seize her and force her forward.

King Alsand leaned down to her ear. "What's wrong?"

"I want to go home."

Her father patted her hand and when one of the Syth guards stepped forward, he whipped out the Lyrinian sword with lightning speed. Everyone drew in a breath and stepped back as they beheld its power. The ring of steel rang throughout the air. It pulsed, audibly, and visibly as the red glow made the air heat and crackle.

Even Koa held her breath as her eyes shot to the Lyrinian blade.

King Alsand's raptor-like glare burned into the guards, warning them to keep their distance. He didn't have to say a word. The red glow of the black blade was enough to make the large brutish creatures rethink their actions.

King Alsand waited a moment longer, making sure that they knew how serious he was. Koa had only trained with that sword once. The power was too great for her now, but one day it would be hers.

She flinched when her father's glare landed on her. "Koa, this is your home."

Koa shook her head, but avoided his eyes. She looked around. The air was stale, not like the fresh, fragrant air of France. The sky was dark, lit only by the Disc Moon that cast different colors across the land whenever the hour changed.

She missed the moon of Earth. She missed the sun, the trees, and the flowers. The Netherworld felt like a nightmare from which she would never awaken. No matter what color the day was in the Netherworld, it was always too dark for her. Koa's father didn't understand her love for daylight, for he had never seen real daylight.

The sun's rays would kill him just as surely as it would kill any vampire, Netherworld or New World. Koa was the only exception and she wished that he would at least try to understand.

"You are half Netherworld vamp, Koa," her father gave her hand a squeeze. "This is where you belong, amongst your people."

"I am also half human."

King Alsand looked down at her and pursed his lips. His eyes hid something from her.

Koa tried to soften her voice and sound as sweet as possible. "Bring mother here, and maybe I won't feel so homesick," Koa reasoned, her green eyes hopeful.

King Alsand shook his head, but his features softened for her. "My darling girl. You will see that this is the place for you. You belong here with your people. The treaty has already been signed." He leaned closer to her ear and whispered. "Your mother cannot come here Koa. She is safe in the mortal world. If we do not fulfill our side of the treaty, she will be in danger. Now, is that what you want?"

Her lips trembled. She shook her head quickly. Just the thought of someone harming her mother made her feel sick. She didn't know what she would do if she lost that sweet, loving, woman.

She looked into her father's eyes.

"Do you understand what I am telling you?"

Koa nodded. She understood, but she still didn't agree with what was happening.

Alsand smiled and stroked her pale white cheek.

"But I don't want to do this," Koa whispered.

Alsand's smile faded, but his eyes didn't turn cold on her as she expected. He knelt down to her level and cupped her cheek.

"I know, my dear girl, but sometimes we have to do things that we don't want to… to protect those that we love."

"May I?" Faun asked of Alsand.

Alsand nodded and Faun gathered her white skirts in one hand and scampered over to fix Koa's long black hair. Koa didn't take her eyes from her father's. She hoped that he would see how miserable she was.

Koa ignored Faun as she examined her face with violet eyes. She was adamant about making sure that Koa's part was perfectly straight and that her hair fell in long ringlets.

"Smile," she said.

Koa twisted her mouth. "I don't want to."

Faun put her hands on her bony hips. She scrunched up the space between her thin brows as she narrowed her eyes at Koa. "Just do it. It's only for a second."

Koa rolled her eyes and faked a quick smile.

"That wasn't so hard, now was it?" Snickering, she gathered her skirts in her hand. "You have red lipstick on your teeth," she said and returned to her place in the procession behind Koa and her father.

Frustrated, Koa rubbed her teeth with her finger. She knew just how ridiculous she looked. Black liner, red lips, and rosy cheeks.

Alsand locked arms with Koa. He leaned close and gave her a kiss on the cheek. He lowered his voice into a whisper. "Remember, never mention that you can walk in the sun. Never."

Koa swallowed and squeezed her eyes shut. "I know, father. You don't have to keep reminding me."

"Good," he stood back to his full height. His eyes widened and he leaned down again. "Or that you can fly."

Koa nodded, her head down. "Yes, I know."

He pinched her cheek. "Good. Shall we continue, darling?"

"I don't know, father." Koa couldn't bring herself to look at her father again. "Is there anything else that you want to remind me not to say or do?" Her eyes were burning from the tears that threatened to gush forth.

Alsand noticed and simply shook his head. He patted her hand.

She hung her head. Once again, they were walking down the black stone walkway that led to the gate and stone doors of the Lyrinian palace.

Koa's heart pattered against her ribcage. She felt like she might have an anxiety attack. So many eyes staring. So much anticipation in the air.

Those golden gates that she'd been staring at for the past hour, as they walked through the entire kingdom, were held open for them and heavily guarded.

When Koa stepped through the gates and entered a massive courtyard of stone. Their path was lit for them. On either side of the carpet were artificial trees of stone and black clay. They weren't real, but they were beautiful. Art.

Even Koa could appreciate the mastery. She examined the sculptures as she followed her escort through the courtyard and to the stone doors that led into the palace. Once inside, light seemed to fill every dark space. Chandeliers, torches, candles, mirrors reflecting the light, and light discs were positioned all over the wide corridor.

It was then that Koa contemplated flying away. She'd thought of it often. It would be her last chance. She took a peek over her shoulder. She could still see the door. She'd just promised her father that she would keep her abilities a secret. She wasn't sure why such things were so important.

She could simply lift herself into the air, and head for the Gate, but visions of her mother being harmed kept her firmly planted to the purple carpeted floor.

Koa felt numb, like she was walking to her prison cell.

Each corridor led to another corridor of a different theme. From one of light and mirrors they stepped through grand archers to a corridor of dim candles and artificial flowers in vases painted with paint that seemed to have a light of its own. There was a corridor with walls filled with paintings and soft music played by a small creature that resembled the one at the Gate. Tunes was what her father called him, but all Koa remembered was how creepy he was. She shuddered as she recalled Tunes' bulbous eyes.

Koa watched it buzz around with short black wings as it blew eerie melodies out of its flute. She tapped her chin and furrowed her brows as she tried to remember what kind of creature it was.

With bat-like wings and rubbery, yellowish skin, she was sure she'd seen that creature in a book from her father's study. Koa spent hours in there, reading anything that she could get her hand on. The Netherworld tomes always intrigued her. Now she was faced with the creatures she'd studied.

"An imp!" Koa shouted triumphantly. She covered her mouth with her hand and looked around in horror. She hadn't meant to say that aloud. Everyone glanced at her with disapproval, but the imp continued playing its flute until they went into the next corridor.

Koa was relieved to find that the maze of corridors had finally ended, and that they were finally in the main ballroom where the prince and the royal family awaited them.

She stepped into the room, from carpet to shiny granite floors and a flood of light and decorations overwhelmed her senses. She didn't want to admit how beautiful it was, but her eyes widened at the spectacle. Hundreds of chairs draped with gold silk lined either side of the alleyway that led to the dais where the thrones stood.

Her heart thumped. She felt something she hadn't expected. Koa's face flooded with blood as her eyes met those of the prince.

No one else mattered. Nothing else existed as Koa's eyes cut through the crowd and down to the set of five thrones as Koa and her father stopped before the platform.

"Princess Evina, 1st Queen Katya, 2nd Queen Lera, your highness, King Greggan, and Prince Jax, behold King Alsand of Elyan and Princess Koa."

Koa heard the introductions but something odd was happening. She stared at Prince Jax with her mouth agape.

He was the most attractive person she had ever seen in her life: piercing dark blue eyes, dark blood-red hair, and a perfectly sculpted chin and nose. Koa felt her face flush as he looked her up and down. Then, he did something that made her grin, despite her previous fears and doubts.

Prince Jax winked at her.

CHAPTER 2

Koa's grin widened. A weight was lifted from her shoulders and she feel light as air, free as a butterfly.

Excitement flooded her small body. She held her head a little higher and practically beamed.

Everyone in attendance could read her expression. Whispers swept through the room as the guests watched the exchange of looks between Koa and Prince Jax. Jax sat at the edge of his seat, his youthful face bright with surprise. Koa wondered if he'd been imagining her as an ugly troll. She never even considered the prince actually being attractive.

Maybe this isn't so bad, she thought as she admired Prince Jax's perfect face. She'd never seen anyone that looked like him, and from the citizens of Lyrinia that she'd encountered so far, Jax probably never saw anyone like her. Growing up in Korea, Koa was kept from others, but everyone had the same dark eyes and black hair.

Koa saw something familiar in Jax's dark blue eyes. She saw mischief, even as he sat beside his father who looked like an evil statue. Koa liked that look. She shared the same craving for mischief. Mischief meant fun was in store. She took her hand from her father's and found herself drawn to the prince. She wanted to speak with him, to share stories, and play games.

He's cute, she thought as she smoothed her dress. Koa never thought she'd be married at the age of twelve, but she suddenly wasn't so opposed to it. *I'm a princess*, she thought. *He is a prince. Isn't it every girl's dream to have a fairy tale wedding*?

Koa didn't try to hide her admiration and her father smiled down at her. "I told you that everything would be all right," he whispered.

King Greggan stood. The entire room quieted. Koa's smile faded. She looked at the man's face and felt instant warnings flood her mind.

He was pale like his son, and shared the same shade of blood-red hair, yet his was long and in a single braid while Jax's was short and messy. King Greggan had a long red beard as well, that he stroked as he looked down at them, as if in thought.

Koa couldn't help thinking that he looked like one of those Vikings that her tutor had taught her about. All he needed was a helmet with horns.

There was something different in the king's eyes and Koa identified it immediately. She swallowed.

Evil. There wasn't another word to describe what she saw.

Koa saw it, and she hoped that her father did as well. She did not trust that Netherworld vamp.

While everyone bowed, Koa and King Alsand were allowed to simply nod their head to the king.

King Greggan clasped his hands before him and looked at the Lyrinian sword.

"Come to bind our kingdoms and return the sword your ancestors stole?"

King Alsand looked up at King Greggan and tilted his head. Koa noticed that this was a heated topic, but her father, being the diplomat that he was, would play this like a game.

"Stole?" King Alsand repeated, feigning ignorance.

King Greggan did not reply, but his dark gaze held a deep hatred for her father that didn't need words. That look made Koa uncomfortable. She'd never seen such hatred before.

King Alsand grabbed the hilt of the Lyrinian sword and withdrew it. King Greggan flinched, but it was such a tiny action that most wouldn't have caught it.

Koa did.

Her father ran his finger along the black blade. "I do believe it is my family name engraved into the sword's metal dear friend. The angels passed it on to my line. You may forget your history," he tilted his head. "I don't blame you… history can be terribly boring at times. But," he raised a finger, "the House of Vangelis once sat on the throne of Lyrinia."

King Alsand looked at Greggan with innocent eyes, but Koa could see the fury silently building behind them. Her eyes went to the Lyrinian blade. It started to glow.

"That is, before the House of Tulach started that little squabble that led to the great divide and forced my family into the Eastern Dominance."

King Greggan's mouth twitched. "Little squabble," he said and nodded his head. He stroked his beard as he regarded her father with silent hate.

"That's right," King Alsand replied. "As I am King Alsand Vangelis, and you are King Greggan Tulach, we should remember our history, lest we repeat it." He slid the sword back into its scabbard. "And my family will keep what is rightfully ours."

"*Rightfully ours*? You sound like such a human."

King Alsand shrugged. "So be it."

King Greggan's gaze went from the sword to young Koa. His eyes lingered on her pale face and she felt herself grow self-conscious. She struggled to keep a straight face and not look away.

She would not show fear. She would not let the vamp king see that she wanted nothing more than to hide behind her father like a little girl. Instead, she held her head high, just how she'd been taught.

Never show fear, her father would say. *Never*.

King Greggan nodded then. Koa wasn't sure why. Maybe he was agreeing with what her father had just said. Perhaps he was admiring her. She feared that both options were false.

"Yes. I believe you're right." His eyes lifted to her father's and he mocked an innocent look of his own. His bushy red brows rose. "So, you wouldn't mind if I marry your daughter, rather than give her to my son, would you?"

Koa's jaw dropped. Her stomach sank. Even Prince Jax was visibly surprised by his father's words. The only person who wasn't surprised was King Alsand.

To Koa's horror, he nodded. She yelped. "No!" She covered her mouth with her hand as her plea seemed to loudly echo throughout the ballroom.

Her father put out a hand to silence her. He looked up at King Greggan.

"If that is your wish, my daughter, Princess Koa of Elyan in the Eastern Dominance will be glad to be your bride. As it states in the treaty—that the angels comprised, mind you—the first born female of the House of Vangelis will be offered to the House of Tulach for peacekeeping. So, the male counterpart is of little concern."

Koa felt her face go red with fury. She shook her head. She bit her lip as she looked into his eyes. Her eyes stung from tears and she risked whispering to him, "Please, father."

King Greggan showed his first smirk then. "Are you sure, *dear friend*? I'd hate to have to break the treaty 'that the angels comprised' due to a misunderstanding and start the war up again."

Koa was nudged forward. She resisted her father's nudge. She didn't want to go. Such an unjustice did not sit well with her. She could have screamed but she knew what would happen if she didn't go willingly. Many people would die. She whimpered and stood before the vamp king.

"Let the wedding begin." King Alsand said and Koa knew that her entire world would end. It was official.

Childhood was over.

"Just one second, friend," Greggan sneered. His eyes were twinkling with malice. "Don't you want to check with the angels first? We have our very own referee here. Let's ask him, if this is agreeable to the treaty."

Koa dared to hope. She'd never seen a real angel, and her interest was thoroughly sparked. Perhaps the angels could save her from this horrible fate. Everyone went silent, and the entire room turned to look towards the back of the room.

Koa followed their gazes. There, in the back, stood two men. One was as tall as a giant and muscular. He didn't wear a shirt, only an iron breastplate that covered his right shoulder and chest, dark pants under armor, and iron gauntlets on each wrist. Scars covered nearly every inch of his bronze colored body.

Koa had never seen anyone with so many weapons. An axe, a dagger, shiny weapons she couldn't identify, and a spear. He looked like a warrior god, but it was the man beside him that held her attention.

The man with the bright blonde hair was tall, but not as tall as the other. He wasn't as flashy either. Only a silver gun peeked from a holster at his side. He was quiet and reserved, but Koa sensed that he was calculating, and perhaps the most powerful being there.

And she was right.

King Greggan's voice boomed. "What do you say, Master Halston?"

Master Halston gave a single nod. Everyone waited in silent anticipation. "I'll allow it."

Koa almost didn't hear the words that came from his mouth, for their eyes locked and she suddenly doubted everything she thought she knew. It was as if he spoke to her with that one look. He urged her to be brave, to trust, to be patient.

Koa had never seen that man before in her life, but somehow she felt inclined to obey. But at twelve, she couldn't help but resist.

And she did.

She turned to run, and before she could get even two feet, her body was held immobile by silver bands. Tears stung her eyes as she looked at her father. His face was paler than she'd ever seen it. His eyes were glossy with tears of his own. But what hurt her more than anything was that he did nothing to stop it. He raised a hand, but withdrew it, and stood by in silence.

Koa's face heated. "You liar," she growled at her father. "I *hate* you."

CHAPTER 3

Now, at twenty-one, Koa remembered the day her life had changed with stunning clarity. Childhood was no longer a blur. The pain returned with full force. When Koa had broken him out of the prison in the Ivory Tower, Prince Jax had returned her memories to her, and now she would have to deal with what she'd always wanted.

The truth.

Her vision of the dark world before her was blurred by hot tears. The truth truly did hurt. Halston had warned her for years. He'd told her that she was better off not knowing what had happened to her during her time in the Netherworld. Koa shuddered at the memories of what Greggan had done to her back then.

Koa wanted to rip herself free and fly after Halston. The look on his face when they'd parted made her ill. She needed to be certain that he would survive. Even though she had her Jax back, she knew that she would not be able to handle the death of the angel that doomed her, and yet became her best friend.

Jax's grip on her waist tightened as they approached the first cavern that led out of Lyrinia. The deafening howls of the Wraith made Koa squeeze her eyes shut and cover her ears with her hands.

"I want to go back!" Koa shouted and tugged her body from Jax's grasp.

Jax wouldn't let her go. He held on and wrapped his other arm around her. "Koa, listen. You cannot go back. This is our only chance to make it out."

"He's right," Evina, his sister, shouted over the howls. "Let Halston do his job. He can handle it."

Koa wiped her cheeks of tears and turned to face the first set of caverns.

"Shadows," she breathed. Memories of the Shadows reaching out to her with their cold hands pulsed in her mind. Halston was not there to protect her from them with the power of his angelic glow this time.

Jax gave her a tender squeeze and whispered into her ear. "I won't let *anything* happen to you, Koa."

His warm breath made her shiver, and she glanced up at him. His face was so close that they could kiss. If she wasn't fearful for her life, she might have kissed him, just out of the passion she felt from having his body pressed to her. His eyes met hers, twinkling in the dim light of the Netherworld's Disc Moon.

With a wry smile, he looked ahead. He gave a nod to the entrance of the first cavern. "Don't worry. We will make it."

The howls of the Wraith were cut off the second they flew into the cavern. The cold seeped through her skin and into her bones. Koa shivered. She wrapped her arms around Jax's neck and buried her face into his shoulder. Black, with a dimly lit path below, the cavern reminded her of an eerie forest at night. The smooth black stone that covered the floor was littered with perfectly spaced discs of yellow light.

A flying beetle the size of her fist buzzed before her face. It examined her. Koa smacked it away and cringed when it let out a loud bellow of pain that sounded like an old man. She watched it dart away and wiped its blood onto her jeans.

Jax kissed her forehead. He spoke softly. "We'll make it. I promise."

Koa nodded but bit her lip to keep from sobbing.

Halston.

The look in his blue eyes as they parted wouldn't leave the forefront of her mind. The Ivory Tower could not be the end of him. She needed him.

Koa looked over at Evina. She rode her disc with mastery, as if surfing along the air. Her red hair flew behind her, and she stood with perfect balance with her arms crossed under her large bosom.

"Watch out!" Koa screeched when she saw a glowing arrow cut through the dark.

Evina veered out of the way just in time. Koa's eyes widened when she looked ahead and saw that there was a squad of guards from the city. Battle-worn soldiers hovered in the air in battle formation. No Scayors or Syths, just vampires that had vowed allegiance to King Greggan.

Jax held her close. "You have any more of those vials from the Alchemist?"

Koa swallowed. Her throat was dry. She shook her head. "No," she whispered. She tensed as she watched the soldiers.

A woman used her disc to fly ahead of the formation. Koa paled. "Second wife," she breathed.

Queen Lera, Greggan's second wife, held her daggers in her hands. "What do you two think you're doing?" She spoke to Evina and Jax. "Traitors to your own kingdom!" She was not their mother. With her black hair and gray eyes, she was covered in the tattoos of Netherworld dialect with the only ink that could permanently stain a vampire's flesh.

No, this vampire woman was not the motherly sort. With her hair pulled into a bun at the top of her head, and wrapped in chains of vampire fangs that she had pulled out from her victims, she was a warrior who lived for battle.

"Just get out of the way, Lera." Jax was calm. He took his arm from around Koa and she stepped off the disc to fly by his side. He took out his daggers, clinked them together, and ignited a red glow that caused the air to sizzle. "I don't want to hurt you, but I will if I have to."

Evina snorted a laugh. She pulled her large curved sword from its place along her back and pointed it at Lera. "Oh no, no. Unlike my brother, I would *love* to make you bleed," she hissed. She waved Lera on. "Just come a little closer."

Lera grinned, but her eyes were not filled with joy, but hate. She clinked her dagger's hilts together and they glowed red as well. She held them ready at her sides. Her eyes went from Evina and back to Jax. "The king doesn't want you dead, but I have been given clearance to stop you at all costs. Do not expect me to show mercy, because I won't."

Koa glanced at Jax and Evina. Neither seemed surprised that their father would have them killed, just to rule in the human world. Koa didn't like how this was going. Her jaw clenched. Fury started to rise within her belly. She did not know if she would be able to control herself. Her hate for Lera was stronger that her patience.

Koa drew her Lyrinian sword and waited. She counted a dozen soldiers, took stock of what weapons they carried, and prepared for an inevitable battle.

Her stomach bubbled with anticipation. The heat and power of the sword coursed up her arm and filled her veins. She felt strong. The sword gave her courage. She wanted their blood to cover the blade. The sword begged her, like an impatient child.

Gimme! Gimme! Koa imagined it saying to her. It did have a mind of its own, and when drawn, it had an unquenchable thirst for blood.

Lera's dark gaze landed on Koa. Her grin faded and her lips curled into a snarl.

"You," she growled. Lera's face seemed to grow dark as she glared at Koa.

Koa flinched at the look of evil in that woman's eyes. Her mouth couldn't form the words that she wanted to say. She wanted to say something snarky like Evina, but her history with the vampire queen was a traumatic one. Instead she looked down at the blade and to Jax.

Jax sensed the tension and moved to put an arm out. Koa looked confused as he pushed her behind him.

Koa raised a brow as Lera licked her daggers. The sharp blade slit her tongue and she let the blood increase their power. "Out of my way, Jax. The half-blood and I have unfinished business."

Koa's heart quickened as Lera flew forward. Lera was so quick that Koa barely saw her form cut through the dark.

Koa simply reacted.

And Koa... was quicker.

Koa didn't mean to do it. It was purely instinctual, but she gripped her sword's hilt with both hands and ducked beneath Jax's outstretched arm. She sliced across the air and through both of Lera's legs with all of the strength within her body. Bone was sawed through and blood sprayed into the air and onto Koa's white face.

The smell of burning flesh wafted into Koa's nostrils, and the sound of Lera's scream thundered in her ears. The Lyrinian sword's blade glowed brighter, redder.

Hungrier.

Koa looked up. There were still at least a dozen more bodies to let it feast upon.

Gimme! Gimme!

Koa ground her teeth as she flew past and looked back at the screaming vampire queen as she reached for her bloodied knees in horror.

The soldiers, Jax, and Evina, watched Lera fall down to the black ground below.

Jax's eyes slowly rose to meet hers. His jaw still hung in surprise.

Koa cleared her throat and nodded to the soldiers. "Well, are we killing them and escaping or not?" Drunk off of adrenaline and the intoxicating power of the Lyrinian sword, Koa dove into the frenzy of battle.

She never looked back, but she heard Evina's battle cry and the clashing of steel against steel behind her.

Koa was never a tidy fighter. She was more of a wild animal, uncaring about how she killed a foe, only that they died as quickly and effectively as possible.

And so, her sword was used as merely an extension of her arm. With wide movements, she flung her arm in a circle and sliced through one soldier's belly. She grabbed the next closest soldier by the back of his head with her free hand and kneed him in the face, shattering his jaw. He fell from his disc and went crashing to the ground.

Koa grinned almost evilly. How dare they try to fight her in her element? No other vampire could fly, and their discs were not as reliable as her body.

She grunted as a dagger stabbed her in the side. Eyes wide with rage, she caught a female vamp's arm and twisted it out of its socket. The soldier cried out. Then, Koa grabbed her by her long hair and flew with great speed higher into the black sky. The soldier's flying disc hovered in the same spot below.

She grabbed Koa by the jaw and shouted at her in a language that she only understood vaguely. Netherworld dialect was burned somewhere in the dark recesses of her mind that she'd tried to forget, but she understood one word.

"Mercy."

Like a cruel executioner, Koa sliced through her neck with her sword. She held the vamp's head by her hair and watched her body fall lifeless below. Then, in Netherworld dialect she spoke to her severed head, bringing its empty eyes close to her face.

"No mercy."

Then, alone above the carnage of what Jax and Evina did to the remaining soldiers, she tossed the head far off like a ball. Hot tears burned her eyes again. Images of what she'd suffered threatened to drive her mad. She tried to push them back into the box of unwanted memories, but they refused to go back. Koa growled and covered her eyes. How many times had she cried for mercy and King Greggan ignored her?

She shivered, cold and exhausted. She wrapped her arms around herself and spoke to the quiet that followed as Jax and Evina looked up at her, done with the battle.

"Halston," she whispered between sobs. Her dagger wound throbbed, but not as much as her head. It threatened to make her black out, but for some reason Koa knew that she could not let herself go. She feared what would happen if she let herself go into that dark place. Sleep was not an option. Not until she and the others were free from the horror of the Netherworld. Not until she knew her loved ones were safe.

"Oh, Halston. Please hurry."

CHAPTER 4

Tristan scratched a long scar that stretched from his forehead, over his right eye, and down to his cheek. "She's only a child."

Halston nodded in silence. His eyes were steady on the poor half-blood princess that was being forced to marry a tyrant.

His gaze went to King Alsand. Even though the king of Elyan stood there without any emotion on his face, Halston could tell that this was a difficult moment. Alsand's only little girl was being taken from him and he had to pretend he was content with it.

The dome-shaped room was brightly lit with elaborate chandeliers, candles, and torches that hung from high above. Carved statues of former Netherworld rulers looked down at them from pillars at each corner. Below, the people of Lyrinia watched Koa from neat rows on either side of the aisle that led to the Binding Circle.

In the center of the circle stood the princess and the king. There was no priest or judge, only a glowing orb that encircled the couple and bound them in a way that could not be undone. Halston knew this to be true because he and Viktor had created it. They'd created many things in order to keep the nephilim in order and peace.

Bells rang. Hundreds of vampires bowed before the new couple as the Binding Circle faded and returned to its place in a secure hole in the ceiling, locked away until another marriage ceremony.

Halston did not bow. As an angel, he only bowed to one, and it certainly was not a vampire king.

King Greggan barely acknowledged him. It was no secret that Greggan didn't agree with being patrolled by the angel class, but he had no choice. Halston could kill everyone in that room if he wanted to. Instead, he was tolerated, a necessary figurehead that monitored their Netherworld dealings.

He wore all white, as was customary for an angel of his position and for such an occasion. With his gold sash and a metallic belt that held his infinity gun, Halston looked like a general, which he was.

Like a foreign dignitary, Halston arrived only when important occasions arose. This, the marriage between the anomaly of a creature and the king of Lyrinia was more important than most Netherworlders knew.

Once everyone came up from their deep bows to the couple, whispers and chatter filled the room. Halston picked out a few of the comments.

Everyone was stunned. They'd all come out expecting a wedding for the vampire prince, not the king who already had two beautiful wives. The gossip would last for months.

Halston tensed. He felt a dark presence, one that he was too familiar with. He put his hand on the handle of his silver infinity gun even though he knew that the special weapon could do no harm to the creature that watched him from the shadows.

Halston didn't look at him, but he knew he was there. He could feel the demon named Bund's eyes on him, burning into his flesh with hate. Halston took a breath. He knew this occasion would bring that demon out of hiding. They both wanted the mysterious, prophesized, half-blood princess... but for very different reasons.

Viktor, now the head of the entire Netherworld Division that they had created together, would be pleased to know that Halston had tracked him down. Still, there wasn't much else he could do. Not yet.

Halston nodded to Tristan. "There," Halston whispered, with a slight nod towards the corridor at the far end of the ball room, right behind the platform of thrones.

"Yeah, I see him," Tristan said. Like a giant, he already stood taller than everyone in the room. He glanced in the direction of the skinny, pale demon that stood in the shadows, watching.

"Keep an eye on him."

Tristan nodded. He hooked his thumbs in his belt loops and scanned the room with his thin, hazel eyes.

To Halston, Tristan resembled an abnormally large human of African and Asian descent, with dark bronze skin and thin eyes. To the vampires, Tristan was a creature created specifically to kill them.

Tristan knew that he and Halston were making all of the vampires in the room extremely uncomfortable, yet he didn't flaunt his status as a top ranked War-Breeder, one of the leaders of his clan.

Most War-Breeders these days lived in an uneasy peace with the vampires, keeping their distance in the separate boroughs of the city.

Still, if at any time a vampire posed a threat, Tristan would be ready. His cool façade would melt and he would become the most terrifying creature one could imagine.

Halston was glad to have such a loyal friend by his side… just in case things got ugly.

"Let's go." Halston glanced once more at Princess Koa as she was shuffled from the room by a squad of handmaids. Something stirred in his heart. He felt pity for the poor girl. It was too bad that her fate had already been decided.

Her face looked sad as she looked back at her father, crying for him to take her home.

Halston jaw tensed. Koa's cries affected him more than he expected. They resounded throughout the entire room, full of misery. Koa didn't seem to care what anyone thought of her in that moment and she fought like a wildcat, calling her father a liar.

Tristan shook his head and made a clicking sound with his teeth. "What a shame. She's a cute one. Too bad she's wasted on Greggan. That ancient bag of bones doesn't deserve her. At least the kid has a conscience from what I've heard."

Halston clenched his jaw and ripped his eyes from Koa as she was dragged away. "That wasn't part of the plan."

He ran his hands through his bright blonde hair, a bit flustered. Halston almost dropped everything and flew over to swoop the girl up. He hated that Greggan asked for his permission. He knew it was a setup, that Greggan wanted Halston to go against the wedding and have the treaty thrown out.

There was a plan. She was to be wed to the young prince. He supposed it didn't matter which of the royal men married her, but this isn't what he wanted. At least Greggan didn't know Koa's secrets. He feared what would happen if the vampire king found out that Koa could fly and that she could walk in the sun, two things which no other vampire could do.

He and Tristan crossed the room. The guests all made a wide path for them. Their eyes widened as they beheld a pure angel, one of their ancestors.

Halston ignored their awed faces. He was disgusted by all of the nephilim of the Netherworld. To him, they were abominations, a constant reminder that his brothers and sisters had disobeyed God and created these horrific creatures.

Then, Halston would remember that he was not without blame. He too had rebelled. He'd followed the traitor Satan from Heaven in hopes of finding more to the world than what he'd seen in Heaven.

Not a day went by where Halston didn't pray for forgiveness or scold himself for being tricked. Fallen angel or not, Halston still upheld the truths and values he had been created with.

Halston would still execute God's will, even if that meant keeping these filthy nephilim at peace in the Netherworld, so that they would not turn their attention to the human world.

Halston's face was set as he made his way to the quiet, solemn, King Alsand. He paused when he saw the tears in the man's eyes.

King Alsand gave a slight bow of his head to Halston, showing the angel respect.

Halston nodded. "You did the right thing."

Alsand frowned. He gave Halston a bitter look. His green eyes were full of pent-up fury.

Halston glanced down at the Lyrinian sword's blade. It pulsed from all of the evil in the room. Halston could feel the blade's desire in his bones, yearning to be set free. The way that blade pulsed was how Halston felt all of the time. It was his duty to seek out and destroy evil.

Why was he orchestrating marriages and keeping the peace? Halston reminded himself that it was necessary. For the greater good. Keep the Netherworld in order. Keep them from the human world. Simple as that.

Halston noticed how Alsand balled up his fist as King Greggan returned to his line of thrones with the royal family. Alsand's eyes shot daggers into Greggan, who sat there with a self-satisfied look on his face.

"I gave my only daughter to that monster." His voice faltered. "My pure, good, little princess to that disgusting creature." A tear escaped the corner of Alsand's eye. He brushed it off and straightened his shoulders.

Halston looked away, giving King Alsand a moment to compose himself. He didn't have the patience for such displays of emotion. His blue eyes scanned the room. Most of the guests were enjoying the reception, drinking and discussing the history-making event that just occurred.

Goblets of carmia, the blood substitute that nourished the blood thriving population, overflowed as vampires toasted to the unification of two powerful kingdoms. Elyan and Lyrinia, bitter rivals, were now at peace.

For now they could relax. No one would have to offer up their male sons to the royal armies anymore if there was peace on this level of the Netherworld.

It was a night of joy, and yet no one seemed to care about what happened next to the half-blood.

Halston clenched his jaw. He shouldn't be worried about her either. She was a pawn. At least, that what he tried to remind himself. He hadn't expected to feel guilty when he looked into her eyes.

"Well," Alsand's voice broke Halston from his thoughts. His eyes were hardened. "What now?"

Halston motioned for Tristan. "We will monitor things from here. You'll go back to the human world and watch over Koa's mother. We'll need her safe and kept from the Netherworld if this plan is going to work."

Alsand nodded. "I've sacrificed my only daughter. This had better work."

Halston gave him a sidelong glance. "It will."

Alsand looked skeptical but kept his comments to himself. "And my son?"

Halston turned to him. "He will rule Elyan in your absence, and I will watch over him as well. Both of your children will be safe. I assure you."

"Give me your word, Master Halston," Alsand's voice lowered. It wavered on the verge of cracking and trembling. "If something were to happen to me, you'd protect them?"

Halston looked away from his eyes, not because he was dishonest, but he hated to see tears in a man's eyes, especially someone like King Alsand.

One thing was for certain, that vampire loved his family. Halston nodded and turned to leave.

"You have my word," he said over his shoulder, and walked away.

CHAPTER 5

Running, face set in determination and untamed rage, Halston reached for his infinity gun. Sweat dripped from his hair and forehead as he ran through the fire-ravaged corridors of the Ivory Tower. Deafening shouts followed him.

The Wraith had been set loose and no one was safe, not even the vampire soldiers of the Royal Guard. Halston rarely paused. The sounds of crunched bones and muffled cries of pain filled the corridor, bouncing off what was left of the walls. Prisoners were awakened, thrilled to be free from their cells, but horrified to hear the screams of agony and the howls of a monstrous creature with no loyalty.

Ahead, there was a pile of rubble. The exit was caved in. Halston looked up. With light emitted from the palm of his hand, he saw through the darkness. Stepping over dead bodies, bodies of Syths, his boot came down in a pile of slush. Someone had exploded and their guts were strewn about.

Halston grimaced.

"Help! Help!" A female soldier called from behind.

Halston looked over his shoulder, watched the armored woman struggling to free herself from fallen stones. The Wraith was not far behind.

Halston sighed inwardly. The soldier was wasting her breath. She was better off shutting up and pretending to be dead instead of drawing the creature's attention.

Thundering footsteps echoed from afar, and Halston bent his knees, summoned a surge of power from deep within his gut, and took off into a burned-out hole in the ceiling. He shot up to another level of the Ivory Tower, one that was dark and smelled of burning flesh. The fire had no effect on him. He landed in the center and ignited his angelic glow.

He held up his infinity gun and pushed a button that opened a lens. Through the lens he could see into the darkness of the hall. Eerie. Quiet. Only the soft echoes of the terror below made their way to his ultra-sensitive ears. Stone walls on either side stretched far down the hall. Steel doors were left sealed. Perhaps the prisoners were too afraid to speak, too afraid to even ask to be free.

Halston raised a brow. *Good, at least some of them are clever*, he thought.

The prisoners were certainly safer inside their cells than out and about. Halston walked softly, holding his gun ready. Every sense was heightened as he listened for danger. If he could only get to the vaults, where the Wraith had slept for centuries, and reset the gates, then the Wraith would be called back and he would be free to follow Koa. If he could not stop the Wraith, then it would continue its massacre of the vampires and creatures in the Ivory Tower, and then turn its attention to her scent. It was the only way. Not even his infinity gun could stop that creature.

"There he is!" A gruff male voice shouted from behind.

Infinity gun cocked, Halston swirled around, identified four armed enemy vampire soldiers in light armor, and pulled the trigger.

A blast, and then a shrill sound, filled the hall. The infinity bullet flew at full speed, hungry, needy, thrilled to be free to fulfill its craving. Like Koa's Lyrinian sword, Halston's infinity gun had a soul and a mind of its own.

Halston bent to his knees and watched as in seconds, the bullet shot through the heads of all four vampires like a heat missile. Silently, he watched, waited, as the infinity bullet, satisfied by the kill, reversed its course and returned to the gun. Halston held the gun ready and with a click, the bullet re-entered. Secure in its home, the bullet was silenced.

Koa.

With each kill, Halston felt a little better that she was closer to freedom. Years had passed and Halston had kept his promise to her father, King Alsand. Many had been killed in the process. He would never forget the day he first laid eyes on the half-blood princess. Nor would he forget how his feelings had grown throughout the years serving as not only her protector, but her boss. He cringed. The screeching that came from afar filled his ears.

The walls and floors vibrated. Rocks and rumble popped and jumped as the Wraith trampled and destroyed everything below. Halston came to his feet and flew to the end of the hallway. He looked both ways at the fork and chose the hall with a door at the end. He flew to the door, opened it, and saw darkness and a staircase leading to the main floor where he could find the path to the vaults. What a maze the Ivory Tower was. Each floor looked the same.

Halston paused at the bottom of the staircase. The Wraith growled like a dog.

Halston braced himself. Energy collected around his body as he saw the large eyes of something unnatural.

Halston stood near the main exit, prepared, waiting. He could not let that Wraith leave and go after Koa. Blood dripped from the ceiling and onto his forehead. Halston wiped it off and glanced up at the gore that was stuck to what was left of the ceiling.

Halston was calm, calmer than he should have been, but at least he knew that Koa was safe. That was all that mattered. He knew that Jax would protect Koa until he could return to her.

Halston didn't reach for his infinity gun. It would not work against this beast. Even as the Wraith thundered down the corridor, Halston examined the damage that Koa had done with the vial that he had given her.

Stone and debris littered the carpet, along with the bodies of countless Syths and goblins that resembled vampire children.

He frowned at the ghastly sight. It was no secret that he never liked the nephilim, but it was his race of fallen angels that had created such abominations.

It was up to the fallen angels to get rid of their spawn.

Halston clenched his jaw.

The things I do for you, Koa. He thought of her face as he sent her away with Jax and his frown deepened. *Jax had better get her to the Gate safely*.

Halston waited. He was patient, even as he was unsure of what he would do to stop the creature. The Wraith was furious, with puffs of smoke coming out of his slime-covered nostrils.

Like a snake with legs, it had a scaly body and a head like a troll with a single horn at the top of his huge head. "Ugly" didn't begin to describe the monstrosity before him.

Two bulging eyes caught sight of Halston, and the red veins of his eyeballs seemed to deepen and stretch as he charged towards the angel before him.

Halston's rank as an angel meant nothing to the creature. Starved for who-knows-how-long, the Wraith knew only that Halston might taste delicious... and that he stood in the way of its main target.

Halston lifted his arms and sent his body into the air. He hovered as the Wraith picked up speed. Halston held his arms out before him and with a push of air, he sent a powerful blast towards the creature.

The Wraith squealed as the shock of the cold air slapped it in the face. It fell to the ground and looked up at Halston with a perplexed look in its eyes. Like a rabid dog, it snarled and came to its stubby feet. With an ear-shattering screech, the Wraith leapt into the air, reaching for Halston with his sharp claws. Halston dove out of the way and sent another blast of air.

The blast sent the Wraith through a wall, and into another corridor. Halston growled and went after it, but paused when he heard robotic voices drifting to his ears from afar. Halston thought a moment. Scayors were coming. He glanced at the creature as it shook its head, trying to regain its senses, and he reached for his infinity gun.

"Put that away, Halston."

Halston's brows rose as he turned to see a little boy peeking over the rubble that was once the front door to the Ivory Tower. Halston flew over to him.

"Roderick? What are you doing here?" Halston was stunned. "You never leave your lab."

Roderick put a finger to his lips. "Quiet down, loudmouth!" he whispered.

Halston landed on his feet. He ran his hands through his blonde hair and shook his head. "What are you doing?"

Roderick grinned. "I told you I wanted to be included in your little games."

Halston glanced over his shoulders. The Wraith was looking through the hole that it had crashed through. Its eyes landed on them. Two quads of Scayors entered the corridor. The tall creatures had black or silver metal covering every inch of their bodies. Halston cocked his infinity gun.

"Put that away!" Roderick ordered. "You know it won't work on that thing."

Halston furrowed his brows and secured his infinity gun in its holster. "Listen, I know what I'm doing."

Roderick huffed and came to his feet. He barely reached Halston's chest and had the face of a ten year old, but Halston knew all too well that looks can be deceiving. Roderick was none other than the Alchemist, the one who had helped him rescue Koa and break Jax out of this very prison only minutes ago.

"You know how to make a big mess. That is all." Roderick narrowed his eyes up at Halston.

Halston began to protest, tell the Alchemist that he needed to go back to his lab and leave matters to the angels, when Roderick spoke quick words, threw two vials and vanished.

Halston looked around, mouth agape as the vials hit the floor. He fell back as a blast of light filled the corridor. As Halston landed with his back against the wall, he saw Roderick reappear behind the Scayors.

Whatever the boy had done sent the Scayors into erratic chaos. Their bodies were electrified. Robotic screams filled the room as they writhed and trembled.

Roderick stood behind them, smiling.

Halston raised a brow. The boy looked evil standing there, enjoying what he liked to call "games." Halston pushed himself off the wall and sent more air to the Wraith. The walls and floor vibrated with its intensity.

While the Scayors were convulsing, the Wraith didn't seem to be affected. Halston closed his eyes and sent more energy into the force of air. The air tightened, collected energy, and turned blue. The instant it hit the Wraith, the creature let out a shrill cry and burst into tiny particles, swirled in circles, and faded into the air.

Halston went to his knees and tried to catch his breath. Lights flashed behind his eyelids as he willed the pounding headache to subside. He'd used a lot of power in such a short amount of time: even angels needed to use caution.

All Halston saw when he tried to calm his breathing was Koa's little face. Those green eyes looked at him lovingly. The corners of her mouth lifted into that small smile that she only gave him.

He felt at peace, and when Halston opened his eyes Roderick was standing before him, his arms holding his red suspenders. Halston leaned to the side to look past the boy. The Scayors lay in a heap of what looked like scrap metal in a junkyard.

Halston lifted a brow and looked at the Alchemist.

Roderick grinned. "That was fun." He dusted his hands and folded them behind him. "What's next?"

CHAPTER 6

With each sunrise and sunset, Eunju thought of the daughter that she had lost.

Tears soaked her cheeks. Only days had passed and nothing could dull the heartache. Nothing could soothe her fears and worry for her only child.

As she looked out the window at the sky, the sun vanished behind the mountains in the distance.

Alsand. She could feel his presence. He was returning, and she knew he would be returning alone. Koa was trapped in the Netherworld for all eternity.

Eunju balled up her fist and pounded the window. The thud wasn't satisfying enough. She wanted the glass to crack and break with a loud shattering sound. She pressed her forehead against the cool glass and squeezed her eyes shut.

Too many emotions. Too much anger. Eunju feared what would happen if Alsand came to her now.

"Lord help me," she whispered. Her heart was broken and in the past, only bad things happened when Eunju was hurt.

She feared what she might do to the vampire king that had taken her daughter from her. She had fallen in love with him, but none of that mattered when it came to the love she had for her daughter.

"Calm down, Eunju," she whispered to herself in a soft voice.

She took a deep breath. Air sparked around her. Green and gold sparks crackled around her. She opened her eyes. Her vision was blurred by shadows. She bit her lip and sucked in more air.

The sound of the doorman opening the door for her husband made her heart thump. The quiet of the manor was all too loud for her ears. The whispers of the staff invaded her mind. She wanted it to stop. She wanted it all to end. Koa was her only reason for living. Without her, everyone should fear for their survival. Without Koa, Eunju might do something… horrible.

Eunju shook her head and wrapped her arms around her body. She needed to control herself. Such thoughts needed to be suppressed. She didn't want to hurt anyone, least of all Alsand. She didn't think anyone else could harm that powerful man, but she knew that she could.

Eunju's hands balled into fists once more. Her eyebrows furrowed. She did not want to hurt him… but if he spoke the words that she was fearing. She would not be able to control herself. That much was a fact.

No one was safe from her power. No man or creature.

It was her blessing. It was her curse.

Eunju loosened her fists and smoothed her long, black, hair. She let out a long sigh. Some of the anger escaped with the air from her lips. The sparks faded into the air and all was quiet, except for the sound of Alsand's footsteps coming up the main staircase of the manor.

Eunju fixed the collar of her white buttoned shirt and smoothed her gray skirt once more. She rolled her neck and closed her eyes.

She wiped her cheeks of tears and turned to face her husband. She looked at him and knew that she could not be angry at him anymore. She still loved him.

She held her breath when she looked upon his face. He looked tired. There wasn't an ounce of vigor in his eyes. She knew then, that he was as distraught by the loss of Koa as she was.

After all, it wasn't his idea. It was that angel's. Halston's. He had devised this plan. Eunju hoped she could trust him.

Before Eunju could stop herself, she was running to Alsand. She wrapped her arms around his neck and sobbed into his chest. He put both arms around her small body and lifted her into a tight embrace. He sucked in a breath and buried his face in her hair.

"My raven-haired queen… I'm sorry," Alsand said in a cracked voice.

Eunju sucked up her tears and looked into his face. She wrapped her legs around his body and held on. "No pet names today, Alsand. It will not work. Tell me what you've done."

Margot, the housekeeper peeked into the library. "Do you need anything madam?"

Eunju shook her head, but kept her eyes locked on her husband's face.

"And you monsieur?"

"We're fine, Margot, please leave us."

Margot nodded, bowed, and closed the door softly behind her.

Eunju held his face in both of her hands. Her brows furrowed. "What happened? Tell me everything."

Alsand carried her over to the sitting area, by Koa's writing desk. This was Koa's favorite room in the entire manor. Eunju pictured Koa sitting in that mahogany chair with her feet crossed on the desk before her, and her face in a large book.

Alsand put Eunju down on the ivory chaise lounge and sat beside her. Eunju could still smell the Netherworld on him. Coal, embers, and a scent that she couldn't describe, but knew it only to be a Netherworld smell.

Eunju wanted to scrub that scent off of him. She didn't want to think about that horrible place.

He wiped his face and shrugged. He was completely beaten down. There wasn't a shred of happiness in his green eyes. There was no doubt that he loved Koa as much as she did. That comforted Eunju.

Eunju sat up straight and folded her hands on her knees, waiting.

Alsand sighed and clasped his hands. "I did everything like I was told. I took her to the Netherworld, presented her as agreed, and..."

Eunju frowned. "And what?"

Alsand looked away. "And King Greggan married her."

Eunju shot to her feet. "What?"

Sparks.

Alsand slowly stood. He held his hands out, urging Eunju to calm down.

Eunju narrowed her eyes. "What?" Her hair blew back as the sparks crackled all around. Alsand gulped and backed away.

"Darling," he said softly. "You must calm yourself."

Eunju knelt and held a hand out. "Why did you give my daughter to that bastard?"

Alsand's voice wavered. "I didn't have a choice."

"I agreed to her marriage to the young prince. Not to the very vampire that started this war."

Alsand's eyebrows rose. He looked up.

Eunju didn't realize that she was floating. She didn't care.

"My love, come back down to me. Let's talk about this calmly."

Eunju shot a green glow, grabbed him with it, and pulled him into the air. Her face was twisted in rage. Alsand was shaking.

"You bring my daughter back or I will banish you all."

Alsand reached a hand out to her. She growled and used the green glow to toss him into a corner. All the tenderness and love in the world could not calm a mother fearful for her child.

Alsand was on his feet in an instant. He did not run, like she expected him to. She glared at him from under her brows.

"Eunju, listen." He spoke calmer than she'd expected considering she'd just thrown him… a vampire king… like a piece of rubbish across the room. He knew the extent of her power, and still, he stayed.

"It did not matter which of them she married. It is not meant to last. Halston has a plan, and I trust him."

"If that vile creature touches my daughter…"

Alsand nodded. "Yes, I know! I thought of that too. And so Halston helped Jax acquire a potion from the Alchemist."

Eunju frowned. "What kind of potion?" She began to slowly lower herself to the floor.

"One that will keep Greggan from touching Koa. He will never have her in the way he intends. It will give Halston enough time to execute the plan."

Eunju landed softly on her feet. The carpet was soft beneath her bare feet, but it was warm, heated from her power. She closed her eyes and stretched her neck. The sparks faded, and her blurred vision subsided.

She calmly sat down, crossed her legs, and looked across the room to Alsand. "Go on. Tell me *everything*."

CHAPTER 7

Raven closed her eyes and sighed.

Eunju.

She missed hearing her real name. To be free from her curse to live as a cat. To have her beloved daughter back. Those were the things she now fought for.

The carnage before her was sickening, but she had to remember why she was there and what they were up against. Still, days of tracking Bund's crimes were beginning to wear on Raven. She only hoped that soon Koa and Halston would return from the Netherworld with the one vamp that could reverse her curse.

"This is awful," Alice said to Raven as she knelt over the little girl's body. "For someone so young to suffer this way."

Alice covered the girl's mangled face up and stood. She had to be careful not to step in the puddle of blood. She shook her head. "It's fairly fresh. I'd say this was probably his first kill of the morning." Alice let out a long breath. "What a damn shame. He's certainly not trying to be discreet about any of this."

Raven followed behind her, saddened by what she had seen. "How are we going to stop Bund?"

Alice flicked a hand and the two detectives who had been investigating the murders woke up from their trance. She sidestepped them and disappeared into the crowd on the sidewalk before they even realized what had happened.

"First, we should tell everyone to keep their children inside, lock their doors, and pray that Bund doesn't become bold enough to start snatching little girls out of their bedrooms."

Raven squeezed her eyes closed. She hated to imagine what happened to the girls that Bund chose. Just thinking that Koa had been harmed by him brought back terrible feelings of sorrow and worry.

Alice glanced back at her. She smoothed her short pink hair with the palm of her hand. "But we can't exactly tell the humans about the existence of vampires and psychotic demons, can we?"

Raven sighed. "I suppose not."

Alice made a face. "You know, I sometimes think ignorance isn't quite as blissful as it seems. Maybe the humans wouldn't be so foolish if they knew that supernatural creatures were targeting them." She gave Raven a look. "What do you think?"

"Don't some of them know though? The kids that go out and become pets know."

"True. But that's only a slim portion of the human population. I wonder what would happen if we just hopped on the television and made an announcement."

"The Netherworld Division wouldn't be a secret organization anymore."

Alice grinned. "Exactly. Halston and I could fight crime in the open, instead of trying to hide it. But oh well. It would never work. The humans are lucky to not have such worries on their mind. I guess that's why we do what we do."

Raven quickened her pace as Alice turned a corner towards a cemetery. "I suppose."

"Indeed, little kitty. I am searching for the powerful, the fearless… the perfect crew." Alice reached in her pocket and pulled out a small device that resembled a compass. Raven wished she was taller, to see its face. She heard a tiny clicking sound and saw a gold light shoot from it and stretch far into the maze-like mausoleum buildings.

"Alice," Raven called, pausing to stare at the light. "What is that?"

Alice lifted a brow. "What? Oh, it's something Halston made for me."

Raven sat on her back legs. She licked her paws. She hated being dirty, and the cold dirt was getting stuck in between her claws.

"I can't wait to see what gadgets he's created for you." Alice smiled, walking in the direction of the light.

Raven lifted a brow and hurried behind. "What?"

Alice chuckled. "You didn't think that Halston would let you into the division and not give you some sort of weapon, did you?"

Raven was speechless. She'd never thought of such a thing. She'd never needed gadgets before, but when she was in her true form, she had enough power to not need the use of weapons.

Raven's fur stood on end. She looked up at the sky. Clouds slowly began to block the sun and the air grew colder. Night would soon be upon them. She felt herself growing a little weary. There was so much evil that awoke when night fell.

"He makes the best toys."

"What is that light that comes out of your compass?"

Alice frowned. "What light?"

Raven nodded towards the gold glow. "The one you're following."

Alice paused. "Oh wow. You can actually see where the compass is directing me?"

Raven nodded. "Why yes. Can't you?"

Alice shrugged. "No. It links with my telepathy, leading me by force to other nephilim."

"Oh," Raven said. Her eyes began to glow and reflect the moonlight as the sky darkened. "I see gold light."

Alice smirked, staring down at her. "Cats. It is kind of cool to be able to talk to you. Inquire about what it is that you see and what not. You'll be an excellent sidekick. In and out of the shadows, there she goes!"

Raven's ears perked up. She thought that she had heard something out of the ordinary sounds that she always heard. Crickets and rustling leaves were her everyday soundtrack, but she was certain she heard a faint scratching sound coming from one of the keeps. Alice quieted and seemed to sense something as well.

Alice lowered her voice. "We'll discuss the whole sidekick thing later. Deal?"

Raven looked up at her, unblinking. "I am not a sidekick."

"Suit yourself." Alice shrugged, whispering. "I am one hell of a superhero."

Raven almost laughed but instead she yelped as she heard a loud crash of stone. She jumped, standing on her tiptoes, her black fur on edge.

Alice put her hands in her pockets. She tossed her pink hair out of her eyes. "Oh sweet. The freak show is awake." She folded her arms across her chest. Raven froze as the large stone door started to creak open. An angel statue loomed down at her, as if daring her to make a sound. Raven held her breath, waiting.

"Don't worry, kitty. It's just Spoons."

"Spoons?" Raven stepped back as a small man crept out of the mausoleum. He was ragged, with shaggy gray hair and large icy blue eyes. He appeared to be over a hundred years old. His spine was curved and his limbs were as thin as rails.

He walked over like a zombie, his feet dragging and his jaw slack. Raven gasped. "Is he… a zombie?"

Alice scoffed with an amused laugh. "No kitty. He's a ghoul. But don't worry, he's pretty tame." She lifted a brow as she noticed the human hand in his fist.

Spoons took a bite, ripping the flesh off the thumb. He chewed and swallowed. "Well, pretty tame, considering…" Alice's voice trailed and Spoons stood a little taller, in an attempt to straighten his back.

Alice gave Raven a sidelong glance. "Good guess though. He does like human flesh as much as a zombie. But I can tell you with about 99 percent certainty that zombies don't exist."

"I hear ya," Spoons drawled in a deep voice. "Talkin 'bout me, like I'm not even here."

Raven shivered when his eyes looked down at her. Spoons frowned. "What is dat?"

Alice grinned. "A kitty cat."

Spoons twisted his mouth. "I don't like dem creatures." He sniffed the air. "Hey. You little lyin bitch. That ain't a cat!" He moved with the shadows, and knelt before Raven before she could run. He had her by the back of her neck, and held her up to his face. He put his cold pointed nose to Raven's belly and sniffed. "What is dis?"

Alice kicked him in the gut. "Put her down," she growled. Spoons dropped Raven and she ran behind Alice. "She's a friend, and that's all you need to know."

He looked up at her. He slowly stood. His gaze landed on Raven who hid behind Alice's leg. "Jus tell me. What is dat?" He scrunched up his nose. "I never smelled anythin' like it before."

Alice stepped to him. "You listen to me, Spoons." She got really close to his face, leaning down to his height. Her voice lowered. "I would love to offer you a deal. You know, get you back in good standing with Halston and all."

Spoons head shot up. "Halston?"

Alice grinned. "Yes. You heard me right. Halston is offering you a second chance. Once upon a time you were the best Navigator any of us had ever encountered."

Spoons backed away. "I don't do dat stuff anymo." He scratched his head.

Raven shuddered as his long nails disturbed a group of spiders that had nested in his hair. They ran along his scalp and into his ears. He didn't seem to mind.

"Come on, Spoons. Do it for me."

He lifted a bushy white brow. "I don't care bout you! Angels! Demons! Lemme lone!" He turned to walk away.

Alice chuckled. She winked at Raven. "Ah come on, Spoons. I was just kidding with you. Come back here." She made her voice soft like a little girls. "Pretty please."

Spoons kept walking.

Alice frowned. "All right. Have it your way. I'll be sure to let Greggan know where you are."

Spoons paused mid-step. He craned his neck around with a terrified look on his face. "G-G…Greggan… is here?"

"He is. And I think he'd love to find you and rip your head off."

"I'm outta here!"

Raven squealed as he transformed into a ragged looking jackal before their eyes. Thick brown fur covered his body. Still, his blue eyes stood out, even though his face now resembled a feral dogs'.

Alice threw her hand out and as he prepared to run, she made him freeze. He growled. His eyes darted from side to side.

"Lemme go! You bitch!"

"Damn shifting ghouls! Why the hell did you get such a cool trick?" Alice huffed and stepped closer to him. She leaned down. Her voice lowered, almost menacingly. Raven's ears perked up.

"Listen here, Spoons. I'm not here to force you to join our side, but really, what is the alternative? You join us and you have a chance of surviving what is coming. No one betrays Greggan and survives. You helped smuggle that girl out of the Netherworld years ago. I know there's something good in you." She stood up and her voice softened. "Even if you try to hide it."

Raven felt her heart pounding. She looked from Alice to Spoons and back again. Spoons' big blue eyes stared at Alice. His fangs were dripping with saliva, and yet he was unable to move to catch the drool, not that he would have otherwise.

"Fine. Just lemme go."

Alice smiled and in an instant, Spoons was loose. He shifted back to his ghoulish figure and looked at Raven.

"That thing right der… smells like dat girl," he whispered.

Alice nodded. "Nice observation. She is Koa's mother."

Raven felt a sting of grief at the mention of Koa's name. She prayed that her daughter was ok. She looked at the two of them. It was a surprise to learn that this ghoul had helped save Koa's life.

Spoons frowned. "What da hell happened to her?"

Alice rolled her eyes. "Enough questions. Can I count you in, or not?"

Spoons spit in his hand and held it out to Alice. "I'm in." He gave her a pointed look as she stared at his hand in disgust. "But no funny business. I help ya kill Greggan and ya leave me alone, foreva. Deal?"

Alice grimaced and shook his hand. She groaned in dismay as she pulled her hand away, mucous stuck to her hand like glue. "Ugh. Deal."

CHAPTER 8

Koa and the others flew for hours, darting through the sky at full speed, afraid that they were still being chased.

The Gate was so close.

Koa's hair whipped around her face as she kept her eyes focused on the final cavern. She did not care any longer that the Shadows waited for her. She only wanted to get home and find her mother.

Koa had rarely seen a world so consumed by the color black. Black skies that were mixed with a constant swirl of gray hovered above her. Black dirt and smooth black stone waited below. Koa missed the color green. She missed home, where trees and flowers filled the landscape.

This rocky, desolate place kept her on edge. The cold in the air seeped into her bones, keeping her tense and uncomfortable. She couldn't understand how anyone could live there.

The Netherworld was horrible; beautiful at times, but horrible nonetheless.

Koa flinched. The sudden howls of the Shadows called to Koa and the others as they entered the final cavern. A sizzle of strange rain erupted from the sky. The sky lit up with green and white lightning that buzzed loudly above and shot into the ground in quick succession. The loud noise filled the cavern.

Koa tensed as Jax's fan flyer started to flicker and buzz. He cursed under his breath. She could fly, but she didn't want him being harmed by crashing to the ground.

"Fly down, darling," he said, pointing to a spot in the valley. The silver river shimmered below. "Our fan flyers are going out. There's an electrical storm coming."

"Good," Evina said. "It'll keep the Shadows away long enough for us to slip out."

They landed and ran at full speed towards the Gate. "Go on!" Jax shouted up at Koa. "We'll catch up!"

Koa flew above and cut through the darkness of the final cavern. There was nothing but rocks and stones. Like a desert, there was very little vegetation, if any. The ground was dry and cracked. She landed before the Gate. She clutched the bars as if a strong wing would lift her, or a Shadow would grab her and pull her away. Koa had come this far. She was not about to be ripped away from her chance at freedom.

She saw the faint glints of Jax's and Evina's weapons as they ran along the black road. Her eyes darted from side to side, and into the dark forest of black trees, as she watched for Shadows. To her surprise, Evina was right. They didn't come out to harass them. Koa couldn't see them, but she knew they were there somewhere, watching her.

Koa looked up at the sky, filled with electricity and a loud roar, and thanked God. Still, she would not breathe with relief until they were free and in the human world.

Evina pulled a long silver key out of her side bag. She closed her eyes and handed it over to Jax. Jax let Koa go and took the key in both of his pale hands. He whispered to it and it started to glow.

Koa's eyes widened as she watched this ancient key glow a bright blue. Jax winked at her. He gently stroked her cheek. Koa was surprised that she no longer felt afraid. She trusted Jax and Evina.

"I told you I'd get us out of here."

"My little brother can do just about anything." She nudged Koa and gave her a mischievous smile. "I bet you're wondering if it was a good idea, helping us escape the Netherworld, aren't you?"

Koa felt a pang of warning and recoiled from Evina.

Jax sighed. He gave Evina a stern look. "Ignore her, Koa," he said. "She's only fooling around with you."

Koa stared at Evina, wondering if the vampire princess really was joking. She shook that feeling of warning off. Halston planned this. She trusted him.

Evina chuckled and cracked her knuckles. "Still suspicious, I see." She shrugged. "I'm not offended. I'd be suspicious too. You're a smart girl, but sometimes you have to open your eyes and see who is helping you. Jax and I gave up a lot to help you escape the first time. This time, our lives and home are at stake. I only hope we can trust *you*."

Koa looked from Evina to Jax and felt a little guilty then. Evina was right. Their homes were at stake just as much as her own. She realized that they had to work together.

"Go on, open up," Evina said. She gave Koa a small smile, a genuine smile this time. It eased Koa's nerves and she returned the smile. This vampire princess was the closest thing she'd ever had to a sister.

Jax stuck the key in the Gate's keyhole and turned. There was a deep rumble and the ground quivered slightly. Jax held the Gate open and Evina ran out. Koa was a little taken aback. Evina ran out as if she feared that someone would change their mind and make her stay behind.

Evina waited for them on the other side, staring into the darkness behind them with her sword ready. Koa glanced at Jax before she followed Evina and stepped through.

A gust of wind pushed Koa out. Koa stumbled onto the ground and breathed in the fresh air of the human world. The black mud was squishy and got all over her. She'd never been more relieved to feel mud between her fingers.

Koa could have cried out with joy.

The smell of trees and wild flowers filled her nostrils and she closed her eyes and smiled. Home. The human world was her home and she had finally returned.

Then, Koa remembered something else about this place. The creature that protected it.

Koa quickly scrambled to her feet. Her eyes darted around, looking for Tunes. He was nowhere to be found. She peered up towards the top of the black Gate and saw the thick fog hovering like a cloud before them.

Tunes had fallen from there when she'd first arrived. Koa wondered with dread if he was up there now, watching them from his hiding place. He enjoyed taunting her.

Koa heard the Gate clink closed. Crickets buzzed and the sound of a faint breeze swept around her. Koa looked up to see Jax and Evina emerge from the Gate. She watched curiously as Jax's eyes beheld the human world for the first time.

His blue eyes were like a child's on Christmas morning.

Koa smiled with him. This was something she used to dream about when she was just a teenager. She'd sleep in Jax's arms some nights and envision the day when she could bring him home to meet her mother.

Back then Koa never thought that such a thing was even possible. Having that dream come true filled her with a flood of joy. Tears stung her eyes when he looked at her. His eyes were clouded with tears as well. He remembered those nights when they'd talk about a fictional future where they could watch the moon over the sea whenever they wanted too.

Koa trudged over to him. She was exhausted and everything hurt, but all she wanted was to hold him. He opened his arms for her and she grabbed his waist. Koa buried her face in his chest and he wrapped his arms tightly around her. It felt right.

There was no doubt that she had loved him with every part of her soul and every thump of her beating heart.

"It's incredible, isn't it," Jax whispered as he rested his cheek against the top of her head. "We actually got our wish."

Koa nodded and wiped a tear from her eye. "I'm like your fairy god-mother."

Jax smiled down at her. Koa almost forgot how worried she was about her mother when he smiled at her like that. She almost forgot that Halston was still in there fighting a Wraith in order to let her go free.

Halston's smile flashed in her mind and Koa tensed. Her smile faded and she dropped her arms from Jax.

He held onto her wrists, giving her a perplexed look. Koa looked down and Jax took her chin in his hand. He leaned down and kissed her softly on the lips. Then, he kissed Koa on the forehead. His lips were cold, not like Halston's, but they still made her skin tingle.

Jax whispered. "Come on, my love. Let's wipe the evil from this world so that our children can have a real future."

Koa closed her eyes. His voice stirred forgotten emotions and she wanted to pull him down and kiss him again. Jax let her go and she felt empty.

She sighed and watched him step over to Tristan. Koa glanced at Evina. She stood there with her hands on her hips.

Evina looked unimpressed. "This is it? This is the human world? It's cold here." She cracked her knuckles and put her flying disc in her belt. It wouldn't work in the human world where there wasn't a Disc Moon to power it.

There was a real moon here, and she stared at it in wonder. She caught Koa looking at her and cleared her throat.

"What now?"

Koa could tell that Evina looked at her with envious eyes. She knew why she was envious. Koa could fly whenever she wanted. Now, in the human world, Evina and Jax were just ordinary vampires.

Jax looked to Koa for answers. "What do we do now?"

Koa shrugged. They were expecting her to lead them. She wasn't a leader. Halston had always been the one giving the orders and making the plans. She liked it that way. Her heart tugged at the thought of him and how he held her. Could he possibly feel the same way? She forced the notion out of her mind and gazed at Jax.

"How am I supposed to know? I thought you and Halston had it all figured out."

"Well then, I know what I want to do first." Evina held up the cloth that covered her lower half. "What are those strange pants you're wearing?" She pointed to Koa's jeans. "I want some. I want to go find some human clothes so that I will blend better."

Evina took a long fingernail and parted her red hair down the middle. She let the long layers cover the tattoos on the left side of her scalp. "How does it look?" She looked at Koa with innocent eyes.

Koa smiled in wonder. She put her hands on her hips and nodded. "Wow. You look…almost normal."

"What about me, Koa?" Jax held out his arms, displaying his pristine black suit. "Do I look normal too?" He smoothed his tie. "I tried to look as human as possible."

Koa laughed. "You look like a banker."

Jax beamed. "Excellent."

Koa shook her head. "I wouldn't call that look normal. You want to blend in. You know? Look like just another ginger."

They both frowned. "Ginger? What is that?"

Koa shook her head, giggling. *I can have some fun with this,* she thought mischievously. She tried to look serious.

No, mother's life is at stake, and so is yours. Koa stopped giggling and sighed. "Nevermind. Just let me take you to the shops. I'll help you blend in."

Evina perked up. "Shopping? Let's go now."

They were like babies, new to the world, and both of them trusted her. She looked up at the sky.

"We'd better hurry. The sun rises in an hour."

Jax and Evina looked up, worried.

"Oh yes," Jax said.

Evina shielded her face as if the sun was already out. "Get us out of here."

A big man stepped forward. Tristan. He was one of Halston's oldest friends. He had scars over every inch of his dark caramel skin. He motioned. "Finally," he said. "You guys decided to show up."

"Oh great," Evina said, rolling her eyes. "I forgot I'd have to deal with you."

Tristan covered his heart with a large hand and mocked a lock of pain. "Vicious woman." He grinned. "I like it. Go on. Tell me more."

"You're still annoying. Where's that wife of yours? I'm sure she won't like you flirting with a vamp."

Tristan's hands dropped then. His grin faded and he turned to walk to the black SUV that Halston had ridden there. There was a sudden sadness that made Koa wonder what changed his attitude.

"Wait," Koa blurted. She looked back at the Gate. "What about Halston? You guys go ahead. I want to wait for him."

Tristan leaned back against Halston's black SUV. His expression was unreadable as he looked up at the stars and folded his arms across his broad chest. "We are talking about the same Halston, right? The Halston I know is indestructible. He will catch up with us."

Evina stepped forward. She walked towards the car. "Well, what are we waiting for? I'm not going to sit here and get burnt to death. Come on, Koa. Golden boy will be fine."

Jax followed his sister. He looked back and reached a hand out to Koa.

Koa shifted her weight to her other foot and hesitated as she looked down at Jax's hand. She wished that it was Halston reaching out to her. She hoped that Tristan and Evina were right. Halston would be all right. He had to be.

She let out a breath and accepted Jax's hand. She stepped into the car after Jax. Tristan closed the door behind them. Koa sat up in her seat and looked out the tinted window towards the Gate. Before long, it vanished into the mist and they drove into the human world.

CHAPTER 9

Koa was trapped in her thoughts. She stared out the tinted window, watching the sky light up. Evina and Jax didn't have long. She wondered where they were going. Where was this safe house that Halston had acquired?

Koa sat up in her seat and pressed her face to the glass when she saw Tristan veer off down a shallow dirt road. She had no clue where they were going.

"Hurry up," Evina pleaded. She rubbed her knuckles raw.

Koa felt bad for her. She'd never had to fear the sun. She always wondered why she had been so lucky. She still wanted to find out what her mother really was. If she was never human before she was cursed, the possibilities were mind-wrecking. She couldn't have been a vampire.

Koa thought deeply. Her brows furrowed.

Could she have been an angel? Koa wondered.

It would make sense. That would explain Koa's ability to fly. But still, Koa had a feeling that her mother wasn't an angel either. She had a feeling that she was something else. Something dark and mysterious.

Koa leaned back in her seat and chewed her nails. She remembered being a shy little girl in South Korea. She lived in a two room cottage with her mother where she spent her days studying books and dealing with the pain of the hunger. She could never escape the smell of human blood, even in their rural village.

While her mother tried her best to keep her safe, she resorted to giving Koa animal blood on occasion, just to keep the cravings at bay. But then, Koa remembered the visits.

They would always be found. Woman would come from far and wide to consult with her mother. Koa would stand in the doorway with curious eyes and watch women sob and beg her mother for help. Her mother would console them, give them hot tea and tell Koa to close the door and go read.

Always obedient, Koa would listen and she would close the door and retreat to her little nook in the back of the house. She'd pull out a worn copy of The Prince and the Pauper, or Little Women, and try to forget her curiosity for what her mother did to help those poor women. It was how they survived, for there were always gifts. Gifts of money, food, and sometimes toys for Koa to play with.

Koa would play with the wooden dolls and never ask what it was payment for. She'd simply be pleased that she had something new.

Koa looked out the window of the car; her mother's image looked back at her. Soft brown eyes and long black hair pulled back with a simple cloth headband. Koa was determined to bring that image back to life. Mother had been cursed to live as a cat for far too long.

But first, she must kill the demon, Bund.

Koa grimaced at her memory of him. His foul breath as he licked her face while slashing her side open with his sharp claws lingered in her mind.

She shivered and tried to forget that image. "Please, Tristan," Koa said after clearing her throat. She glanced out the window to see the clouds lightening into a faded yellow. "Hurry."

"Don't worry. I know where I'm going. This used to be our old safe house, back in the early 1600's, before we started reforming the Netherworld." Tristan's eyes met Evina's. "Before *your* father was even born."

Koa's mouth parted when they drove out of the narrow road surrounded by ancient trees that provided a canopy of green. The road opened up to a large clearing. A church stood before them. She grabbed the seat cushion to settle herself.

Old but beautiful, a single tower stretched above the squat church, with its bell still intact at the top. It was clear that the church had been abandoned for decades. Weeds and grass overtook the walkway. Purple flowers littered the ground in huddled groups, making the land look enchanted somehow.

The sky above was a mixture of blue, orange, and yellow. Sunrise.

"See, looks just the way I remember it."

Koa opened the door the instant Tristan stopped. She stepped out and felt daylight start to come over the back of the church. Tristan hopped out and motioned for them to follow.

"Hurry! Get inside." He ran towards the large double doors set beneath four curved arches. He used an old key to open them. Jax and Evina didn't hesitate. They shielded their faces and ran right on Tristan's heels.

Koa stood in front of the SUV. The smoke was already coming from the back of Jax and Evina's exposed necks. They winced from the pain as Tristan worked the lock. The instant the door was opened enough for them to fit, they ran inside. They disappeared into the darkness and Koa breathed with relief.

She was finally alone. Koa tilted her head up and beheld the magic and purity of a sunrise. The orange clouds opened up to allow the sun its grand entrance. Once again the vampires were forced to flee to their hiding spots.

All except one.

Tears trailed down her face as she watched the sun's light come over the church's roof.

The light bathed her face with warmth. Her bottom lip trembled and she closed her eyes. Her head threatened to explode. Halston was gone. Her mother was being hunted by a demon. Greggan wanted her for some horrible purpose. And then, the memories. Koa had them back and she wanted nothing more than to forget once again.

Too much, Koa thought with a wince. "Too much!" Koa shouted.

She gasped when someone touched her shoulder. Her eyes popped open and she caught Tristan by the wrist.

Tristan towered over her like a giant, but his face showed a look of concern. "You all right?"

Koa nodded. She let go of the iron gauntlet around his wrist and quickly turned her back on him. She rubbed her eyes dry. She'd had enough of feeling helpless. She was emotionally drained, tired, and hungry. Hunger always came first.

She held her hand out behind her. "Keys."

"Where do you think you're going?"

Koa turned on him with intense eyes. "I need to feed. Is that a problem?"

Tristan held his hands up to calm her. "Calm down. I was just curious." He fished the car keys out of his pocket and dropped them into the palm of her hand.

Koa closed her fingers over them and stepped through knee-high grass to the driver's door. She needed Lindley. Her pet had the one thing that could soothe her pain and give her a moment of peace and clarity.

Blood.

Koa opened the door and hopped inside. She turned the ignition and rolled the window down. She gave Tristan a look and forced a half-smile. "Thank you for everything, Tristan. I know I am a handful, but now I remember what you all did for me years ago."

Tristan folded his arms and nodded. "It was nothing. Don't mention it." He smiled back.

"Modest," Koa teased and he shrugged.

"I've been called many things, but never modest."

Koa laughed lightly, too tired to do more than that. "Let them sleep, will you? I'll be back by nightfall."

Tristan nodded. Koa backed out and speed down the dirt road. Her heart thumped. Her fingers curled around the steering wheel. She looked up at the rearview mirror. Tristan stood there with his arms crossed, watching her.

Koa shrieked when something dark flew from the church and opened the passenger door. Koa covered her mouth as she saw Jax sit in the seat beside her. His speed was incredible. Her heart still raced, even though she knew it was him. Smoke came from his sun-damaged skin as he sat there. Once he closed the door, he was safe from the sun's rays.

The smoke faded and he gave her a lopsided grin.

Jax put a hand on her thigh and gave it a tender squeeze. "I waited for you in that prison for years. I dreamt of your beautiful face every night." He stroked her cheek with his thumb. "I finally have you back and I'm not going to let anything happen to you again. You're not leaving my sight."

Koa didn't say anything. She pictured the day they'd met and felt that same excitement she'd felt as a child. She nodded her head as their eyes locked on one another.

Jax fastened his seatbelt and looked at her with a mischievous smirk. "Show me this Wryn Castle."

Koa returned the smirk. Despite her worries and fears, she felt a little excited to show Jax her world. There was so much for him to see and experience. Now they could do things together. She nodded and drove them from the abandoned church.

Koa needed to feed, and apparently, so did Jax.

CHAPTER 10

Blood dripped from the ceilings. The floor was flooded with it. Greggan's boots sloshed as he stepped from the last stone step and onto the slick concrete floor. He had to resist the urge to slide his finger through the delicious smelling nectar of human blood. He was more dignified than that, but it was a rare thing to taste real human blood back in the Netherworld—though he was no longer a prisoner of the Netherworld.

No, the human world was finally open to him, and he had grand plans to make a few... *changes*.

Greggan's blue eyes gazed up at the hanging bodies. He grimaced at what he saw.

Children. Little girls.

Greggan looked over at Bund and gave him a look that made the skinny demon lower his eyes.

"Why so many? Do you really need this many?" His hand pointed to the cluster of little girls. There were fourteen.

Bund shrugged. "Ya said I could have as many as I want. I was hungry."

Greggan stroked his long, crimson, red beard and narrowed his eyes. He saw one of girls start to stir. She bucked against her shackles and tried to pull herself up. Her mouth was sewn closed.

"Ey," Bund called to the little girl. Her blonde hair was slick with blood. The blood turned it into an odd brownish color. "Stop ya fussin. I'll pull ya down when I'm ready for ya."

The girl whimpered. She looked to be about twelve. Greggan stared at her. She was the same age that Koa had been when he'd married her. His fingers curled into a fist.

The girl was tall for her age and slim, like an athlete. She was the oldest in the group. Her large brown eyes went wide. She flickered them to Greggan, looking at him pleadingly. A strange sound came from her throat. It was a muffled scream.

Bund growled. Before Greggan could say anything, Bund snatched her throat out with one clawed hand.

Greggan watched as Bund ate the girl's bloody larynx. Good thing the other girls were still knocked out. There would have been quite a panic if they'd seen what just happened.

Greggan clenched his jaw and shook his head at Bund. The demon could be so sloppy and impulsive, two things that Greggan had never been accused of being. But Bund was a necessary evil. He needed this demon to keep Halston out of his affairs. He closed his eyes and tried to forget about the overwhelming smell of blood that surrounded him.

Greggan opened his eyes and the entire basement filled with the screams of the little girls as he made the room fill with fire. Bund stood in the flames and growled at Greggan.

"Why'd ya do that? They was mine!"

Greggan felt the flames heat his face as he stepped into the fire and approached Bund. His eyes narrowed as he looked into Bund's dark blue eyes.

"We came to frighten the humans," Greggan explained. He began walking up the cellar stairs. "This will get their attention."

"What do ya think I was doin?" Bund snarled at Greggan, his fangs sharp and covered in blood. "I'll kill ya if ya do that again. Lemme do things my way, or I'll eat your black heart while ya watch."

Greggan paused. He felt a shiver run through his body at the demons tone. Bund could kill Greggan, but Greggan had something the demon wanted. Something he needed. He must be reminded of that fact.

"I think we both know that would be unwise." Greggan exited the cellar then, but he could feel Bund's eyes following him.

Outside, Lera, his second wife waited for him. Her pale face seemed to glow under the moonlight. He loved seeing her hair free from her usual braid. Her long black hair seemed to float around her face with the breeze. Lera looked more like a witch from folklore than a vampire. She was pale and beautiful, but there was no mistaking the coldness in her eyes.

Greggan loved her for that. Lera stepped forward and bowed to him.

Greggan reached beneath her chin and pulled her face up to his. He kissed her forehead and she smiled. Second wife was his favorite. There was no mistaking that. This vampire queen would do anything for him. She would die for him, without question.

Greggan ran his hands through her hair and she rested her face in the palm of his hand.

"Lera, my sweet," he called.

She looked up with eerie violet eyes. "Yes, my king?"

"Are you ready for some fun?"

Lera's eyes brightened. Her fangs curled into a grin. Out of two small scabbards, she pulled out dual daggers. "I am. I'm ready to destroy that little half-blood."

Greggan kissed her forehead and nodded. "Good girl. Me too."

Lera clinked her daggers silver metal together and the sound vibrated along the earth. "That little bitch cut off my legs. I want to cut off her head." Her hair curled into one long braid while she clinked the daggers together, preparing their Netherworld blades.

Greggan folded his hands before him. She stood there in her light armor. Black pants with silver gaiters. A black corset and silver breastplate. It was all slim, and light, so that she could move with grace and agility. Lera was one that he could count on. Vicious and almost as cold as he was, she would get the job done right.

Lera tilted her head. She licked the blade of each daggers, slicing her tongue so that a small drop of blood would spill onto their blade, making them let out a slight screeching sound that fully woke them up.

"What would you have me do, my king?"

Greggan looked up at the sky. The moon was bright. The night was young.

"There's someone I want you to visit tonight."

Lera's eyes darkened with mischief. "Who, my love? Koa?"

Greggan looked off into the horizon, listening to the screams of the burning children in the distance. "No, not yet. In time. Tonight, I have another target for you. An angel," he said and Lera grimaced.

"Name it and I will kill it."

Greggan grinned. "Good girl. Find the angel named Alice. Kill her, and bring me the black cat."

CHAPTER 11

Wyrn Castle looked like a castle out of a gothic tale. Black and eerie. Towers reached into the dark gray clouds and the moon shimmered along the stone. This was the castle from every horror movie. There were rumors of ghosts and witches. No one came anywhere near this place. No one except the few enlightened humans that were willing to sell their blood, and the registered "reformed" vampires that were willing to pay for it.

Koa liked it that way. She liked the Vampire Registration System. The VRS, and the Netherworld agents that executed its rules, were the only things keeping vampires in check.

Vampires could now live a "clean" life, free from killing. Simply pick a human, feed from them, and pay them for their service. Koa knew that it sounded odd at first, almost like blood prostitution.

Koa didn't like to think of it like that. When Ian had been her pet, she had paid his college tuition, housing, and gave him money for whatever else he needed. Vampires had money. There were countless ways to make it. You'd have to be a dumb vampire to be poor and unable to afford a pet. Such things just didn't exist. Koa was well off because of her father's fortune, but even if she hadn't inherited his wealth, she had a list of ways to make her own.

Jax followed Koa with a look of suspicion. "Humans really come here to let us feed from them?"

Koa nodded. "Yes. If you can pay the price."

Jax looked at her. His red brows furrowed. "What if you cannot pay the price?"

Koa shrugged. "You offer your services. Think of it as bartering. Some humans like having a vampire bodyguard. They always find a way to work it out."

Jax still didn't seem convinced. "You expect this to last?

"Why wouldn't it? Everyone is happy."

Jax shook his head. "I have a feeling they won't be for long. Father would never go for something like this. No one tells father what to do. He didn't come here to live under your rules. I'm pretty sure he came here to rule all of you."

Koa sighed. She knew he was right. She remember too clearly how Greggan was. She shoved back the memories of how her Netherworld husband had treated her. She hated to admit how right Halston was… once again. He warned her that some memories were best left forgotten. Koa wondered if she could give up the memory of Jax's love and devotion to her, just to forget how cruel Greggan had been to her.

Her stomach grumbled and she took Jax by the arm, leading him to the front doors where the guards were stationed.

Black suits, slicked back hair, blacked-out shades, and pale faces set in stern resolve, the guards gave Koa a nod before opening the door for her. Koa smiled at them, glad that no one questioned her guest. Koa couldn't recall them actually ever saying a word to her before.

On the other hand, once the double doors closed behind them, and they entered the grand hall, Greta grinned a smile as bright as sunshine and squealed in delight when she saw Koa and her date.

"Miss Ryeo-won!" Greta, a blonde human from Sweden, clasped her hands in glee and came from her post behind the front desk and skittered over to Koa with her high-heeled black stilettos. "Welcome back! We were worried about you after your abrupt exit last time."

Koa looked over at her. "Why were you worried?" Koa tried to hide the suspicion from her voice, not that Greta would have noticed.

Greta looked flustered. Her smile turned a little unsure and she giggled an odd melodic sound. "Why, well, you just flew off and left your pet all alone." Greta wrung her hands. She looked from Jax to Koa, as if he might help her answer the question.

"The poor girl was in hysterics that you didn't say good bye or give her instructions on what to do next. We had to let her stay here in your usual room. She said that she didn't have anywhere else to go, that her friends had left her."

Koa winced. She had forgotten about Lindley when she rushed off to the Netherworld. Lindley was her pet, she was supposed to take care of her.

Koa sighed. "Is she here?"

Greta nodded. Her bouncy blonde hair shook with her overenthusiastic nod. "She is! Absolutely. She refuses to leave the room!"

Koa nodded and walked past Greta. "My guest and I will go up now. Tell Lexi I'd like to speak with her in an hour."

Greta's smile returned. "Absolutely, Miss Ryeo-won."

Koa and Jax headed towards the hallway.

"But who shall I put down as your guest, ma'am?"

"Just put down John," Jax responded. He winked at Koa and folded his arms across his chest. "John Smith."

Greta nodded. One look from Jax made her freeze in her spot. Both of her hands dropped to her side and her eyes followed Jax as her smile faded and her face drained of color.

Jax smirked and followed behind Koa. Koa glanced back. Greta was still standing there, watching after them with a glazed look in her eye, as if hypnotized.

Koa raised a brow. "You're good," she said. "But I can glamour better."

Jax chuckled as they approached the elevator. "And how exactly is your glamour better?"

Koa shrugged. "Mine is less obvious." She nodded towards Greta. "How long is she going to stand there like that, with that dumb look on her face?"

Jax walked over to Greta and pulled her hair from over her shoulders. He tilted her head and ran his nose gently across her skin. Greta didn't flinch.

"How does this work, my love?" Jax asked. "Can I taste this one?"

Koa shook her head. "No! That's not how it works at all." She looked around to see if anyone was watching. "Stop that! You're embarrassing me."

Jax chuckled to himself. He turned to face Greta, snapped his fingers, and turned back to Koa. Greta shook her head, as if waking from a trance. She looked confused for a moment, then turned to return to the front desk. She was just as bubbly as before.

Koa couldn't help but be impressed. "Not bad. Not bad at all, sir."

Jax gave her an exaggerated bow and his most charming smile. "It is my goal to impress you, my love." He stood to his full height and scooped her up in his arms. He pulled her face close to his and kissed her full on the lips.

Koa was stunned by his sudden actions but gave in to the intensity of the kiss. His lips were soft and full and his tongue wet and sweet. When he set her back down on the carpeted floor Koa was left breathless. She looked into his eyes and felt her heart pitter patter.

He leaned down to kiss her neck and whispered in her ear. "Take me up to your room and I'll remind you of just how impressive I can be."

Koa couldn't help but blush. She did something else she rarely did. She giggled and had to look away.

Jax took her hand and laughed. "Come on. Let's go."

Koa still couldn't speak. Imagining a night with Jax made her nervous. She led the way to the elevator and once they were inside she stood on the opposite side. Jax leaned against his side and grinned at her.

Koa could barely look at him without blushing a bright red. She focused on the numbers as they glowed on the way up to the floor on which she had a private room. She felt hot and pulled her hair to one side and over her shoulder. She risked a side long glimpse at Jax and he was still staring at her. He winked and she quickly looked away.

Koa felt like a teenage girl again, and she did not like it. She shook her head and stood up straighter.

Stop acting like a fool, Koa scolded herself.

Once they exited the elevator, Koa led the way down the narrow corridor to her usual room at the end. She swiped her card and with a deep breath, she opened it to loud music and an energetic blonde sprawled across the bed. She was naked and her white skin stood out against the black covers. She was laid facedown and completely still.

Koa ran to her, fearing the worst. Her face flooded with blood as she grabbed Lindley by the arms and pulled her to her feet. Lindley groaned. Koa could smell the alcohol on her breath and in her hair. It seemed as if Lindley hadn't showered or done anything but drink since she'd left her.

Tears filled Koa's eyes. She felt horrible for leaving her pet alone like that. She hugged Lindley. "Sweetheart. Are you all right? I'm back. I've come back for you," Koa whispered to her. She pulled her short blonde hair from her face and tried to look into her eyes.

Lindley groaned again and peeked at Koa through narrowed eyes. A small trace of bright blue looked back at Koa and Lindley's eyes widened. She burst into tears and wrapped her thin arms around Koa's neck. She kissed Koa with dry lips all over her face, sobbing uncontrollably. "Master! Master, you're back!" she cried.

Koa held her and rubbed her hair tenderly. "I'm sorry for leaving you, Lindley."

Lindley continued to cling to Koa and sob. "I thought you would never come back! I thought something had happened to you, that you'd died!"

Koa couldn't help her own tears. She and Lindley had only been together for a month, but they never left each other's side, and they'd bonded over those four short weeks. She knew Lindley, inside and out, and had come to love her like family.

She had to be more responsible. Koa shook her head at her own foolishness and leaned over to press the black button on the wall. Within seconds there came a knock on the door.

Koa nodded for Jax to open it and there stood two human women in their black uniforms. Simple black dresses and hair pulled back in single blonde braids. Koa motioned for them to come forward. Joan and Julia were their names. They were specially designated for Koa's floor, and she had only needed them once before, but Koa never forgot a name.

"Julia," Koa called. "Please, find something nice for my pet to change into. Joan, could you run her a nice bath?"

Both girls nodded and went to work. Koa gave Jax a quick look as she stroked Lindley's blonde hair. "Don't worry, darling. These nice girls are going to take good care of you while my friend and I get a little supper."

Lindley shot up. Her face twisted. "You aren't going to leave me again, are you?"

Koa hugged her close. "Of course not, sweetheart. I will be right back after supper, and we will cuddle tonight and talk about all the adventures I had when I was away."

Lindley's face brightened. A look of wonder was brought to her face. "Adventures?"

Koa held her by the shoulders and smiled. "Yes. Just like in a fairy tale."

Lindley wiped her face. "Yes. I would like to hear all about it."

Koa nodded. "You will."

Joan stepped into the doorway of the large bathroom. "Bath's ready."

Lindley gave Koa a last look. "I'll see you soon, right?"

Koa nodded again. "You don't worry about a thing. Enjoy your bath and let Julia and Joan know if you need anything. Anything at all. I'll be back shortly. I promise."

Lindley smiled weakly and nodded. She followed Joan into the bathroom and the door was closed.

Koa sighed and glanced at Jax.

"Well," she began. "Let's eat, shall we?"

Jax grinned and stepped aside. He held the door open for her and gave a little bow. "After you."

CHAPTER 12

Still unsettled by Lindley's present emotional state, Koa had a hard time relaxing during supper. She sat across from Jax in one of the dining rooms on the main floor of Wryn Castle. Lit by only tall jars filled with candles set in the center of the table, shadows danced across Jax's face. His eyes rested on her as he drank from a goblet of fresh blood.

"I must say," Jax began. "These New World vampires have it pretty good up here." He drank another sip. "Human blood is much more delicious than carmia."

"But much harder to get."

Jax shrugged. "But you guys seem to have it all figured out. Thanks to the angels and your Netherworld Division, the vampires here don't even have to hunt."

"Don't get too comfortable."

Jax raised a brow. "To think. Just yesterday, I was in a cell in the Ivory Tower."

"You weren't exactly in chains, eating crusts of bread and gruel." Koa drank her goblet down. She licked her lips. "Even though you were a prisoner, they treated you like a prince."

Jax chuckled softly. "I suppose it wasn't all bad. Lonely is all. Years of loneliness. You weren't there. I thought of you every day. I worried about you."

Koa's face softened. He reached a hand across the table and she rested hand in his palm. He stroked it in between both of his.

"You have no idea how happy I am just to be here with you. I would have gladly stayed in the Ivory Tower if only I had a way to see you and know that you were all right."

Bells rang and all of the diners turned their attention to the doors that were raised open at the end of the dining hall. Koa looked away from Jax. She was glad for a distraction. She never knew what to say when he spoke of his love for her.

They watched the servers walk through the room in two rows, as if in a choreographed dance. While each table for two was set in rows, the beautiful servers walked through the rows with their wrists exposed. Each woman or man had seductive smiles, reassuring the guests that they were willing humans, and not forced to be there.

Koa knew all too well that there were humans out there who thought of a vampire pet's life as a glamorous thing. Young men and women came in hordes to Wryn Castle in hopes of being selected for one of the many positions at the castle as well as the other establishments in the VRS.

As the two lines of humans paused at her table, Koa nodded to Jax to do as she did. She took the wrist of the girl before her and drank. Jax did as well. He eyed the pretty brunette and put her under his alluring spell. Koa paused as she watched him.

Before Koa could protest, Jax had the girl in his lap, sucking the blood from her neck, then her mouth. Koa lifted a brow as Jax wrapped the girl's legs around him and went in for a passionate kiss. A moan escaped the girl as she straddled him and pressed her exposed bosom into his chest. Blood dripped from their kiss and Koa swallowed.

Her cheeks flushed. Something stirred in her and she was embarrassed. She came to her feet. Jax lifted a brow at Koa's look of disgust but continued to kiss and drink from the girl.

Koa shook her head and walked away from the table and towards the exit. She half expected him to come after her, but when she looked over her shoulder, he sat with the girl straddled around his body and continued to feast.

Koa growled and pushed through the doors. She ran her fingers through her hair and forced herself to calm down. She did not have the time or energy to worry about such trivial things.

She made her way to one of the sitting rooms and dialed the old safe house up on her watch.

A voice immediately responded. A hologram of a pretty woman with brown skin and shoulder length brown hair pulled up. Her brows were drawn together in worry.

"Koa! What happened? Are you all right?"

Koa nodded and slumped into a leather chair. "Yes, Micka. I'm fine. How are things at the safe house?"

"It's fine. Where is Halston?"

Koa rubbed her temples. "Still in the Netherworld, I suppose." She had half hoped that Halston would have answered her call. She knew it was a long shot, but she had to try.

Micka sighed. "That's unfortunate. Victor sent a message earlier. It wasn't pleasant."

Koa sat up, alarmed. "Victor? What did he want?"

"He wants Halston to report to him at headquarters right away."

Koa stood. "That doesn't sound good."

"When the boss wants to see you, especially one like Victor, it rarely is," Micka said. She shifted in her seat. She lowered her voice. "I think Halston is in some sort of trouble."

Koa's brows furrowed. "But why? He did nothing wrong."

Micka shrugged. "I don't know. I just have a bad feeling."

Koa pursed her lips and nodded. Her stomach immediately felt unsettled. She wrung her hands. She wasn't even sure if Halston was alive, and now she had to worry about him facing trouble from his superior if he returned. Koa looked up when she heard the door to the sitting room open. She watched Jax enter the room and close the door behind him. He waited patiently, waiting in the shadows.

Koa sighed and glanced at Micka. "Please, keep me posted."

Micka nodded. "Is that him? The prince?"

Koa met Jax's eyes and answered. "It is. Goodbye, Micka," she said and cut the connection by pressing a button on her watch.

Micka's image faded and Koa was left with an awkward silence as Jax simply stood there, watching and waiting.

Jax walked over to her. She remained silent as he took her hands and laced his fingers between hers. She refused to shy away this time. She looked into his dark blue eyes and noticed something she hadn't paid attention to before. Around his iris was what appeared to be a clock, with Netherworld numerals, a minute hand, and an hour hand.

Captivated, Koa went onto her toes for a better look. Her lips parted as she studied his eyes in wonder.

Jax closed his eyes and Koa felt cheated.

"Why did you run off?"

Koa pursed her lips. She felt as if her answer was a stupid one. She knew it was foolish, and so she wanted to keep her reasons to herself.

"I don't know. I didn't like seeing you kiss that girl."

Jax lifted a brow. "You? Jealous?" He wrapped his arm around her waist and pulled her body to his. "Now, that doesn't sound like the Koa I know. She was simply an appetizer."

Koa held her breath, looking at his mouth with fevered need. Her breaths became labored for no reason at all, except she wanted him, and he was fully aware.

Gently, he kissed her forehead.

Koa closed her eyes, shaking.

Jax picked her up with one arm and carried her to a desk set neatly with stacked magazines, books, and stationary. He pushed the things aside and sat her upon the cold wooden surface. Koa leaned back on her elbows and watched him. With a hand cradling the back of her head and his other holding her bottom firm, pressing her body to his groin.

Koa wrapped her legs around him and craned her neck up for more of his delicious kisses.

Nothing else mattered when Jax kissed her. Soft kisses turned to greedy kisses as Jax sucked her tongue and bit her bottom lip. Koa closed her eyes and moaned, nearly delirious with desire. She was hungry, but this time it was for something other than food or blood. She wanted Jax like she'd never wanted anything else in her life.

His hand, cold but soft, slid up her shirt and cupped her small breasts. Koa gave in and wrapped her arms around his neck, pressing herself against him, grinding.

Jax's tongue traced down from her ear to her clavicle. He nibbled on her ear lobe, and Koa felt heat and desire fill her body.

Koa reached for his belt buckle, intent on satisfying this animalistic craving, when her watch buzzed.

They both paused at the sudden sound.

Koa, flushed and haphazardly dressed, felt her entire body pale of color and go numb when Halston's image appeared beside her.

He looked them over, made no indication that he cared about what he witnessed, and rested his serious eyes on Koa.

"Halston," Koa croaked, hopping off the desk to fix herself.

"Meet me at the Gate in the morning. I should be there at 9 am sharp."

Koa nodded. "Of course." She smoothed her hair. "Are you all right?"

Halston looked from her to Jax. "9 am sharp," he repeated and cut the connection.

Koa felt her heart sink into her stomach. She couldn't even look at Jax as she flew from the room and went up to keep her promise to Lindley.

All that went through her head as she waited in the elevator was Halston's words. "9 am sharp," she said with a nod. All desire had gone out the window the instant she saw Halston's face. "I'll be there, Halston. I'll be there bright and early."

CHAPTER 13

Koa entered her cottage and was welcomed by an eerie quiet. She only had a few hours before she needed to meet Halston at the Gate, and after a night with Lindley, she wanted to check on her former pet, Ian, and hoped to see her mother as well. Jax returned to the church the night before after Koa's abrupt departure. She wondered just how awkward things would be when she returned. It almost didn't matter.

Halston was safe. That's all that mattered. Now, seeing if Ian and her mother were doing all right would ease her mind further.

The drapes were still closed and everything was still.

All she heard was the ticking of the grandfather clock at the end of the corridor right off the stairwell landing. She stepped inside and her heels clicked along the stone floor.

Home. She had missed it. Still, it would never replace her father's manor, where she had spent most of her life. Koa had lived in many different places: South Korea, America, England, and the Netherworld, but she missed France the most. Her memories there were all of good times.

Koa felt a shudder run up her spine as she thought back to her time in the Netherworld. There was no doubt that the Netherworld was the worst of all the places that she'd lived. She didn't blame Halston for erasing her memories of that time. But now, they were all back, and she could not escape them.

Koa smelled something.

A familiar scent. Her eyes scanned the room. A terrible sense of fear and trouble filled her. Someone had been there, someone she never wanted to see again. And then. Koa remembered where she had smelled that scent before and was taken back to memories she wished she could forget.

There were hundreds of bedrooms; each with its own private bathroom. Dozens of kitchens. Nine dining halls. Seven grand ballrooms. Five libraries; one for each wing, and another massive one for the guests.

The Netherworld was Koa's prison, the Lyrinian palace her cell, and yet, she found a way to make it bearable. As she sat on the steps watching the hordes of creatures pass her by, Evina played with her hair.

Koa sighed as the vampire princess finished the long braid she made with Koa's black hair.

"Done."

Koa pulled the braid over her shoulder and looked at it. She'd never had her hair braided before. She smiled at her friend.

"Thank you," Koa said.

Evina shrugged. "No problem. You almost look like a Netherworlder now." Evina traced something on Koa's face. Her blue eyes narrowed as she examined Koa.

Koa chewed her lip, feeling odd under Evina's gaze. She couldn't help it. There was just something in the Netherworld vampire's eyes that made her feel exposed and uncomfortable. Even her father's eyes made her feel like hiding sometimes.

She thought of Jax. Her lips curled into a smile. Whenever he looked at her, she would blush, but Koa never turned away. She hid a grin from Evina. She looked forward to sneaking away with him again. It was all she had to look forward to.

Evina nodded. "Yes, I can see it now." She kept tracing shapes onto Koa's face. "You just need a few tattoos, right across your cheekbones."

Koa made a face. "Never."

Evina tilted her head. "Come on. Give it a shot. It will look amazing."

Koa shook her head as she looked at all of the tattoos that Evina had on her neck and at the corners of her eyes. They may have looked intriguing and beautiful on the vampire princess but Koa was certain that she'd look like a clown with tattoos on her face.

She turned up her nose. "Like I said… never."

Evina pushed her shoulder and shrugged. "Suit yourself, but the people will never accept you unless you start to act and look like us."

"That's fine with me."

Evina grinned. "Oh come on. We should start making sketches. I know just the artist."

Koa sighed and watched Evina pull a silver pen out of her purse and clicked it twice. The sound of tiny bells ringing made a few of her lady's maids and escorts glance over from their stations with vague interest, but once they saw what Evina was doing, they returned to looking ahead with expressionless faces.

Light collected around the tip of the pen and stretched outwards until hundreds of little blue dots seeped into the air. The dots combined and slowly transformed into identifiable shapes.

Evina frowned at the pen, shook it so vigorously that her black curls bounced around her face, and clicked it again. "This dammed thing needs to be looked at. It's awfully slow," she complained under her breath. "Jax's pen never does this."

Koa's mouth parted in wonder as the image of a pale male face floated across the air. His brows were too big and bushy for his skinny face, but they furrowed as he looked back at her.

It was as if the ghostly artist could actually see her. She twisted her mouth.

No. It's not possible, she thought. Apparently anything was possible in the Netherworld. Koa's cheeks paled as the artist drew strange characters onto a piece of parchment. Her face started to appear on that very parchment, with an intricate tattoo around her left eye.

Such an anomaly intrigued Koa. The image was outlined in silver and clung to the air like a ghost. It couldn't be real, and yet he seemed to see her, or knew her face well enough to draw it.

Koa rubbed her face. She didn't want to admit that the tattoo actually looked interesting. Instead, she frowned at Evina. "I'm never getting a stupid tattoo on my face." She gasped as the image floated through the air and hovered before her face.

The artist seemed to sneer at her but disappeared the moment Evina clicked her pen and tucked in back into her silver side purse. With the interesting images gone, Koa went back to ignoring her lady's maid, just as she had been doing all day.

"Come on, Koa. You can only reject your role as Netherworld royalty for so long. You'll have to get on eventually." Evina didn't seem to notice that Koa was intentionally ignoring her. "Perhaps something red. As I recall, it looked quite nice on you—your wedding dress."

Koa cringed; she wanted to forget her wedding day.

Evina spread her arms out towards the passing creatures. "Right now you look human." She gave Koa a sidelong glance. "And that's the last thing you want to look like in the midst of creatures that would love to take a bite out of you."

Koa gulped and looked down the narrow staircase at the crowded citadel. She was thankful that the tall gates at the bottom of the staircase separated her from the vampires, War-Breeders, Syths and Scayors. She'd been in the Netherworld for four years, and the citizens still frightened her.

"Come on," Evina coaxed. "Just one tattoo. Father will be pleased. Your sixteenth birthday approaches and..."

Koa felt a chill. She shot Evina a look that made Evina purse her lips and look away. Koa couldn't hide the hurt in her eyes. "Don't say it."

Evina covered Koa's hand with her own. She spoke softly. "Forgive me. I nearly forgot."

Koa stared at her, trying not to let the tears fall from her eyes. Evina lowered her head. Her voice came out cracked.

"I truly am sorry, Koa. I look at you like the little sister I never had. Sometimes I pretend that you are just that, and not my father's third wife."

As if on cue, Lera, second wife to King Greggan stepped between them. The skirt of her red gown brushed across Koa's face. Koa pursed her lips and glared up at the vampire queen.

"Watch where you're going," Koa warned.

Lera grinned, showing off her fangs. She knelt down to Koa's face. Grabbing her by her chin.

Koa tensed. She wanted to push that woman down the stairs. The smell of rosemary was strong. Lera seemed to bathe in it each day, for it followed her and lingered even when she left a room.

"Or what, little bug?" Her voice came out like a purr. Her violet eyes were full of hate despite her smug grin.

Koa didn't know what to say. What could she do?

Lera laughed lightly then. Koa was afraid of her. She'd seen Lera do things that she couldn't explain. Netherworld vampires have odd powers.

Evina, Jax, Greggan, Lera, and Lysett all had a certain skill for which they were known in the kingdom, and Koa still wasn't used to living amongst a bunch of beings that would be considered superheroes—or super villains—back in the human world.

Lera's violet eyes bore into Koa's. Koa pulled her head back and held her breath, afraid of what the vampire might do. She'd seen Lera chain a servant to the floor once, and had her guests strike the poor young vampire girl with fire whips.

"You walk around here like you're better than us." Lera sneered at her. "But you are not. You are a bug beneath my boot, and I will squish the life out of you if you get in my way. I am King Greggan's favorite, and I will remain that way. Do you understand?"

Koa couldn't help herself. Even though she was afraid, she sucked her teeth and made a face at Lera. "You think I want him?"

Lera tightened her grip on Koa's chin and Koa snatched her face away, flailing the back of her hand at Lera's face, except Lera caught the blow with one hand and Koa's throat in the other. She squeezed. The squad of Syths stepped forward.

Evina was on her feet, with one hand on Lera's shoulder.

Lera hissed in Koa's face. Koa struggled to breathe.

The Syths bowed. "With respect, Queen Lera. We have orders to not let anyone harm the Queen Koa, not even you. Forgive us."

Lera ignored them, but somehow Evina's hand on her shoulder made her pause.

"You'd better listen and take your hands off of her," Evina ordered. Koa was so surprised by the authority in the princess' voice, even she shot a look at her, despite being unable to breathe.

Lera looked from Evina's tattooed hand back to Koa's face. "Remember my words, *little bug*. Either way, he will kill you." Her voice lowered to an almost inaudible whisper. "But if, for some reason, he doesn't, *I will*."

Lera released Koa, shrugged Evina's hand off her shoulder, and pulled a black disc from her belt. She opened her disc. Like a fan, the electronic device opened and hovered before her. She hopped onto it and with one last glare, flew away.

The smell of rosemary wafted into Koa's nostrils and as she was brought back to the present, she knew: Lera was not dead.

She had been there. In her home.

CHAPTER 14

Koa panicked. "Raven?" She needed to see her mother.

The smell of Lera lingered and she couldn't help the immediate sense of dread. She tore through the house like a maniac. She flew up the stairs, her breaths quick and her heart thumping. With each door that she swung open and found empty, the fear intensified.

Her skin crawled. Her face drained and she began to sweat. Breathless, she went through every room in the small cottage.

"Ian?"

Nothing.

She landed on the floor at the bottom of the staircase. She rubbed her temples and groaned. She was exhausted. She still hadn't slept. For some reason, Koa was afraid to sleep. She couldn't place why. Perhaps she wasn't comfortable sleeping until she knew Bund was dead and Greggan was either sent back to the Netherworld, or dead as well.

Koa walked past the stairwell and went towards the kitchen. Her shoulders fell. She breathed with relief when she saw Ian sitting at the table writing in a notebook. Koa almost felt at ease when she saw his charming smile. Something familiar. She needed that.

"My god, I was worried." Koa was happy to see her first and only sire. Once her pet, she loved Ian like a brother. She couldn't see herself turning another human into a vampire, especially since she had turned Ian almost completely by accident.

One night, full of rage for being fired by Halston from the Netherworld Division, she had drunk way too much of Ian's delicious blood and nearly killed him. She only turned him because she knew she couldn't live with his death on her memory.

She walked to the cabinet at the back of the kitchen and grabbed a coffee mug. She would have never recovered from the depression if Ian had died on that night.

"*You* were worried?" Ian repeated. "I had no idea where you were! You just disappeared for days."

Koa glanced back at him. She was touched that he was concerned. It felt good to be missed. She admitted, she had missed him as well.

She sighed. "Long story." She looked around the kitchen. If Lera had been there before, she couldn't possibly be there now. The sun's light filled the room.

Koa almost felt safe.

Almost.

"Have you been to see Lindley? She was in pretty bad shape."

Koa nodded silently. Lindley's miserable face would linger in her memory for days. She had already resolved to take better care of her.

"She really bonded with you. I don't know if I even bonded as completely as Lindley did." Ian drank some juice. "You left me plenty of times, and I never had such a mental break."

"I took care of her."

"Did you?"

Koa sighed. "Yes. I set her up in a nice flat in Kensington. She has a pretty generous allowance as well." Koa gave him a look. "She's fine."

Ian cleared his throat. "Funny how money can buy *most* things. I wonder if it will ease her troubled mind though. You did leave her again."

"Well, Ian, when I picked her she told me that she wanted to be taken care of. I did that. Enough of the criticism. I can't take her everywhere with me, can I?" She started to prepare coffee, angrily ripping open a new box of sugar packets. "Where is Raven? Have you seen her?"

"Not in a couple of days. She vanished a little after you did. What's with you women? Don't you know I'm like a child? I cannot be left alone, unsupervised for too long."

Koa frowned. That didn't make her feel any better. She needed to see her mother.

Where could she be?

She turned the coffee maker on and turned to Ian. His youthful face was even brighter as a vampire. She leaned against the sink and rubbed her temples. Where could Raven be?

"That's odd."

Ian's eyes widened. "A mother for a cat is odd."

Koa shot him a look. Her face reddened. "Don't call her that. Not even in public."

"Oh yes," Ian said. "I forgot."

She thought of all the times her mother had told her that same thing. She also remembered calling her mother in front of the demon, Bund. She'd ruined their secret, and now Greggan knew that her mother had been cursed to live as a cat. And now, Koa knew that the curse was the only thing that had kept Raven safe from the vampire king's agents for so long.

Koa felt a pain in her stomach. She was worried. She missed her mother.

Ian glanced past her. He nodded to the open window. "It's a beautiful day, isn't it?"

Koa followed his gaze. Birds were chirping, the sun was shining, and a nice breeze wafted into the kitchen, bringing a sweet scent of freshly cut grass.

Koa shrugged. "Yeah, I guess."

Ian cracked a grin and stood. He was taller than her, and thin. His black hair was still messy was ever, but his hazel eyes were his best feature. He nodded as he approached her.

Koa's brows furrowed. "What are you grinning at?"

Ian shrugged, but that goofy grin was stuck to his face. "I just want to get a closer look at this lovely day. I mean, the sun is magnificent, wouldn't you say."

Koa frowned and looked up at him. He had such a nice face. The sun highlighted his freckles and the tiny speckles of green in his eyes.

He leaned in closer. She expected him to kiss her when realization washed over her.

"What the…" She gasped. Her eyes widened. The sun shone directly on Ian's face.

The sun is shining, she thought.

"Ian!" Koa screamed. "Get back in the cellar!"

Ian grabbed her shoulders. He brought his face close to hers. His grin widened even more.

"Took you long enough to notice."

Koa couldn't believe what she was witnessing. She shook her head. "No. This cannot be right." She stared at him, mouth agape. "I must have done something wrong." She covered her mouth with her hands. "You must not be a vampire."

Ian chuckled and leaned against the counter beside her. "I assure you, I am. I've been craving blood every night since you turned me, and I've been feeding from my new pet, Emily, ever since I chose her at the ceremony back at Wryn Castle."

Koa shook her head. "No Ian. You don't understand." She ran her hand through her bangs, getting them out of her face so that she could get a better look at her sire. "Vampires cannot walk in the sun! That's just how it is."

Ian gave her a look. His mischievous smile never faltered. "Really? And yet *you* can walk in the sun."

"Yes. But I am different. I'm not a full vampire."

Ian nodded. "I see. You created me, Koa. I must share that with you then. It makes perfect sense. Doesn't it?"

Koa began to speak but closed her mouth. Ian was right. He was her first and only sire.

"Holy Hell," Koa whispered as she reached over to touch his face. His skin was still smooth, although cold to the touch. She missed his warmth, but she would rather have him alive than have to bury him.

"You're right."

She cracked a smile. "I've never turned anyone before. You are my first. I now see why Greggan wants me. He wants whatever trait my mom passed down." Koa looked at the floor. Her smile faded. "Damn."

"What's wrong?"

Koa covered her face with her hands. "This is not good."

"No, it's great! I don't have to hide out in the daytime. I can be like you. I can finish school, and live a normal life again." Ian frowned. "I thought you'd be happy."

Koa shook her head. Her stomach was full of anxiety. "Imagine a world with vampires roaming the streets in the daytime. The Netherworld Division wouldn't be able to monitor them. The humans wouldn't have a chance. That is what King Greggan wants."

Ian frowned. His wavy, black hair fell over his eyes and he ran a hand over it to pull it back. "Who is King Greggan?"

Koa sighed. She motioned for Ian to follow her out of the kitchen. "I fear you're going to find out very soon."

She had to get to the Gate to meet with Halston. Koa took Ian's hand.

"You're coming with me. Halston *has* to see this."

CHAPTER 15

Tunes fell from the sky once Halston approached the Gate. A squat little creature, Tunes resembled a goblin. His skin was scaly and dry, and when he wasn't glamouring himself, he was completely bald. Tunes peered at young Roderick with bulging black eyes.

"What's *he* doing here?" Tunes looked up at Halston. His eyes narrowed and he scratched his scabbed over scalp. "You're just letting all kinds of creatures out, Master."

Halston gave him a stern look. "Open the Gate, Tunes."

Tunes nodded. He glanced at Roderick once more. The boy smiled at him. Tunes had no idea just how powerful Roderick was. Tunes played a note on his silver violin and then used the bow as a key.

A loud clinking sound resonated throughout the entire valley on the other side, as well as the dark cavern of Shadows behind Halston.

He looked over his shoulder. The Shadows were being obedient. They hadn't been so obedient when he'd brought Koa there days ago. Now, they were bowed low for him, as if frozen.

Halston entered the human world and breathed in the fresh air. It smelled like home, and yet this was not really his home. Roderick recited rap verses behind him like a poet recites his best work. Halston looked down at him with a side grin, amused.

Somehow, when Roderick rapped it just sounded right, like he had discovered a new language. That was when Halston realized the power in the boy's words. Roderick had found a way to combine his spells with the music he had grown to love.

The Alchemist, grand wizard and immortal being, loved human culture above all things. Halston couldn't help but grin as he watched the grass grow taller at Roderick's words. The flowers bloomed bigger, the air smelled sweeter, and Halston felt oddly joyful.

Roderick looked up at Halston, and still rapping, he winked.

Halston shook his head but chuckled. He was tired, but somehow he felt certain that he'd made a good choice letting the Alchemist come along.

The rapping stopped, and all was quiet.

"So," Roderick said, looking up.

In the light of the sun, his face was almost translucent. Halston had never seen anything like it before. Roderick almost looked like a ghost.

"That's what a real sun looks like?" Roderick spoke softly, in awe of his first glimpse of the human world.

Halston followed his gaze. The sun had the most power in their world. It was beautiful and humans took it for granted. The sun protected them from vampires.

"It's even more beautiful than you said." Roderick looked around in wonder. His childlike face smiled. "Pictures don't do it justice. Why didn't you bring me here sooner?"

Halston looked down. A new form of vampire had now arrived. Greggan wanted Koa for one thing, and that was to produce vampires that could dwell in the sun.

"I agree with you," Halston said, nodding. He checked his watch. Koa should be heading back to the safe house with Tristan and the others by now. "Pictures don't do it justice."

Roderick looked up as the sun's light spilled through the canopy of trees above. Halston froze. Roderick became almost completely translucent. Roderick took a step forward, and cried out. He seemed to hit an invisible wall that made his entire body flicker, disappear, and reappear.

Halston reached out to the boy. "Are you all right?"

Roderick cringed. He held a hand out and touched the invisible wall. Once again, his body slowly began to face. His voice seemed to come from far away. "Halston! Pull me back!" Half of Roderick's body was sucked into the wall. The boy's cried filled the valley that surrounded the Gate.

Halston moved quickly. He grabbed Roderick's arm and yanked him from the force that seemed to pull back.

Halston knew then that he would not be able to bring the Alchemist along.

Roderick seemed to know it as well. He fixed his clothing and felt his face, making sure it was still there, and not fading any longer. When he gazed at Halston, the look of disappointment on his young face was heartbreaking.

"Roderick," Halston said. His shoulders slumped. He was disappointed as well. They could use the help of someone like Roderick. There was no one else in existence that could do the things that boy could do. Besides that, he had grown to like Roderick, almost like a younger brother.

Roderick sighed. "You're just going to leave me here, aren't you?"

Halston looked away. The tears in Roderick's eyes bothered him. He already had enough worries and heartbreak. The look on Koa's face when he had to leave her haunted him every second of the day.

"You have to stay. Somehow, the human world rejects you. I don't think you were ever meant to leave the Netherworld."

Roderick's face twisted with sorrow. "But why? I never harmed anyone. How is it fair that vampires get to roam free and I am stuck in that horrid place?" He pointed at the Gate as tears trailed down his cheeks. "All I ever wanted was to see a real human. Please. Help me."

With a sharp lump in his throat, Halston put a hand on Roderick's small shoulder. Seeing the boy look so devastated cut to his core. He tightened his jaw, and tried to look brave, for Roderick. "I'll find a way to let you out one day Roderick."

Roderick looked up at him with big brown eyes. He looked hopeful.

"But right now, I have more important things to worry about. I hope you understand. If I don't there might not be any humans left."

Roderick's face darkened. He pursed his lips and gave Halston a look that made him looked significantly less like a child and more like the being that creatures all over the Netherworld's many levels feared.

Roderick turned back towards the Gate. "We shall see."

Halston wanted to say more but the words wouldn't come to him. He watched Roderick return to the Gate and speak to Tunes. Tunes glanced at Halston questioningly.

Halston nodded and Tune's opened the Gate. Roderick stepped inside and looked back at Halston one last time.

Halston held his breath. Roderick's pale face shone in the dark as he grabbed the bars of the Gate. Then, he vanished into the darkness, and Halston was left alone.

"Halston," a familiar voice shrieked with joy.

Halston didn't turn right away. He smiled to himself, thrilled to hear her voice again. Everything he did seemed to be for her. But somehow he felt as if he could not let her know that. He could not let her see that she meant so much to him. And so, his smile faded into a stern look as he turned to face her.

There she was, standing in the sunlight with her hair gently swaying in the light breeze. Her eyes were creased at the corners as she beamed at him. His heart thumped in his chest. He wanted nothing more than to swoop her up in his arms, swirl her around, and kiss her like she'd never been kissed before.

Instead, his shoulders slumped and he looked past her, at her sire. Seeing him stand behind her… in the sun, changed everything. It was exactly what he was afraid of.

"Koa," Halston said with a nod. He walked past her without another look and made his way to his car. "Keys."

Koa, devastated, tossed his keys to him and got in the back seat without a word.

Ian, confused by what just happened, sat in the passenger's seat, filled with the excitement of a little boy on a quest for adventure.

Halston had to hide his hands as they shook. He wanted to hold her so badly. He took a deep breath and got in the car, turned the ignition, and started for the church safe house.

He risked a look back at her through the rearview mirror and saw the glassy look of tears in her eyes. His heart broke at that look, but this time, he would put duty first. The humans needed him more than Koa did.

"*So*, who are you anyway?" Ian asked.

Halston looked ahead. Koa shushed Ian.

"What? I haven't been introduced!" Ian exclaimed. "And what was that creepy gate you came out of?"

CHAPTER 16

Alice surveyed the massacre. The sun rose, and so they were safe… for now. A cool dawn and faded sunlight shone down on an old farmhouse that was burnt to the ground.

All of the livestock had been slaughtered. Cows and sheep lay scattered around the grounds as if someone had simply run through the fields, cutting them down with an axe. The flies buzzed around the bodies with glee. What a feast had been laid out for the vultures and scavengers.

The poor family had been murdered, bled dry, and pinned to stakes in the ground for all to see. Two young women around the ages of twenty and twenty-five, a boy of about ten, and the mother, father, and grandmother. All dead, all with their eyes ripped out and mouths sewn shut.

It seemed that no matter where they went, that death and destruction had already made an appearance. Raven felt as if she was going to be sick. She'd seen so much in her long life that she should have been prepared for this.

The smell of burnt flesh lingered in the air making Raven gag. She looked up at Alice with tears in her eyes.

"More children?" Her heart beat in her chest like a tiny drum.

She yawned. Raven was weary from running around with Alice from crime scene to crime scene. There was no rest for the pair. They were tracking a demon, and would not stop until they found him.

Alice nodded. Her face was serious, angry, and pale. "That bastard," she growled. "I will pound his ugly face with my fist and chop his skinny body into tiny pieces."

The firemen were frozen as Alice and Raven looked over the damage. An old house had been burned down. It was apparent that the fire had started in the basement and destroyed everything.

But with Alice's gadgets she had surmised that there had been fourteen young bodies. She could actually view the scene with absolute clarity. Raven imagined what would happen if the humans had their hands on such technology, just how many crimes would be solved. With the device in Alice's hand, she pulled up the scene, and they watched Bund hang the girls by their heels.

They watched him taunt and tease them, feed from them, and then, they watched Greggan enter the room and set it on fire. The only thing that was missing, was the sound. They had no idea what was said between Greggan and Bund, but it was clear that the demon was not happy with Greggan's actions.

Raven stood on a stone step and watched Alice look over the ashes and remains of the old farmhouse. A buzzing sound drew her attention. Alice raised a brow and looked down at her watch. She pressed a button and shot to her feet when Halston's image pulled up before her.

Raven ran over to get a better look. She was too afraid to hope or feel joy yet. She needed to hear what he had to say. Halston was fine, but where was her daughter?

"Well," Alice began. She folded her arms. "Took you long enough, Mr. Boss Man."

Halston looked around at the burnt logs and piles of rubbish and ash. "What happened here? Any luck with tracking Bund's whereabouts?"

"While you were off playing around in the Netherworld, rescuing damsels and breaking princes out of prison, Greggan and Bund haven't wasted time with making the humans fearful to leave their homes. It is a real shit show out here, Halston. Greggan made an announcement on the BBC that he is making a change to this world. He told the humans to stay in their homes until the "transition" is over. He says that he wants to take the VRS from a secret agency to a global scale. No human will have a say, and that they will all be at the mercy of vampires."

"What a fool." Halston didn't look surprised. "Meet me at the old church as soon as you can get here. I'll wait for you two."

Alice raised a brow. "Oh, will you? I'm honored."

"Viktor wants me to report to him at headquarters. I need you to look after the others while I'm gone."

"Like a *babysitter*?"

"Where is Koa? Is she all right?" Raven cut in.

Halston nodded. His face softened when he looked down at Raven, as did his voice. "She's fine, Raven. She will be here at the church when you two arrive."

"We're on our way," Alice said.

Halston gave a nod. "Take care, you two."

Alice nodded. "We will. You do the same."

Halston's image faded as he cut the connection and left Alice and Raven in silence.

Alice rolled up her sleeves and took a deep breath. "We'd better get a move on then."

Spoons came sniffing along, in the form of a jackal. He stepped in the center of what used to be the basement and dug his nose in the ash.

"Not even a piece of meat left for me," he growled, disappointed.

Alice rolled her eyes. "Stop complaining. I let you eat that body back at the library crime scene. Shouldn't you be full for a couple of days?"

Spoons looked up at her, with the same ice blue eyes that he had in his true form. It looked strange on a jackal. "I'm always hungry."

"Well, tough luck."

Raven put a paw on Alice's leg. "Can we head to the church now? I need to see Koa. Please."

Alice smiled and picked Raven up. She nuzzled her neck. "Of course. We'll go there now." She looked over to Spoons. "Do you still have his scent?"

Spoons nodded. "I do. Where the two of you's goin?"

"We are headed to the safe house to meet with Halston, you keep tracking Bund until I meet up with you again."

"Right, leave me to do all da work. Jus like ya angels. Lazy bastards."

Alice let out a long breath and shook her head. She ran up the stone stairs with Raven in her arms and into the cool afternoon. A group of onlookers had appeared, confused by the frozen firemen and the damage to their neighbors' farm.

One of the teens stood before the stake to which one of the farmer's daughter had been nailed. His face was white as a sheet of paper and his breaths came fast. He was on the verge of an anxiety attack. A few moments longer and the kid would surely start screaming his head off.

Alice cursed under her breath and sat Raven down on the grass. "Go on, hun, stand back."

Raven did as she was told. She knew what Alice was about to do. She'd only seen the angel do it a couple of times, when their cover was almost blown by a few nosy humans. Freezing cops and police officers was a simple task for Alice, but when other humans came into the mix and actually saw what she'd done, it took more than a little freezing of their muscles and minds.

Alice stepped before the two older women that stood at the gate, a smile on her pretty little face. The women looked at her with fear, and stepped back.

"Hey ladies, what a lovely day it is, isn't it?" Alice lifted a hand and the teen boy was lifted from the ground. She tilted her neck and he yelped as she sent him flying across the field and dropped him beside his family. She dusted her hands and looked them over.

"So, is it just the three of you then?"

"Y...yeah." The women held onto one another and the boy scrambled to his feet to join them in their frightened huddle.

Alice nodded. Her smile remained friendly, and soothing, but it was too late, the humans had already seen too much. "Good. Now," she ran her hands through her short pink hair and clicked her teeth. "Let's say we play a little game."

Raven's eyes widened as she stood far away and watched Alice levitate off the ground. The woman started to scream but Alice muted their voices somehow. Then, she started to glow.

Rings of light encircled her body, crisscrossing and shooting up and down from her feet to the top of her head. The women and the boy watched her with stunned awe. They knew it then, that she was an angel, and their faces softened into looks of wonder.

Raven was unsure of what they saw, but their faces went from contorted horror to looks of joy and relief. Alice's angelic glow softened against the humans faces and bathed them in feelings of happiness and serenity that would have a completely opposite reaction to any form of nephilim. It was why Alice told Raven to step away.

Raven lowered her head as she watched. She was a nephilim, a supernatural spawn of the fallen angels. Not vampire, or Syth, Jem, or anything she'd ever seen or read about; Raven was a new breed. Even so, Alice's angelic glow would have killed her.

Raven was reduced to tears as she thought of how the beauty of what Alice did to the humans would have burned her from the inside out and sent her into episodes of agony until she was nothing but ash.

It was then that Raven felt her first wave of doubt. The angels were there to clean up the mess they began centuries ago. They were to either eliminate or find a way to separate the nephilim from the humans. There was no changing that both she, and Koa, were nephilim.

Neither was exempt from the wrath of God and his agents.

CHAPTER 17

Returning to the church with Ian in tow and Halston leading the way, Koa assumed that she would feel at ease now. She had imagined smiling and feeling full of joy to have her best friend back. However, her stomach was in more knots than she thought was possible. She felt sick, on the verge of vomiting.

The entire ride, Halston was in a strange mood. She'd expected a completely different reunion. She expected hugs and tears of joy, not the cold, stern, greeting she'd received.

Ian's constant chatter and non-stop questioning did little to break the tension. Koa began to wonder what happened to Halston in the Netherworld. What made him turn cold on her?

Am I the crazy one? Koa wondered such things as she walked into the church for the first time. So much wood. The walls were wooden as well as the pews. Ian stepped inside and sat his backpack on one of the pews. He folded his arms as he looked around.

"I can already feel it, Koa," he said with a nod. A smile spread across his face and Koa frowned.

"What, Ian? Why are you smiling?" She leaned against the wall and watched Halston go through the door that led to the lower level and the catacombs. He never looked back at her. She shook her head as an unsettling feeling flooded her.

What did I do wrong?

Ian sat on the back of one of the pews and faced her. "We are going to have a blast, you and I. And that surly blonde dude."

Koa shook her head and cracked an uneasy smile. She lowered her voice as she leaned closer to him. "Halston is no 'dude.'"

Ian laughed.

Koa laughed as well. "And I'm not sure if we're going to have a blast. I don't think you know how serious this all is. We are not playing video games here."

Ian folded his arms. "Oh but I do. I saw that BBC thing that's all over YouTube. That Greggan guy made an announcement about changing the VRS and a bunch of other stuff. He claims he's a king and plans to rule over all the vampires while making the humans feed us."

Koa stood and stepped closer to him. Her face paled. "What?"

Ian nodded. "Yeah, you haven't seen the videos? They're all over the place now. I even embedded it into my blog."

Koa took Ian's hand and pulled him along behind her. She went over to the door Halston had disappeared into. The brass handle was rusted and scraped her hand as she turned the knob.

She paused at the top. Darkness welcomed her. The staircase trailed deep into the Earth. The darkness below made her uncomfortable. Koa knew that only horrible things happened in the dark. A flood of fear crept onto her, making her skin tighten and her throat swell. Bad things entered her mind.

Memories.

Not just the memories of the things Koa had seen and done with the Netherworld Division, but the memories that Jax had returned to her. The Netherworld had nearly killed Koa. She struggled to force those memories from her mind. Standing above a dark staircase threatened to cripple her.

Koa's shoulders slumped. She had to get over her fear of the dark and her fear to face her past. The things that had been done to her in the Netherworld.

Koa swallowed. It was strange being half vampire and still afraid of the dark.

She clenched her jaw and pulled Ian along.

"Hey, what's the rush?" Ian asked from behind. "I can walk without you holding my hand."

Koa let go of his hand and glanced over her shoulder. Her brows furrowed. "I'm sorry," she apologized.

Ian shrugged. He smiled. Such a warm friendly smile was a gift to her in these times of fear and doubt. She was glad that she brought him along.

"It's fine. I was only joking. You can hold my hand whenever you want." Ian winked and Koa snickered.

She turned back to the dark stone corridor and caught sight of a row of doors. On either side were large wooden doors, but Koa could hear voices coming from the door at the very end.

"I just need you to tell Halston and the others what you just told me about that BBC video."

Koa walked quickly to the final door and pushed it open.

Tristan greeted her with a stern look. Koa noticed that the door lead to another hallway, one with lights. Tristan was just about to leave. He nearly blocked all of the light as his large body seemed to fill the entire doorway.

He looked over Koa's shoulder and gave Ian a strange look. "Who is that?"

Koa put her arm around Ian's waist. Pride shone on her face. "My sire. Ian, meet Tristan."

Ian held his hand out. Tristan lifted an eyebrow and stared down at Ian's hand. He gave Koa a sidelong glance. He gave her a sidelong smirk. Mischief twinkled in his eyes. "I didn't know you had it in you."

Koa poked Tristan in the abdomen. His stomach was as hard as stone. "Yes you did," she grinned.

Tristan chuckled and looked Ian over, either ignoring his outstretched hand or unsure of just what to do with it.

"Where are the others?"

Tristan nodded to another door. "Just through that door."

Ian finally lowered his hand and gripped the handles of his backpack.

"Where are you going?" Koa asked Tristan.

He pulled a cylindrical bottle out of his leather side bag. He held it up before her face. His already narrow brown eyes narrowed even more as he looked at her through the glass. "Going to bottle up some sunlight."

Koa raised a brow but didn't question it. Anything was possible with Halston's inventions. "Have fun with that," she said and walked over to the other door. "Come on, Ian." She expected to be greeted by a damp, cold, basement.

Koa looked around in disbelief. She should have known better. The basement was oddly modern. Gadgets, electronics, sleek furniture and prototypes of Halston's inventions were everywhere. It was a lovely sight that reminded her of Halston and their time as partners. She did a 360 and stepped back when she saw Jax. He glanced up from a giant tome that he was reading.

His blue eyes lit up when she looked at him, and his quiet confidence made her look away. There was something about the way Jax looked at her that made Koa feel self-conscious. Whenever those blue eyes rested on her, she felt as if he were studying her, and it made her uneasy.

With a nervous nod, Koa acknowledged his presence and quickly crossed to the other side of the room. She didn't want to think too much of the night they kissed. She felt guilty, as if she'd betrayed her feelings for Halston. She didn't have room in her head to worry about such things right then.

Evina sat on the edge of a white leather sofa, and filed her nails with a knife.

"When can we leave this place?" Evina came to her feet and held her hands in the air while turning in a circle. "You mentioned shopping…"

Koa leaned against one of the stone columns and folded her arms. "Talk about priorities, Evina," Koa said. She avoided Jax's eyes. He was still watching her. She saw him sitting in front of Halston's computer station in her peripheral vision.

"You brought someone with you," Jax said, closing the tome and coming to his feet. He approached Ian like a curious child. He spoke about Ian as if he wasn't standing right there. "21 years old." He looked at Koa. "Freshly turned." He shot a look back at Ian. "Another day walker."

Koa's jaw dropped. "How did you know that?"

"You're making a habit of underestimating me. Which is fine." Jax smiled and turned from Ian, who was content with exploring all of the gadgets lying about. "I enjoy surprising you."

"New vamp?" Evina eyes brightened and she followed Ian. "Come here," she ordered him.

Ian paused and raised a brow to Koa. "Should I listen to her?"

Koa laughed. "I would."

Evina pressed her bosom to Ian's chest and laced her fingers through his black hair. He swallowed hard and his cheeks flushed as he looked at her. Her face was close enough to kiss and Ian seemed visibly uneasy.

"Not bad, Koa," Evina whispered as she touched his cheeks and ran her finger over his full lips. "He's not bad looking. Not bad at all."

Koa watched Halston who typed away at a computer station. He seemed to be in another world and she did not want to disturb him.

Evina turned on her heels and came grinning over to Koa. "Can I have him?"

Koa scrunched up her brows and glanced over at Ian who still stood there completely still with a strange look on his face. She gave Evina a look. "Don't even think about it."

Evina chuckled. "Stingy." She pointed at Koa with a long finger and red manicured nails. "You cannot have all of the attractive guys, Koa. First there's my brother, then there's Halston, *now* a new guy. Come on, share a little."

Koa's cheeks burned red. She tried to hide her embarrassment from Evina's comment and walked over to a glass cabinet stocked with liquor. She had to admit, Halston had everything covered with this safe house. It was like a bunker full of everything they could possibly need if they needed to lay low.

She sat on the counter top and opened a bottle of carmia. She drank it down and opened a bottle of tequila.

"Drinking so early?" Halston asked without looking up.

Koa shrugged. "To help me sleep."

"The War-Breeder seems to be sweet on you," Koa tried to change the subject. She drank a shot of tequila. Her favorite.

Evina scoffed. She faked a laugh. "Please. Do I look like I'm interested in a War-Breeder? Netherworld royalty do not intermix with the other races. No thanks."

Koa shrugged and downed another shot of tequila. She sucked in a breath. "Suit yourself. Big man like that, fairly attractive considering the scars, and he likes you. Why not give him a chance? Because Ian, and Halston, are off limits." She immediately regretted that last statement. She swallowed and felt her cheeks burn with embarrassment.

Jax frowned at hearing it, but didn't say a word.

Surprisingly, Evina kept her mouth sealed as well. They both looked at her with knowing eyes. Koa cleared her throat and poured herself another shot.

Her arm froze midway to bringing the shot glass to her mouth when she heard something come down the stairs. The sound of tiny feet.

Koa smelled a familiar scent, one that brought her to her feet and made her set her shot glass down.

"Mother," Koa shouted. Tears instantly filled her eyes and she squealed with delight when her mother ran to her. Koa ran to her and Raven leapt into her arms. Koa fell to her knees and closed her eyes. She embraced her mother and wept with joy.

Raven purred. She was soft and warm, but their embrace would never be the same as when her mother was free of her curse.

"My dear Koa! You made it back to me again."

Koa nodded and let the tears fall into her mother's black fur.

"I did!"

"Halston kept his word, again." Raven pulled back and looked at Koa with big, green eyes. "I knew he would. He always does what he says he will."

Koa squeezed Raven to her bosom again. "I missed you, mama." It felt so good to have the freedom to call her that again.

"I missed you too, dear."

Koa smiled and sat on the floor stroking her mother's fur.

A young woman came down the steps. She was a pretty girl. She stepped into the room with a wide smile. Koa looked her up and down. Tall, long legs, pink hair. She had big gray eyes and looked to have been blonde from the highlights in her pink hair.

There was something about her. An air of superiority. Koa could tell this mysterious intruder should not be taken lightly. Koa moved her mother aside and came to her feet. She brought her hand to the hilt of her sword.

"Well, this is a lovely reunion," the woman said. Her gray eyes scanned the room with a look of approval. "Halston. Brother," she said warmly.

Halston finally stopped working on his computer and stood.

"Welcome back, Alice," Halston said with a nod. "And you as well, Raven."

Jax and Evina gave her a quick bow. "Master Alice," they greeted in unison.

The girl made a sound with her tongue. "Oh, children. You don't have to call me master. We aren't in the Netherworld anymore. No one's watching… I won't tell."

Evina and Jax both looked at her and nodded. They looked afraid of her.

Alice turned her gaze to Koa. She approached her and Koa tensed. She looked confused when she hugged her.

"It's great to finally meet you, Koa. I've heard so much about you." Alice took the shot glass that Koa had set on the countertop and tossed the tequila into her mouth. She licked her pink lips and winked at her. "Where's the lime?"

Koa's mouth parted. Her eyes widened with realization. "You're Al? I mean Alice? I've heard of you," Koa said slowly. "You're a legend."

"Oh sweetheart." She gave Koa a fond look. "You're much sweeter than your reputation lead me to believe. How nice of Halston to finally let me meet you."

Koa nodded, unsure of how she felt about the statement about her reputation. She looked Alice over once more, intrigued by her sense of style. She couldn't believe how pretty Alice was. As an agent that preferred to be called Al when in the field, she could have easily have passed for a model. But of course, there wasn't an angel that Koa had met that wasn't attractive.

"Well you know how Halston is," Koa said.

Alice clasped her hands before her and looked up at Halston with inquisitive eyes. "So, Mr. Boss Man. I saw that giant War-Breeder outside filling vials with sunlight. Nice touch, I must say. Now, we have a prophet," she nodded to Jax. She pointed a finger at Evina. "A temptress."

Her gaze fell on Koa. "The half-blood and her mysterious banisher of a mother. Two angels, one of which is a pretty awesome metal-mind." She tossed her hair, referring to herself. "Spoons is our navigator."

Jax grinned. "You found Spoons?"

Alice nodded. "Did you doubt me?"

He shook his head and Evina smiled as well.

"Amazing," Evina said.

Alice turned to Halston. "Well…that seems to cover just about everything we need. We seem to have a pretty nice team put together. When do we start killing enemy vamps and banishing demons?"

"More importantly," Koa cut in. She walked over to Raven and picked her up from the floor. "When is Jax going to break my mother's curse?"

Koa looked from Halston to Jax. Halston stood from his desk chair.

His jaw tightened as he stepped over to Jax. The tension in the air was thick as they shared looks of loathing.

"Why don't you tell everyone what you did?" Halston said.

Koa felt her stomach bubble with anticipation. This is what she'd been waiting for. She could only imagine how Raven was feeling at that moment.

Jax looked past Halston and with a straight face, absent of emotion, spoke. "I can't break the curse. Only the Alchemist can."

Koa's face heated. She shook her head. "What?"

"The Alchemist gave me the spell to help your mother stay safe from Bund."

"And failed to mention that the Alchemist warned him that the spell was irreversible," Halston added.

Jax glared at Halston, who was a few inches taller than him. "I was getting to that."

"I can't believe it," Raven said.

The disappointment in her voice broke Koa's heart. All she wanted was to protect her mother and break her curse. It never occurred to either of them that Raven would be forced to live as a cat forever.

Halston turned to them. "Let's not lose hope now. I'm working to bring the Alchemist to this world. We will find a cure."

Koa hugged Raven close.

"It'll be all right, sweetheart," Raven whispered to Koa.

Koa only felt mildly comforted. She couldn't help but glare at Jax. She felt cheated somehow. She was under the impression that helping Jax escape the Ivory Tower would solve all of their problems.

Of course, Koa thought. *Nothing is ever easy.*

CHAPTER 18

Koa waited outside. Her hopes for a quick cure for her mother's curse were dashed. Now, they would have to find another way to stop Bund.

She chewed her nails as she watched for Halston. She stood far off into the forest, watching the churches door for him to exit. This was the moment she'd been hoping to have since they'd reunited. Just to have him alone, to find out what happened in the Netherworld and why he was acting so strange. She needed to know.

Halston stepped of the church's back door shortly after he told her to wait for him outside. She heard his boots crunching on dead leaves as he approached. Koa wasn't sure if she should be the first to speak or not. She decided against it and sat on a tree stump with her hands in her lap.

Her chest filled with hope as she watched him walk closer to her. He looked as perfect as ever. Not a single wrinkle or blemish tainted his sun-kissed complexion. His white blonde hair was a little disheveled and his bright blue eyes were a little dimmer than Koa remembered.

It worried her. There was something new in his gaze. There was a weariness that she wasn't used to.

"I didn't mention it earlier," Halston began.

Koa detected a small measure of nervousness in his voice.

Peculiar, she thought.

He glanced at her, and then at the sky, folding his hands behind him. In the clearing, the sun seemed to shine only on him, like a spotlight. Koa watched the sparkle of dust motes float around him in that perfect light.

He continued. "But I am glad that you made it out of the Netherworld safely."

Koa dared to smile. "I am glad that you made it out as well. I was worried about you."

Halston rested his gaze on her. His old mischievous smile hid in the corners of his mouth. "How many times have I told you not to worry about me? I am *your* boss. You're not mine. Leave the worrying to me."

Koa twirled the ends of her hair and nodded. "Yes, I forgot. Sometimes it's hard. That's why I prefer for you not to leave me like that. Don't do it again."

Silence stretched between the two as Halston looked her over and seemed to mull over her words. The silence wasn't an awkward one. They were comfortable within it. They didn't need words to fill in the blanks. They both seemed to know what needed to be said. And yet, neither said the obvious.

Koa began to wonder if it really was that obvious. "You won't leave me again, will you?" She sat on her hands, anxious for an answer.

Halston cracked his knuckles and sucked in a breath. "Yes, actually. I have to. I need to head to headquarters soon."

Koa came to her feet. She raised a brow. "Viktor?"

Halston nodded. His eyes landed on her and she felt encouraged to come closer. And so she did. She crossed the space between them and stood directly before him. She felt bold. She felt fear.

He reached out to touch her and Koa saw the fear in his own eyes. She held her breath. When he withdrew his hand, her chest deflated. All of the pent up anticipated vanished.

"Take me with you," Koa blurted. She took his hand in hers and pressed his palm to her face. She was tired of waiting and wondering.

Halston's eyes widened. Koa tilted her head to rest her cheek in the palm of his hand. It was warm. She missed his warmth. His touch wasn't cold like Jax's.

Koa refused to let him look away. To her surprise, he didn't. He raised his other hand and cupped the base of her head. Koa held her breath and closed her eyes as Halston rested his forehead against hers.

"I can't take you with me, Koa," Halston whispered.

Koa lowered her voice as well. "Why? Is it because Viktor doesn't like me?"

"No. Viktor doesn't like anyone really," Halston assured her. "He barely likes me, and we're brothers."

Koa looked up at him. She wrapped both arms around his waist and buried her face in his chest. "Please, Halston. I don't think I can handle being away from you again. I'll worry too much."

Halston laughed softly. He took her by the shoulders and held her out at arm's length. He smirked. He stroked her cheek. "What did I tell you about worrying about me?"

Koa smirked as well. "What did I tell you about leaving me?"

Halston sighed. His smile faded and he folded his hands behind him and turned away.

Koa's hands dropped to her sides in disappointment. She hated it when he turned his back on her. And so, she walked up to stand beside him. They both looked back at the old church.

She thought of the catacombs below. Dark. Creepy. Quiet. Jax and Evina would be safe from the sun there. They were probably sound asleep by now, preparing for the night ahead.

Koa's brows furrowed. She realized that she still hadn't slept. She wondered if she would be able to do so now that she knew that Halston was all right.

"I'm not leaving right away, Koa. There are a few things I need to take care of before I leave for Egypt. You can come with me."

Koa's eyes brightened. "Yes, I'll go anywhere. What do we have to do?"

Halston sighed. "We need to warn Lexi of Greggan's arrival."

Koa's smile faded. "Why? Is she in danger?"

Halston shook his head. "I don't think so, but she is Greggan's sire. He's sure to come for her. And she knows too much about you."

"Her loyalty to me is nothing compared to her loyalty to her master."

"I know," he said. "But we can try. I also want to make sure the humans there will be safe from what Greggan has planned."

"I was just there, and Lexi didn't come when I requested her," Koa said as she thought of how odd that was. One of the Wryn clan's leaders, Lexi had a crush on Koa and always spoke to her whenever she spent time in her castle.

Halston's jaw clenched. "Maybe he's already gotten to her."

"All right," Koa said. She checked that her sword was in its baton state at her side. "Let's go tonight. Let's not waste anymore time."

Halston stroked her cheek. Koa instantly felt warm all over at his touch.

"There's that fire I missed," Halston said softly. He withdrew his hand and checked his watch. In an instant he went back to being an authority figure.

"Tonight then. Let me brief the others first."

Koa stood there and watched as Halston started back for the church. She sat on the ground and smoothed the spot on her cheek where Halston had touched her. A smile came to her face. There was so much to do. They needed to kill Bund, Greggan, and break her mother's curse, but Koa decided to add one more thing to that list. She and Halston would be together.

Whether he knew it yet or not.

Part Two:

Netherworld Enemies

CHAPTER 19

"Tell me," Greggan began. He touched the rich velvet drapes and examined the tapestries. When he turned back, Lexi was on her knees, a blank look on her face. Silver barbed wire was wrapped around her neck but she did not flinch. She was indeed stronger than he had anticipated.

That made Greggan proud. She was one of his first sires, one of the first humans to whom he had passed the vampire strain in the ancient times.

Greggan remembered those wonderful days as if they had just happened moments ago. He was a young vampire back then. Young and full of ambition. He'd been free to roam the night and feast on human blood whenever he pleased. That is, until the angels came and forced them back into the Netherworld.

The Netherworld was created to give the vampires a home of their own, but to Greggan it had always felt like a prison. That's what it really was. While most of the nephilim had been vanquished by the great flood in Noah's time, the vampires and the other races found salvation in that very prison.

He sat down in his chair and rubbed his temples. His eyes looked across the room at Lexi. She was stoic.

"What do you know about the half-blood?"

Lexi didn't hesitate. She couldn't if she wanted to. As his sire, she could never hide anything from him. She looked up and her eyes watered for the first time. Greggan lifted a brow. After all of the torture, it was mention of Koa that made her resolve falter.

Lexi cleared her throat. She found a spot on the wall and fixated her dark brown-eyed gaze on it. She refused to look at Greggan while she betrayed a friend.

"She's filthy rich," Lexi began softly. "She used to live in France, but moved here only weeks ago. I don't know where she lives now. She comes about once a month to Wryn Castle to feed from her pet."

"Who is her pet?" Greggan interrupted.

Lexi shrugged. She flicked a worried look at him and looked away almost too quickly for him to notice. "Just an American girl. No one special."

Greggan nodded. "Come now, everything about the half-blood is special to me. Don't be shy. Tell me, do you know where this American girl is?"

Lexi swallowed. She shook her head of mahogany brown curls. "I do not know where she is, Master. Koa set her up with a new home somewhere in the city of London."

Greggan motioned for Trinity to come from his post against the exit. Trinity walked forward. He was a large Scath, cloaked in black to hide his hideous features. He had patches over both of his eyes. He stood behind Lexi and yanked her head back by a handful of her hair. To his surprise, Lexi did not struggle or cry out. She took the pain like a warrior.

"What is her name? And do not think to hide anything from me."

"Lindley Price," Lexi said through clenched teeth.

"What does she look like?"

Lexi dared to glare at him, even with her neck strained and her head held back. Greggan could see her veins pulsing with restrained anger.

"Why? What does it matter? She has nothing to do with anything."

Greggan made a signal to Trinity. Trinity pulled Lexi down to the floor, straddled her, and held a wooden stake over her heart.

Lexi paled. She swallowed and looked up at the ceiling. She knew that unlike her Netherworld ancestors, she was a New World vampire, one that was once human and turned… not born with the vampire trait. And that meant that once staked, she would not recover from such a fatal blow.

Trinity ripped the front of her black collared button-down blouse, exposing her full breasts. He pressed the sharp end of the stake into her milky white chest.

"Pardon my outburst, Master. She is about 5-foot-3, blonde bob, blue eyes, Southern American accent, petite, pretty."

Greggan nodded to Trinity. "Track her and bring her to me. Alive."

Trinity stood and left the room as silently as he had appeared. Greggan watched him vanish like a shadow. He drank a cup of fresh blood and watched Lexi lying on the floor. Trinity's appearance was effective. She was clearly too frightened to move.

He ran his finger around the rim of the cup and watched her chest rise and fall with her breaths.

"Get up," Greggan called with a tug of the silver wire that was wrapped around her neck.

She screeched as the wire tightened with the force with which he pulled her. She was brought to her feet by his tug alone.

His interest was sparked when he saw her mascara drip onto her cheeks. He'd made her shed tears.

He pulled her closer and closer until she was right before him. Her thighs stopped at his knees. She rubbed her eyes roughly with the back of her hand and breathed deeply. She avoided eye contact.

Greggan was almost disappointed that he had broken such a stoic vampire clan leader so quickly. It was amazing what forcing an individual to face their mortality could do.

Greggan sat up and put a hand on each side of her slim waist. Her silk blouse rested on his knuckles as he ran a hand across her belly.

He pulled her into his lap and she let out a little whimper.

"You're a quick learner, Alexis Cabane." He chewed on her soft skin with his teeth, leaving puncture marks on her breasts.

Lexi looked up at the ceiling with fresh tears in her eyes. She nodded. "Thank you, Master."

"Good. After we're done here, I need you to make me a list of every vampire clan in the country."

All the vitality had drained from her face. She was nothing more than a slave now, and she knew it. "Yes, Master."

CHAPTER 20

When they went back inside, Halston was no longer a friend, but Koa's boss. In front of the others, he would never be anything more than that. He simply nodded to the others and sat in front of his computer station. Everyone turned silent and watched him, waiting for him to say something.

Koa sat on the counter top and watched him, just like the others. The tension in the room was palpable. They wanted to know what they had been brought there for. What was the next move for this team of supernatural agents and soldiers?

"Halston," Alice called.

Halston held a hand up, silencing her. He went back to playing around with his computer system. There were five different flat computer screens encircling him, and he seemed to be studying each of them simultaneously.

Alice rolled her eyes. "Oh yes, you're in deep thought. Pardon."

They watched him, as patiently as they could until he stopped typing, swirled around on the swivel chair, and faced them.

He folded his hands in his lap and gave them each a look.

His gaze landed on Jax. His face was unreadable. "Jax, tell us about your latest prophecy."

"A grand ball."

Everyone but Koa kept a serious face. Koa laughed. "Why is that relevant to our plan?"

Halston unfolded his hands and put them on the arms of his chair. "Because Jax is a prophet. Every dream he has is important to our plan."

Koa made a face. "But a ball? Really?"

Jax nodded. "Yes, grand ball, like the one my father threw when you were presented to us. With vampires and humans together as equals. Except he isn't the one throwing the ball. He is not invited, and yet, he will be there."

Halston came to his feet, and made a perplexed face. "So he's crashing parties now?"

No one replied. It was apparent that he was asking himself that question.

"Not what I expected, but it's something we can work with."

Koa hopped off the counter top. "What are you thinking? Wryn Castle?"

Halston shrugged. "It could be at one of the many clan castles. Wryn seems the most likely."

"We need to warn Lexi and the others then," Koa said.

"Good thing we already planned on paying Lexi a visit. Are you ready?"

Koa nodded. "Yes."

"He'll likely exterminate them, and assert himself owner of their territory." Halston checked his infinity gun. He charged it by feeding some of his angelic glow to it.

"But Lexi, and the others, they never harmed anyone. They set up a system that keeps vampires fed and humans alive," Koa explained. "The system works, it has for centuries. How can Greggan come along and ruin it?"

"Koa, do you think he really cares about this 'system'?" Alice asked softly.

Evina shook her head. "Father cares about nothing, except being on top. The vampires up here, the turned ones, they are inferior to him. They are children and he is their father. The vampires up here carry part of our bloodline," Evina explained. "To King Greggan, they are his property, and if they don't cooperate, he will not think twice about killing them all."

"Who is King Greggan?" Ian asked. He looked alarmed. "He's going to kill Lexi and the other Wryn members?"

Koa walked over to him and sat on the arm of the sofa. She put an arm around his shoulder. She suddenly realized that she had put him in danger by turning him. She had inevitably put Ian on the wrong side of this war. Her stomach churned with dread. She touched his cheek. Ian was no longer warm. He was as cold as ice.

"I warned you about going there, Koa." Halston sighed and nodded to Ian. "Now we have a baby vamp to look after, amongst everything else on our plate."

"I had to do it, or he would have died."

Halston lifted a brow. "Always an excuse."

Koa bit her tongue. She understood that Halston had to be the authority figure. She didn't want to be insubordinate in front of everyone. She just hated being scolded. She would keep quiet now and address it in private later.

To her surprise, Spoons arrived. Koa watched him from the window of the church. The ghoul refused to come inside, so Halston and Alice had to go out to speak with him. It was still dark out and the upper level of the church was without electricity.

The ghoul was interesting to Koa. She'd seen them before, but Spoons was different. For a ghoul, he seemed to function at a slightly higher level. The fact that Alice was able to convince him to work with them was impressive.

Ghouls had no allegiance, no loyalty, and yet this one was tracking Greggan and his crew for them. She wanted to go out there and hear what he had to say, but Halston had her stay inside. So Koa trusted him, and waited.

Just as quickly as Spoons had arrived, he transformed into a ragged jackal and ran off into the dark woods. Koa leaned back on her heels at the sight. She'd never seen a ghoul do that before. Alice shot into the sky and Halston came back towards the church.

Halston opened the door and peeked inside. "Come on."

Koa nodded gleefully. She was ready for action. She ran to the door and slipped through with a quick wave to the others.

Once outside, Halston reached a hand out. She looked at it and a smile crept onto her lips. She took the hand and he gave her small hand a squeeze. "You handled yourself well in there," he said.

Koa laughed and slid her hand out of his. She leapt into the sky. "You underestimate me, Halston!"

He peered up at her and smiled. With a blast of air, he met her in the sky.

She was exhilarated. They hadn't flown together in ages. He motioned for her to follow, and together they made their way high into the clouds where they could fly undetected. The cool wind wrapped around her as if welcoming her back. She sucked in a cleansing breath. It felt good.

The Wryn clan needed her. A good friend needed her. Koa was eager to actually be of some use again. She was happy to have her Halston back.

CHAPTER 21

They flew for what felt like hours and Koa realized just how long it had been since she'd slept. Still, her adrenaline pumped through her veins and kept her awake. She was ready. She could sense the danger and it thrilled her. With Halston anything was possible, and she feared absolutely nothing.

She almost forgot the severity of the situation as they flew through the night sky towards Wryn Castle. The wind swept through her hair as she tried to keep up with Halston. They flew high above the clouds, where no one would see them. Koa sniffed the air as she flew. The clouds were dark and she could smell rain.

Koa smiled. She didn't want this time together to end. Jax was left behind with his sister and Tristan. She was glad for a small break from him. She needed to figure out exactly what she wanted and how she felt about him.

One thing was certain. She loved Halston, no matter what. That certainty gave her a sense of freedom. As they flew closer towards Wryn Castle, Halston began to slow his speed. He paused and hovered in the air. He held a hand out for Koa.

Eagerly, Koa accepted his hand and let hers slip into his grasp. He pointed to the castle. It stood on a rocky hill with its back against the dark sea. Waves tumbled and rolled and crashed against the rocks as the wind picked up. At first glance, Wryn appeared to be the same as always, but Koa could feel that something was wrong. She pursed her lips.

"See that?" Halston whispered as he held his hand out to point towards the front of the castle where the tall gate stood.

Koa narrowed her eyes and leaned forward. She gasped when she saw the dead bodies impaled on the sharp points of the black gates that enclosed the castle.

"We're too late," Koa breathed with horror. Thunder boomed loud in her ears. The rain followed, slapping Koa in the face as the wind seemed to direct it right towards her. Koa couldn't help but get the sense that the storm was trying to push her away from Wryn.

Halston didn't reply, he flew full speed to the castle and Koa had to use all of her energy to catch up. She fought the wind and rain and struggled to keep up.

Halston's speed was much greater than hers and he landed on the lawn right inside the gates. He darted towards the door of the castle too quickly for Koa's eyes. She breathed heavily as she ran to him.

Before she could catch her breath, he pushed the doors open and what they saw made Koa's blood turn cold.

Inside the doors of Wryn castle was a young man. No. He wasn't a man at all. He had the face of a young man of no more than twenty but Halston and Koa both knew the truth. He stood in the middle of the foyer with nothing but the silence and the darkness. The demon that killed her father, threatened to kill her mother, and promised to keep her as his pet for an eternity of torture waited before Koa and Halston.

Koa froze.

Bund stood there, pale, tall, and with a wicked grin on his face.

Koa's scream caught in her throat. He was the one creature that truly horrified her. His face was white as snow and almost translucent. He stood there with blood all over his clothes and face. His black hair was wild and fell over his face.

Even though he grinned, Bund seemed to be in another world. His eyes were glazed over and it was unsure if he even noticed that Halston and Koa had entered the room.

Koa touched Halston's back. He held a hand up, silencing her. Koa put a hand on her sword's baton.

"Well hello there, Halston. Finally decided to join in on the fun?"

Halston ignited his angelic glow and a surge of light pulsed from his body. Rings of golden light crisscrossed his body in circles, like hula hoops.

Koa stepped back from the heat so that she wouldn't get burnt. Bund's gaze darkened as he looked at Halston. "Always a show off." He pursed his lips. He held his arms out with his palms facing upward and his body slowly went into the air.

Halston stepped further into the castle and his angelic glow cut through the darkness all around. Every dark corner was illuminated by his light.

Koa finally saw the blood and bodies of some of the vampire staff.

Bile came up Koa's esophagus and she gagged when she saw Greta's body pinned to the wall behind her desk. Her skin had been ripped off from the neck down.

Koa balled up her fist. She bared her teeth. Greta did not deserve such a death. None of the people or vampires in Wryn castle did.

She watched Halston. Bund watched him as well.

"These vampires dared to challenge me," Bund said. He turned in a circle while in the air. "I do like playing with them though. I enjoy the looks on their faces when I drop the act." He chuckled. "I cannot wait to reveal my true intentions. I hope you're still alive to see what I have planned."

"When are you going to stop this, Bund? I'm tired of watching you play these games. What do you want?" Halston asked. "Why are you here?"

Bund laughed then. It was more of a cackle than a laugh. It started off jovial, but became more bestial and seemed to echo off the walls of the entire castle.

Koa's eyes darted around the room, searching for a brunette with shoulder length curls. None of the bodies fit the description, and she could not smell her cinnamon lotion.

"Where is Lexi?" Koa shouted.

Bund's gaze fell on her and his grin faded. Black veins appeared on his pasty white skin. His lips curled into an evil snarl, and he revealed sharp fangs. He pointed to Koa with one long finger.

Koa shuddered. She felt as if he saw into her soul. She felt an overwhelming sense of dread and fear when his eyes met hers. They were blue from what Koa remembered, but now, they were inky pools of black.

Koa's throat seemed to tighten. It was as if his cold hands had wrapped around her throat, and squeezed.

The corner of his mouth lifted into a grin.

"Her," he hissed. "I want *her*, Halston."

Koa's throat went dry as she drew her sword. She knew already from a previous battle with Bund that her sword would not work against him, but she needed something to give her strength, or else she feared that she'd embarrass herself in front of Halston by running away like a scared little girl.

"Yeah," Bund said as he clasped his hands and tapped his knuckles on his thin lips. He looked to be deep in thought as he watched Koa. "Give her to me, and I'll leave. I won't harm another person. I swear."

Koa let the power of the sword pulse into her. It was all that kept her feet planted to the ground. She feared what Halston would say. She didn't know what she wanted him to say. She did not want to suffer an eternity of pain with Bund, but she also didn't want more innocent people to die. Perhaps it would be best to just give in to his demands.

"Why do you want Koa so badly?"

Bund shot a glare at Halston. His face twisted into rage. "You know why!"

Koa winced. Bund's voice boomed throughout the entire castle. He was angry. Koa wondered what could have made him so angry so quickly. There was a sinister mystery to that demon. Something was not quite what it seemed to be. Koa was sure of that much. She was just too afraid to find out what it was.

"You already know that I can't let you take her," Halston said.

Koa breathed a sigh of relief. *Better to leave the big decisions to Halston*, Koa thought.

Bund shot down towards Koa with a snarl. Halston was faster. He met Bund in the air with such speed that Koa blinked and missed it. Before she knew it, Halston had Bund by his neck. He sent shards of fiery light into Bund's body like electricity.

Bund howled and Halston tossed him across the room. Bund was sent flying backwards but controlled his speed. He laughed again as the flames seeped into his skin. "Hot," he laughed. "I like it hot. Reminds me of home, Halston."

Halston increased his angelic shield and his eyes turned golden with his inner light.

Bund clapped his hands at seeing this.

"Yes!" He cheered with a wild grin on his face. "Gimme a fight. Gimme a challenge! Good angel versus naughty demon! Too bad we don't have an audience to witness this momentous occasion." He flew over to the body of one of the vampire servers. He picked her up and held her to his body in a firm embrace. He held her hand up and spun her around as if they were dancing. His maniacal laugh made Koa cringe.

"I'm sick of these weak vampires," he said while he continued to dance across the stone floor with the dead body. He dipped her and thick, black, blood fell from her mouth. "Why'd we make 'em anyway?" He stuck out his long, rubbery, tongue and licked the blood from the corpse's mouth. He winked at Koa.

Koa gulped.

Halston had both hands balled into fists as he glared across the room at Bund. "I didn't create them, Bund. You started it. You and the others. I'm just here to clean up your mess and send you back to your traitorous master."

"My master gave me a few gifts, Halston." Bund ripped the corpses head from her body, opened his mouth, and defied the laws of physics by swallowing her head whole.

Koa cringed.

Bund licked his lips and with a snap of his fingers, ignited his own glow. It wasn't an angelic one. No. Not anymore. He'd given up his halo centuries ago. He'd traded in God's favor for Satan's. With that, came a demonic glow. Black, and like a thick fog, it cracked with black sparks and surrounded him just as Halston's did.

He placed his hands before him and the sound of thousands of screams filled the room.

Koa dropped her sword and covered her ears. She didn't have a choice. The sound was so jarring that she felt she might go insane. She fell to her knees and caught a glimpse of a shadow form between Bund's hands before she lost all sense of direction.

Blood covered her hands as it seeped out of her ears and the piercing sound shook her eardrums making her scream from her gut. A jolt of pain seared through her heart and forced her arms and legs out until she was laid flat on the cold stone foyer.

Her eyes widened and she saw nothing but black.

Koa's breath was ripped from her and she was certain that she was dying from the inside out. Blood came out of her mouth, eyes, ears, and nose, and all she heard was the screams.

The pain was too much that she almost welcomed death. Almost.

CHAPTER 22

Halston fought to break through Bund's demonic aura. He knew what he was doing and the horror of having Koa linked to that demon made him consider doing something completely wrong.

He had to protect her. He'd promised her father. But even more than that, he refused to let the only woman he'd ever loved suffer a form of demonic possession. Bund would not have her.

Bund cackled and continued his assault on Koa's soul. "How does it feel, Halston, to be helpless against *my* power this time?"

"Leave her out of this!"

Bund shot a glare at Halston. His hands continued to build upon his inner power and collect energy from the dead bodies all around.

"While you've been running around for centuries, trying to help these weak humans, I've been feasting on their souls and becoming stronger."

"Stop this," Halston shouted. Sweat beaded on Halston's forehead. He tried to pump more power into his shield so that it could penetrate Bund's. To his dismay, Bund's dark shield grew larger and larger, forming a smoky bubble around his body, and pushing Halston further away from him.

Bund ignored Halston's orders. His power lifted Koa's seemingly lifeless from the ground.

"Want to know what I learned after all of these centuries on Earth?" Bund grinned. "Vampire souls make me even *stronger*."

Halston growled with frustration. He realized that his only chance was to get Koa's body out of Bund's range.

He flew as fast as he could, grabbed Koa's arm, and slung her over his shoulder. Bund chased him. Halston flew away with Koa, higher into the dark sky. Bund may be stronger than Halston in some ways, but Halston still had an edge on the demon because of his speed and agility.

He flew high into the clouds as the storm raged on. Before long, Bund could no longer see them. Halston could no longer feel his presence. They were safely out of the demon's range. As if God knew that Bund was on their heels, the storm picked up. Rain fell in torrents. The wind howled loudly. Heaven was very angry.

Bund would never be able to find them. Halston said a silent prayer and turned his attention from fleeing, to finding shelter where he could revive Koa.

He knew a place nearby. It would not do to go to any of the inns or hotels. Instead, Halston took Koa to a cavern. He put her body down and touched her face. Her skin was nearly blue. Her eyes were wide open, but there wasn't a shred of life within them.

Halston held her face in between his palms. He dripped water over her as he closed his eyes and focused on using his inner glow to heat her just enough to not burn her flesh. Halston was never much of a healer. That was more of Micka's job. He wished he could get Micka out there to help.

To his utter joy, Koa sat up with a start. She screamed. Halston frowned and covered her mouth with his hand. She kept screaming, a scream that meant she had felt the demon's presence in her soul. Halston could only hope that Bund had lost the link before completing his devious plan.

Koa fought him. She was obviously still locked in a state of terror. He held her close, firm, but gentle.

He smoothed her wet hair. "Calm down, Koa. It's all right. He's gone. It's just you and me." He spoke softly to her until her muffled screams behind his hand ceased.

He removed his hand and she turned to him with glassy eyes. Tears dripped down her cheeks and she wrapped her arms around his neck. "Oh god, Halston!"

He shushed her. "You're safe now, Koa," he said. "I shouldn't have brought you along. I should have known that Bund would be there." His brows furrowed in frustration. "I let my anger get the best of me, and almost lost you again."

Koa pulled back and wiped her eyes with the back of her hand. She sniffled. "Don't blame yourself. I wanted to come." She put her hand over her heart and looked off behind Halston. "What was he trying to do?"

Halston hugged her close. "He tried to link you to him."

"What does that mean?"

"It's a form of demonic possession where he can make you do things or listen to your thoughts and know where you are."

Koa shivered. "Did it work?"

Halston barely heard her question. She spoke so softly and the storm thundered so loudly outside the cavern.

He was afraid. There was no way of knowing if Bund was successful. His silence gave Koa the answer she'd been fearing.

"Oh god, Halston."

"Now calm down, Koa. I didn't say it worked. It's just that I can't really tell. You can though." Halston's eyes searched her. "How do you feel?"

Koa kept her hand on her heart. She felt her heartbeat and it reminded her of a hummingbirds wings. It beat way too fast. She drew in a long breath and tried to calm herself.

She tried to concentrate. Koa was silent as she searched herself for answers. She expected to feel an unwelcome presence. "What am I looking for?" Koa asked as she opened her eyes. "What does it feel like?"

"Can you feel Bund's presence? Do you feel anything odd?"

Koa was silent for a moment longer. She finally shook her head. "No. I feel fine." She looked up at him with hope in her eyes. "I'm cold."

Halston nodded. "Let's get you somewhere warm." He started to stand and help Koa up, but Koa shook her head.

"No. I can't even stand." She felt weak and as if she'd been beaten. She rested her head on Halston's arm. "I'm so tired, Halston."

Halston cradled her head and nodded. "All right. It's going to be just fine." He stood and looked down at her. She was probably drained from what Bund had attempted. The storm didn't look as if it would lessen. "I'll build a fire. We can stay here for the night."

Koa nodded and scooted to the wall of the cave. The moonlight made her look eerie as she gazed back at him with her ethereal green eyes. Halston made a fire in between his hands and formed it into a ball.

Koa watched him curiously as he set the golden ball of flames in the center of the cave. It hovered over the cave's floor and illuminated the small room. Koa smiled. The fire heated the entire mouth of the cave. "It's like magic."

Halston felt his heart soar at her smile. It was that smile that she only gave to him.

"Impressive," Koa said.

Halston shrugged. "It's nothing."

Koa scooted closer to the fire and pulled her shirt off from over her head. She closed her eyes as she warmed her hands. Halston avoided looking at her in only her bra. This was not the time to let his desire take over his intelligence. He had to think of a way to stop Bund.

Koa's mother seemed like the only solution, but Jax was unable to reverse the curse. He glanced over at Koa as she sat on her heels. She wrung her shirt out of the excess water and placed it flat beside the fire. She did the same with her long dark blue hair, twisting the water out.

She was so small, and slim, with tiny breasts beneath her black lace bra. Halston squeezed his eyes shut.

Stop, he said to himself. *Just stop. This is not the time.* He put his head in his hands and tried to focus on what his next move would be. It hit him. He sat up. He needed to find a way to bring the Alchemist to this world. Halston didn't smile at his idea. He already knew that Viktor would not be pleased. It worried him to think of what Viktor had planned.

"Halston," Koa called, breaking him from his thoughts.

Halston raised a brow and looked over to her. "Yes?"

Koa nodded to him and pointed to his clothes. "You should let your clothes dry too. You'll catch a cold."

Halston made a face. "You're just trying to get me naked, aren't you? You know I cannot get sick."

Koa giggled. She shrugged. "Can't say I didn't try." She winked at him and lied down on her folded arms.

Halston smiled as he watched her. His smile slowly faded as he realized how much trouble Koa was in. Seeing her face as she looked up at the ceiling confirmed that she had a feeling that things were about to get much worse. She had an uncanny sense for danger. She was trying her best to pretend to be fine.

That was when Halston paled. Koa had lied to him.

Bund had been successful.

CHAPTER 23

Raven licked her paws as she watched Alice train the new vampire on how to defend himself. Raven sat up and raised a brow. It was almost comical watching the lanky young vampire try to block Alice's blows.

To be fair, Alice was an angel with centuries of experience. Ian was just a geeky southern boy from the United States.

"Good thing you're a vampire now, kid," Evina said between laughs. "Because Master Alice is kicking your ass."

Alice swept her feet underneath Ian's legs and knocked him to the floor. He fell onto his bottom with a yelp. Alice reached a hand down to him. She smiled.

"You'll get better," she assured him.

Ian accepted her hand and she pulled him up effortlessly. He winced as he rubbed his bottom. "Geeze," Ian said. "You girls are tough."

Alice and Evina laughed. "We're not girls, Ian," Evina said. She winked at Alice.

"That's right," Alice said. "We're superheroes."

Ian nodded and cracked a smile. "I'll vouch for that. Just teach me how to be awesome like you, sensei," he joked and even bowed before Alice. Alice ruffled his black curls.

"Why are you so cute?" Alice asked with a grin.

Ian shrugged. His smile brightened the room.

"You almost make me feel guilty for knocking you on your ass."

Ian simply laughed.

Raven liked that about Ian. He was always positive. She wasn't sure about him when Koa first brought him back home after turning him into a vampire. She had been certain that he would only get in the way and get himself killed. She sighed. There was still plenty of time for that to happen.

She stood and walked from the room. She didn't want that to happen. She didn't want any of them to get hurt, especially the boy that had just begun to grow on her.

The church was cold, even for Raven who was always too warm. She hated the musky smell and the damp air. She'd never been a fan of old churches. Raven paused when she thought she heard something call her name. Her ears perked up.

Even in the darkness of the stone corridor, Raven could see quite well. It was one of the benefits of being cursed to live as a cat. The corridor was empty. There were pebbles and dirt on the stone floor and closed doors lining the walls. At the end of the hall was a door that was bolted shut and boarded with wood.

Raven was certain that was where the sound came from. She took a step closer and froze. A cold breeze made her fur stand on end.

Raven screeched when Alice knelt down beside her.

Raven felt her heart pound nearly out of her chest. Alice gave her a look. "What are you up to, kitty?"

Raven breathed in relief. "You startled me."

Alice rubbed her fur, smoothing it down with her soft, delicate, touch. "Sorry, it's a habit. I have to be light on my feet." She smiled and picked Raven up. "At least I know I can sneak up on a clever kitty such as yourself."

Raven looked towards the bolted door. "What's in there?"

Alice followed Raven's gaze. She stroked Raven's fur, almost as lovingly as Koa would do. "Dead bodies mostly. No ghosts or demons." She kissed the top of Raven's head. "Don't worry. You're safe with us, Eunju. It's just a temporary safe house."

Raven looked up at her with large green eyes. "Alice, you have to stop calling me that."

Alice smacked her forehead. "Sorry, I keep forgetting! I like Eunju so much better. It reminds me that you're so much more that a cat, and a pet name."

Raven didn't know what to say. She rested her head against Alice's chest.

"I like to call you Eunju because it gives me hope that you'll be human… well whatever it is that you were… once again."

Raven sighed. "Perhaps you're right. Bund and Greggan know that I'm cursed now."

"Don't worry. Soon they won't be a problem anymore. We have a pretty good team of supernatural soldiers here."

Raven smiled. "Yes. We do. I just wish I could be myself again and help."

Alice started to carry her back towards the others. "Halston will think of something. He always does."

"You really think so?" Raven asked. She dared to hope that she would have her body back.

"Of course," Alice said. They entered the room where the others were still training. Raven watched Jax. She whispered to Alice.

"Can we really trust him?"

Alice lingered in the doorway.

Jax looked over at them, as if he had heard. Raven's heart quickened. She'd almost forgot just how well vampires could hear. She cringed. Of course he had heard her. He looked at her for a moment and then went back to reading. He was quiet and always seemed to be in deep thought, or calculating. Raven had an unsettling feeling that he was planning something.

"*Haven't I taught you better than that*?" Alice said, but this time she spoke directly into Raven's mind.

Raven couldn't help but smile. How could she forget why Alice was called a Metal-Mind?

"Pardon me," Raven replied. *"It will take some time getting used to this."*

"After all we've been through… all of our adventures?"

Raven laughed. *"I must admit, this is nice."*

"Now, back to the question at hand. Can we trust the vampire prince?"

Raven frowned. *"What do you think?"*

"I think his actions will answer that question for us. He does love Koa."

"Perhaps too much."

"What do you mean?"

"I detect an air of obsession from him when Koa is around. He's always hovering."

Alice stroked her fur. *"At least we know he won't betray Koa."*

"We shall see," Raven said. She stared at Jax, unable to take her eyes off of him. *"There's something about him that I don't like."*

"What? That he cursed you? You know he did it to protect you."

Raven looked up at her. *"Do I?"* She narrowed her eyes. *"And now he suddenly can't reverse it."*

"These curses are always dangerous business. We will find a way to reverse it. And then you can banish that demon back to Hell."

Raven nodded. She glanced back over at Jax. She flinched when she saw that he was gone. Her eyes searched the room for him.

"I hope that happens sooner than later," she whispered aloud.

CHAPTER 24

Koa woke in the middle of the night when a howling wind chilled her exposed feet. Her body felt weak and sore as if she'd been beaten. She groaned in pain as she sat up. She shuddered and rubbed her arms when another wind came in through the cavern's opening.

Her teeth chattered and she crawled closer to Halston's hovering ball of fire. She looked at her watch. It was only four a.m.

She purred in delight as the fire warmed her entire body. She touched her shirt to see if it was dry and sucked her teeth that it was still too damp to put back on.

Halston's soft breaths drew her attention. She looked over at him and felt a guiltiness fill her gut. She'd lied to him. Her shoulders slumped as she closed her eyes. Something did indeed feel out of place. There was a heaviness in her chest and shoulders, an unearthly presence.

Koa swallowed and spoke inside her head. "Whatever you are, you need to leave. I will not let you stay. I will find a way to get rid of you."

Nothing. No reply. Only a slight coldness filled her veins, making her shiver again. Koa wanted to cry. She was afraid. She felt vulnerable and helpless.

Koa moved closer to Halston. Something drew her nearer. Perhaps it was a desire to feel safe. Halston always made her feel that way. She needed him more than anything now.

As she looked at him, she felt an intense desire to touch him. He slept with one arm bent under his head and the other at his side. Halston's shirt was crumpled against the wall of the cave, leaving his chest exposed. Through tears, she smiled to herself. He listened to her suggestion after all.

He must not have been cold, because he slept exposed in the cold night air and away from his fire.

Koa swallowed as she looked at his perfectly formed abs and his smooth chest. Her heart pattered against her rib cage. She crawled closed to him and hovered above his sleeping body. She watched his chest rise and fall with his breaths and saw his golden lashes twitch with whatever dream he was having.

Koa couldn't help herself. She watched his mouth and licked her lips. She wanted to kiss him, but was too afraid. Instead, she traced Halston's lips with her finger, softly, almost too gentle to even feel his skin beneath her finger.

Koa almost forgot how Halston was a light sleeper. Halston stirred at her soft touch. He opened his eyes with alarm. Bright blue eyes searched her face, seeing traces of her tears, and he looked around the cavern. "What is it? Is something wrong?"

Koa shook her head and smiled down at him. "No," she said as she wiped her eyes. "I was just admiring your cute face."

Halston looked perplexed for a moment, but after noticing the longing in Koa's eyes, he grinned. "Cute?"

She giggled and paused when he reached for her wrist. Their eyes locked and Koa trembled at his touch. She wanted him. She needed him to know that, before it was too late.

She drew in a breath when he kissed her fingers. Such a gentle, innocent, action caused her mind to turn to dirty thoughts. He kissed her wrist and tugged her down to him. Her hair fell over his face and shielded their kiss from the world.

She'd dreamt of this moment for so long, ever since she kissed his on the day he'd found her drunk in a park. That kiss didn't compare to what she experienced right then. His mouth was sweet and his tongue caressed her own.

Koa's eyes fluttered closed as Halston laced his fingers in her hair and brought himself up to his elbow. Koa found herself on her back as Halston positioned his firm body in between her legs. She was breathless when he pulled away from her kiss.

Koa's entire body tingled with joy. "Halston," she breathed.

He kissed her again and held her close. "You lied to me, Koa. I know it."

Koa felt new tears sting behind her eyes. "You know me so well."

"I will fix this, Koa," he assured her. "I promise you that."

Koa nodded. "I know you will."

Halston held her firmly. His eyes searched hers. "Good. Because I swear that I will set all things right. Bund and Greggan will not win."

She looked up at him and felt a surge of courage. "I love you," she said. She couldn't keep it in any longer. She needed him to know. If she died during this mission, she couldn't leave this world with that secret between them.

Koa's lips parted in surprise as he looked away from her. She could see the glistening tears in his blue eyes. Her voice cracked. "I'll understand if you don't feel the same way."

He shushed her and held her hand to his face. He closed his eyes letting a sparkling tear escape the corner of his eye. He kissed the palm of her hand.

"I love you too, Koa," he whispered. "I always have." His eyes met hers and she felt weak at the look of devotion in his eyes. Jax's words could not compare to what she saw in Halston's eyes. "I always will."

Koa smiled and wrapped her arms around his neck. "It's a good thing we're immortal then," she said. "Because I want to love and be with you for all eternity."

She craned her neck up to kiss him again.

He paused and put a finger to her lips. He raised a brow and searched her eyes as if thinking about something. Koa could look into his eyes for hours. The blue was so pure and bright that they were the only indication that Halston was not human. There was a depth to them that human's simply did not have. Koa could get lost within them.

"What about Jax?"

Koa shook her head. "What about him? What we had was a childhood romance, Halston. At first I wasn't sure how I felt about him now. But, trust me, I am certain that I do not love Jax in that way anymore. I care about him, of course. He'll always be my first love, but I cannot see myself with him as an adult. I only have room in my heart for you."

Halston embraced her in his strong arms. This time Halston's kiss went from gentle to greedy. Koa could feel the love and passion radiating between their bodies. He finally let go of his reservations and devoured her mouth.

Koa felt her body heat and her heart race as his hands caressed her thighs. His kisses went from her mouth and to her ear.

A moan escaped Koa's lips and she reached her small hands into his pants.

Halston tensed.

Koa paused. She looked up at him with concern. "Do you want to stop?" she asked. She'd almost forgot what he was, and what this meant.

Halston was silent for a moment. Koa didn't want to stop. She took his silence as acquiescence and unbuckled his belt. She watched his eyes as her fingers worked his buttons loose. When she slipped her hand into his pants and gently grabbed his hardened manhood, Halston closed his eyes.

Koa had no idea what she was unleashing, and she didn't regret being so forward, once he pulled her hand from his pants and pinned her hands above her head with one hand.

"Koa," Halston whispered in her ear. "You weaken me."

Koa nodded. "I know. But I want you. I've never wanted something so badly in my entire life." She closed her eyes and sucked his earlobe.

Halston used his other hand to take her pants off. He pulled them over her knees and over her feet, and tossed them away.

Koa shivered at the cold, but when Halston gripped her thighs and kissed her belly, she grew warm all over and no longer noticed the wind that swept into the cavern. Her back arched and her eyelids fluttered closed as Halston licked higher and higher up Koa's soft inner thighs.

Her mind filled with blurry blissful thoughts as Halston made her body feel such pleasure that she'd never imagined.

Her love. Her Halston. He filled her and she felt an explosion of euphoria better than any drink of human blood she'd ever tasted. She almost forgot where they were and Halston covered her mouth with his to suppress her cries of delight.

Love never felt so good.

CHAPTER 25

When morning came, Koa and Halston were still wrapped in an embrace. Koa rested her head on Halston's arm as he laced his fingers in between hers and kissed the back of her hand.

"Don't you just love how morning seems to chase away all of the evil of the night? All of your sins and misdeeds seem to fade away when the sun shines its cleansing light."

Halston smiled at her. "I've never heard you talk like this before," he said and kissed her forehead.

"I've never felt this way before."

Halston squeezed her close. "Me either."

Koa beamed. "Never?"

Halston shook his head. "Never."

Koa primped and grinned. "Well," she said. "Aren't I special?"

Halston laughed at her and pulled her into another passionate kiss.

"I love you," Koa said.

Halston's pause made her worry. He looked deep into her eyes and cradled the back of her head with his hand. "I love you, Koa," he said in a lowered voice full of such sincerity that it made her shiver.

"Wait until I tell Galena," Koa whispered with a grin.

Halston tensed.

Koa frowned at the serious look on his face. "What?"

"There's something I've been meaning to tell you," Halston said.

The tone of his voice made her wary. She raised a questioning brow.

"Galena is dead," he told her as he sat up to put his shirt back on.

Koa felt a cry get trapped in her throat. Galena hadn't been a close friend or anything, but they had worked many missions together. Galena had been a Russian woman that joined the Netherworld Division shortly after her parents were murdered by vampires.

Koa went numb. Why was she surprised? Being a Netherworld agent was a dangerous job.

"How?"

"Bund," Halston answered.

Koa pursed her lips and shook her head. "I hate him."

Halston didn't reply. He came to his feet and picked up Koa's shirt. He handed it to her. "He will pay for his crimes."

Koa took her shirt and slipped it over her head. Her cheeks were red with anger. She tried to calm herself as she came to her feet. All of her sweet feelings of love and joy were replaced with bitter hate. Bund seemed bent on ruining their lives. She could not understand why she was targeted. Why did he want her?

The feeling of cold filled her veins again and she glanced over at Halston.

He didn't notice the look on her face. "We need to head back to the others."

Koa nodded. She wanted to hug her mother again, before something bad happened. Koa couldn't tell Halston, but she felt her own end coming. She felt something odd. Was it a sense of duty? She actually thought of surrendering herself to Bund, just to protect her mother and the innocent people of Earth.

They flew back to the church. When they arrived, the sun was bright in the sky.

Halston landed and waited for Koa to do the same. She held onto his waist, knowing that he was leaving her.

"I need you to do a few things while I'm away," Halston said. "Go with Jax to the Oracle. Find out what you can about breaking your mother's curse."

Koa nodded.

"Then, I need you to go to Lady Colleen in the vampire colony of St. Baron's Court."

Koa shot a look at him. "Seriously?"

Halston nodded. "Yes, it'll be fine. She'll be expecting you."

Koa made a face. "And what exactly am I to do there?"

"Tell her we need her help. Bring Evina along. Evina knows all of the rules and decorum for such a meeting." He looked down at her. His face was serious. "I need you to make sure Lady Colleen and the vampire colonies are on our side."

Koa still looked confused. "But why would a vampire ever want to be on our side when Greggan is offering them free human blood?"

Halston leaned in. "Because it will not be free. Nothing, and no one will be *free*."

Koa shook her head. "I don't understand."

"Greggan will try to dominate this world just as he has the Netherworld. He probably wants to make himself emperor or something. And we both know how he rules. Many vampires will die at his hands, as well as humans. The world will be enslaved by him."

Koa sighed. She imagined what that would be like. She had seen the cruelty of his dictatorship. "But we won't let it come to that."

Halston nodded. "Good girl." He smiled again. "That's right."

"Then you better not take too long coming back to me then. I'll try not to screw things up too bad before you return," Koa said, only half joking. She'd made plenty of mistakes already.

Halston reached out for her hand. Koa's hand slid into his with ease. It felt right.

He gave her small hand a squeeze turned to her. His eyes locked on hers and he stroked the back of her hand with his thumb. "I won't be long. I promise."

Koa nodded, stomach full of butterflies. "And I'll try not to worry."

"You must not forget, you're a Netherworld agent. You better start acting like it again."

Koa cracked a grin. "I somehow recall someone firing me."

"Oh yes," Halston said. "I like to think of it as more of a suspension."

"Really?" Koa's grin widened. She batted her eyelashes at him with an exaggerated look of feigned innocence. "Are you saying that I'm reinstated?"

Halston made a skeptical face. "Sure… reinstated but under probation."

Koa laughed and nodded. "Whatever you say 'boss.'"

Halston pulled her in for a kiss that caught her off guard. She savored the warmth and taste of his mouth and moaned with yearning. She did not want the kiss to end. She did not want to break apart from him again.

When he finally set her back on her feet, she was dizzy and drunk off of her love for him. She knew she had a goofy grin on her face, but she didn't have the strength to hide it.

He smiled at her warmly as he stroked her cheek. "Be good," he said.

Koa nodded. "Only for you."

Halston kissed her forehead and turned to the old church.

Koa stood there and watched as he walked away from her. It was daytime, but she was sure she saw someone watching from the stained glass window. She tensed. Her eyes narrowed as she tried to make out who it was. Even though she couldn't be sure, she had a feeling that she knew who watched her. Someone had seen her kiss Halston.

Koa swallowed and turned away to hide the look of worry on her face.

She was certain that it was Jax and couldn't explain why she felt as though cold water had been splashed on her face.

CHAPTER 26

Svorn held out a hand and watched in wonder as droplets of rain fell into the palm of his large, white, hand. "Water? From the sky?" Svorn lowered his cloak and exposed his bald tattooed head to the rain.

"Remarkable," he said in Netherworld dialect. "What is this place, Master?" He nodded up to the black castle that stood at the top of a craggy hill and looked to Greggan with deep-set black eyes.

Greggan stepped forward. He held his arms out and breathed in the fresh sea air. It was magnificent. The rain was refreshing and something he'd missed since his first journey to the human world centuries ago. The Netherworld could never compare to the beauty of the human world. Greggan grinned. Soon, it would be all his.

He looked up at the grand castle. It would make a fine home. He'd had the Syths and his vampire soldiers remove the rotting corpses from the pikes of the gate. Bund had done as he was told and killed all of the vampires and left the human pets locked in the Keep. But still, he had gone too far with displaying the bodies like trophies. As always, Bund took things a dozen steps too far.

Greggan put a hand on the big Syth's shoulder. "It is our new home. Our head-quarters."

The Syth backed away when Bund flew out of the darkness and landed before them. Svorn fell back in line with the other Syth's, bowing his head to the demon.

Bunds eyes brightened and an evil grin spread across his bony white face. He rubbed his cleanly shaven chin. "It's all cleaned out of greedy vampires. I feasted on their souls. Hope ya don't mind if I ate a few of the pets…"

Greggan looked away from the demon. He hated being surprised all of the time, but Bund wasn't one for punctuality or following all of Greggan's orders. He would need to find a way to control the demon better. For now, he would remain cordial. He had no other choice.

Greggan's brows drew in as he wondered if Bund knew that. By the look on Bund's face, he doubted it. The demon was easily manipulated.

"You've done a fine job, Bund. Good work."

Bund scoffed. "Did ya doubt me, *your highness*?"

Greggan held the collar of his black trench closed against the chilling wind that swept in from the crashing sea. He noticed the disdain in Bund's voice when he said your highness, but chose to ignore it. "Of course not. Come now, we're all getting what we want here. I want you to do something else for me."

Bund lifted a brow. He lifted himself from the ground and glided across the cool night air with more grace than Greggan thought he had. He landed before Greggan and sniffed at his coat like a dog.

Greggan looked down at him and twisted his mouth in disdain. Bund's pale skin was illuminated by the moonlight. Greggan could see his bones and his black veins through his thin flesh.

Bund stopped sniffing and gave Greggan a look. "The Netherworld scent fades from you. You're startin' ta smell like a New World vamp. You stink."

Bund glared at him. Even Greggan was put off by Bund's eyes. Hollow, a deep blue like the sea at night, and deep-set. But there was much more within the eyes of a demon. A knowledge that they could see into your soul and that they could do horrible things to you without warning.

"That's to be expected," Greggan said. "Go and take care of business, and you won't have to smell me."

"What do ya want?" Bund asked. He came to his feet and stood a foot taller than the vampire king.

Greggan patted the demon's shoulders, put off by the demon being so close to him. "What you've been waiting for, of course. Time for a little fun, my friend. Has the girl fallen asleep yet?"

Bund closed his eyes for a moment. Smoke shrouded his face. A thick, black cloud, surrounded him as he searched. When he opened his eyes, a smirk came to his thin, rubbery, lips.

"Yes."

Greggan nodded. "Then, you know what to do."

Bund cackled then. Not like a man, but a monster, a beast from the darkest depths of Hell. The smoke covered his entire body. He folded his arms across himself and fell backwards as the smoke gently carried him to the ground.

Greggan watched with amazement as Bund's thin body was wrapped in the smoke. It laced around him until you could see nothing but small traces of his clothes and face.

Bund's body slowly sunk into the earth. The ground opened and swallowed him up. There wasn't a trace of the demon.

Greggan relaxed. The tension in his neck and jaw settled and his shoulders slumped. He stared at the ground and knew that Bund was gone, but he could still feel his presence. He looked forward to the day when the demon would be trapped in the Netherworld.

He stroked his red beard and thought of how grand that would be.

Soon, he thought. *Very soon.*

Lera was out tracking the angel, Alice, and Koa's cursed mother. Bund would keep Koa occupied for a while. He thought of what Bund would do to the half-blood and chuckled. She would pay for leaving him. She would wish she'd never betrayed him with her son. Jax and Evina had turned against him because of her treachery. His chuckle faded and he glared at the ground.

"Make her pay," he said to the dirt, hoping that Bund could hear him. "Bring her to the brink of insanity. Kill the bitch's spirit. Make her beg to be returned to me." He didn't realize that he had balled up a fist. His fist was covered in flames.

Greggan stared into the red flames for a moment. They licked and consumed his entire hand, and yet he felt no pain. All he felt was rage. He only wished he could see her face while Bund tortured her.

Soon, he reminded himself again. Greggan let out a slow breath to release his anger.

Now all, he had to worry about was Halston. He grimaced. That would be his biggest challenge. The rest was easy to him. But Halston worried him. He needed a plan. A small smirk came to his lips.

He had an idea. Greggan clasped his hands and looked towards the castle. Bund would be kept occupied for a few hours, and he could take over the VRS just as he'd planned. The humans were falling under his spell already. Their leaders could not resist his glamour, and their fear of the killings kept them in their homes.

Of course there was a little opposition. It was to be expected. Greggan had plans for the Netherworld Division. Big plans.

He motioned for his quad of Syth's to come forward. "All right, Svorn, Ulia, Yohan, and Rikie, let's make ourselves comfortable."

CHAPTER 27

Koa stood outside of Jax's room. She wrung her hands as she stared at the mahogany wood. She worried about what would happen when they were face to face. She knew that he had seen her with Halston, and decided that she might as well face the subject head on.

Koa knew that he was her first now. For years she had thought that she was a virgin and that she was saving herself for Halston. Having her memory back presented her with quite a few problems.

Was it possible to love two people?

Koa closed her eyes. She shook her head. *No*, she thought. She had already made her choice.

Koa clenched her jaw. It was time to get serious. There were innocent humans being punished and while she felt helpless about helping them, this was one thing that she could put right. Time would only make the situation fester.

She knocked twice and stood back. She couldn't let Jax see her weakness around him. She put on a courageous face.

Jax opened the door and stood before her. Koa pursed her lips when she saw him in nothing but the new boxers she'd bought him. He looked her over, leaning against the door's frame.

Koa's face flushed. She willed herself to keep her eyes on his face. Not his defined abs or the toned muscles of his arms. She bit her lip.

Jax reached his hand out and stroked her cheek. "Is everything all right, my love?"

Koa moved away from his hand. "Please, don't call me that."

Jax took his hand back. He looked hurt. "Why not?"

Koa couldn't form the words. She couldn't say it.

Jax pursed his lips and gave her an inquisitive look.

She shook her head. Her stomach churned with anxiety. She was sure he could see her face flushing with embarrassment.

"It's nothing. Nevermind." She started to walk away and he caught her by the forearm.

He pulled her close and leaned down to her face with intensity in his eyes. "What is wrong with you? You're acting all strange."

Koa swallowed. She feigned ignorance. She hated to act dumb, but sometimes it was just easier. "What do you mean? I'm fine."

Jax shook his head. "Stop pretending, Koa."

Koa's face paled. "What do you mean?"

Jax ran his hand through his red hair and sighed. He leaned against the door frame and gave her a pointed look. "You know that I saw you kiss Halston."

Koa tried to keep her face free from expression. She shook her head, too afraid to speak. She feared that if she said anything she might croak.

Jax leaned closer to her, his face growing annoyed. "Are you going to lie to my face? I thought you were better than that. At least tell me the truth now so that I can move on."

Koa's lips parted. She couldn't believe that his words hurt her a little. She felt a little selfish for wanting Jax to fight for her.

Her shoulders slumped. She swallowed against the dryness of her throat. She looked in his eyes. "You're right. I'm glad that you're here," Koa said softly. "And I cherish our memories as teenagers, but it would be best if were friends."

Jax scoffed. "Typical spoiled little brat." He shook his head in disgust. "Whatever you want, Koa. Let's be friends."

Koa put a hand on his arm. "Listen. It's for the best. I care about you and don't want you to get hurt." Koa realized that she sounded as if she was pleading.

Jax removed her hand from his arm. "You're so noble, Koa. You *care* about me," he said sarcastically. "I think this conversation is over."

Koa stood there with a stunned look on her face as Jax closed the door. She didn't know what to do. She considered knocking on the door and smoothing things over. She decided against it. Breakups were never easy, but that was Koa's first time. It felt awful.

Koa sighed as she walked back towards the room she would catch a little sleep in. Her head pounded. She didn't feel any better about what she had done.

It's for the best, Koa told herself over and over, but it didn't make her heart feel any better.

While Jax and the others rested up for the night ahead, Koa took a quick shower. The water was cold and left her shivering even after she stepped out of the old rusty tub. Koa cringed. She hated rust, dirt, and grime. The stone floor was cold and cracked beneath her feet.

She glanced at herself in the old mirror and saw nothing but a blurry reflection. Her hair was flat against her head and her face was clean of all eyeliner. Koa rarely looked at her natural reflection anymore. She was reminded of a pure childhood that was far gone now.

She sighed, and left the bathroom. She quickly ran down the hall to the small room that she would sleep in. If Halston hadn't told them to stay together, she would have been happy to get a hotel room somewhere closer to where the Oracle lived.

Koa slipped on a T-shirt and looked down at the meager bed that were made with a wool blanket. Koa made a face and just lied on top of the blanket. She only wanted a few hours. Just enough to take the edge of her fatigue off.

Her night of passion with Halston had worn her out. She smiled at the memory. She needed to rest and have enough energy for all that she and the others needed to do once night came.

She lied there staring at the door for a moment, listening to the silence. Then, she turned off the light on the nightstand.

The room went black.

Koa closed her eyes.

Only minutes passed and until Koa felt something soft tickle her ears. Koa wiped at her ear, thinking that a bug had crawled onto her.

She tried to clear her mind. Too many thoughts ran through her mind.

Koa sucked her teeth and slammed her fist into her pillow. She didn't see sleep coming to her. She sat up in her cot and glanced towards the door.

Koa's ears perked up as she heard a faint whisper. She tensed.

The rooms before the catacombs didn't have windows to let in any light. This one was bare, except for her cot, a small lamp, and a simple nightstand.

Koa imagined one of the keepers of the church sleeping in that same room ages ago. She wondered if they were as afraid of the dark as she was. Not only were there dead bodies from the Middle Ages in the catacombs, but there were also rooms that had been sealed shut in the deepest floor of the old church.

Koa held her breath. She listened. The others should have been up and preparing for their trip to the Colony. Koa and Jax would need to visit the Oracle first, but she was nervous about going to the infamous Lady Colleen and asking her for help.

Koa sucked in a breath as her eyes darted around the dark room. She was certain that she heard a voice call her name. "Who is there?" Koa whispered.

She strained to listen, but heard nothing.

She couldn't hear the others, but she could feel something drawing near. Koa's throat tightened. She wasn't sure how she knew it, but something evil was there with her. She froze, too afraid to turn around, but she knew it.

She could smell him. She'd never forget his scent. Or his low chuckle.

Bund was watching her.

Koa could feel his eyes boring into her back. The fear clutched her, and held steady. No amount of counting could ease her fear. Koa did count however. She did it whenever she was really afraid. When she was a child, she would count to herself in bed whenever she felt the hunger gripping her. On the nights when she was hungry for blood, she would have the worst nightmares.

"*Koa,*" a voice called from the dark recesses of her mind.

Koa's shoulders slumped. A whimper escaped her lips. Koa knew it then. She wasn't awake.

No one was there to hear her scream. No one was there at all. She was trapped in a nightmare, alone.

With a demon.

Her heart screamed when he appeared before her. Pale face, sharp teeth, and black veins pulsing in his face and neck. He growled, low, like a wild beast.

Koa whimpered. This was one battle she'd have to fight alone.

Koa reached beside her bed. She gripped her Lyrinian swords cold scabbard and pulled the blade free. The clinging sound of metal rung as the Lyrinian blade was set free. Koa sucked in a breath as the power of the sword filled her. She shuddered at its intensity. Rarely had it ever felt such evil.

The Lyrinian blade squealed, loud, like a banshee as it sensed Bund's evil presence. The blade wanted him, but Koa knew, not even her sword could stop that demon.

Bund vanished.

Koa gasped. She swirled around ready for him. She found herself alone in that tiny room once more. She stood there her sword before, her feet apart, and ready for a fight. As her eyes darted to every dark corner of that room, they adjusted. They landed on the door's brass knob.

Koa wasn't ready to face him. She wanted to wake up and run for help. Their last encounter nearly killed her. She'd never fought anyone like him.

She closed her eyes and sighed. "God, help me." A small measure of courage quenched her fear. She wasn't sure if it was the power of her sword, or if God really had answered her prayers.

Koa ran to the door, turned the knob, and nearly fell out into the dark corridor of the church. The silence heightened her fear. The stone walls reminded her of a tomb. The jumped when the door to room slammed shut behind her. She pressed her back against the stone wall and looked down towards the stairs that lead to the others. Koa knew they weren't there. Still, she had nowhere else to go.

The temperature dropped and Koa looked before her to see a puff of her own breath. She rubbed her bare arms with one hand to fight the gooseflesh, and held her sword with the other.

"Where are you, you bastard?" She almost didn't recognize her own voice. It came out weak, like a child's.

Such cold and darkness left her feeling exposed. Koa had never seen a real ghost, but she was certain that if they did exist, that this would be the kind of place to encounter one. Still, not even a ghost frightened her more than a demon.

As Koa crept through the catacombs, she prayed. One of her greatest fears was of demonic possession. Would Bund do such a thing? He wanted her. But she wasn't sure why. She held her heart with her free hand and turned her blade diagonally across her body, as if shielding herself from him.

She walked rapidly through the stone corridor, rushing for the door to Jax even though she knew he would not be in this nightmare to help her. She had never felt fear such as she did then. She ran and whimpered when the sound of footsteps followed her.

Koa swirled around, eyes wide, and searched her surroundings with her eyes, they strained in the dim light and her ears struggled to listen in the death-like stillness. All she could hear was the sound of her very own quick breaths, as her heart beat faster and her body began to tremble.

"Stop it, Koa. Everything is fine. You just need to wake up." She tried to convince her mind of something that she knew wasn't true. Everything inside of her issued warning. That cold feeling that filled her veins reminded her of what Bund had done to her.

The darkness was maddening. The presence she felt, but couldn't see, tormented her. She heard the slightest sound and as she turned, a terrified gasp escaped her lips. Before her, eyes glaring, mouth in a wicked, arrogant grin, was the grim face of Bund.

She stumbled back as he was suddenly so close to her they could kiss.

"Ah, I see you've been waiting for me, little princess." He walked towards her as she backed away from him. Koa shivered as the air grew colder and colder. She tried to look brave, by glaring at him, but the violent trembles of her flesh betrayed her courage.

"I've been waiting for you, my dear." Bund's dark blue eyes never left Koa's.

Koa cried out as he reappeared behind her. His arms held her immobile in a tight embrace.

He nuzzled her ear, closed his eyes, and smelled her hair. "You still smell like home," he whispered.

Koa closed her eyes, grimacing.

"Did you really think bringing that prophet here would change anything, Koa? You all are goin' to lose. Your friends, your family, will all die, and then, it will be just the two of us."

"What do you want from me?" Koa was too afraid to move.

"I just want to enjoy this night." His breath was warm on her neck, yet, it sent chills up her spine. "I just want to taste you. Your screams will please me. Your struggles will arouse me. Come love, let me have just a bite."

She stomped on his foot, with all of her might, and sent her arm up to jab him in the jaw with her first. She spun out of his grasp, and with an angered grunt, she swung her sword at him. He chuckled as it went through his body.

Koa put her sword away, sliding it into its scabbard. The Lyrinian blade would not work. Bund only smiled and caught her off guard with a forceful kick into her side, she yelped and swung at him, catching his ear with a closed fist.

Bund's laugh resonated throughout the catacombs. "Weak little girl. You'll take all the fun out of it, if ya can't do better than that."

Koa growled, and in a blink of an eye, elbowed him in his jaw. Something snapped in his face and his eyes widened with anger and shock as blood began to drip. She watched as the bone in his jaw healed itself.

Bund smiled. An ear-shattering scream escaped her mouth as he lunged into her with full force, crashing through the railing and sending them both airborne. They fell forever, finally, onto the landing of one of the staircases, beside her sword.

Her eyes shut tightly in pain. She cried out as her head hit the thick-carpeted floor with the strong impact and he remained atop her, holding her down with his weight. His eyes were full of hate and he was relishing in her agony.

She tried to move under him and he began to laugh. Its resonance was low and deep in his throat, as she reached for her sword, not two feet away. He slammed her reaching arm down and pulled it close to her body.

"Come on, Koa," Bund hissed. "Where's that scream? Let me hear it, won't you?"

She squirmed under him as he used his own powers to lift his sword from the ground and he caught it with his hand. He lifted it over her, directly above her heart, and rested the tip under her breast. A tear rolled off the side of her cheek. She had failed so soon. What would everyone do if she was dead?

Could I die in this nightmare? Koa's mind was a torrent of fear and agonized screams, but she would not let him have the satisfaction of hearing her scream. She started to wonder if this was real, because the pain sure felt real.

Her eyes squeezed closed as he grinned over her, his expression ghastly and evil, as he began to slowly sink the blade through her shirt and into her chest.

Her heart skipped a beat as she felt cold water lapping onto her pinned body. Her eyes darted about. She realized with acute terror that she was no longer in the church. Gray empty faces were surrounding her and Bund.

It was like being in a cold dark cave. She heard wails and weeping of little girls in the distance. She felt she had gone mad when she noticed a familiar face amongst the quiet, pasty faces of the beings surrounding her. There in the crowd was Lindley.

Koa screamed. She reached out. "No! Lindley," she cried. "No!"

She heard a deep rumbling laugh coming from above her, her eyes meeting those of Bund's. She didn't want to die.

Am I dead? Koa wondered. Then she felt such a pain as she'd never felt before as he leaned down over her and began to slide the sword deeper within.

Her eyes widened and she gasped at the intense pain. Dark blood began to gush out of her mouth, choking her.

"Just once, lass, and I'll stop," he promised licking the blood from her mouth.

Koa couldn't breathe. She began to suffocate. Blind fear entered her eyes. It took everything within her not to scream.

CHAPTER 28

Raven wept over her daughter's body.

Evina held onto Koa's head with both hands as Koa screamed and thrashed. She looked up at her brother with panic in her eyes. "I can't wake her. Something's wrong. It's as if there is a wall, blocking me from entering her mind."

Jax held Koa's hand. His features were twisted in worry. He leaned over her face and whispered to her. "Koa. Wake up, please. I'm sorry." He kissed her forehead.

Raven wondered what he was sorry for. She was prepared to claw his face to shreds if he had something to do with Koa's present state.

Raven heard Jax whisper to Koa. "Please don't leave me, Koa. I'll never stop loving you."

Evina put a gentle hand on Jax's shoulder and urged him to move aside. "Move back, Jax. Give me some space to work." She closed her dark blue eyes and focused.

Raven had never seen a temptress at work. The black Netherworld tattoos on Evina's arms seemed to crawl along her white skin as she channeled power from her mind to Koa's. She spoke to Koa, softly.

"Fight it, Koa. Come back to us."

Koa kept screaming. Her eyes were squeezed shut in a pained expression. She was drenched in sweat.

Raven joined Koa in screaming when blood seeped out of the corners of Koa's mouth.

Jax shot to his feet and turned to Alice. "What is happening?" He ran his fingers through his red hair and looked down at Koa. "Is she dying?"

"He has her," Alice said from the doorway.

"Who has her?" Jax asked with furrowed brows.

Alice looked at Koa with concern in her eyes as she leaned against the doorframe. "Bund." She folded her arms.

Everyone sat up and stared down at Koa. Their faces paled and the room fell silent, except for Koa's whimpers.

"There's nothing you can do." Alice shook her head. "A demon's grip is almost unbreakable."

Evina shook her head. Red hair cascaded over her shoulder and brushed Koa's face. "I can do this!"

Jax held her hair back. "Go on, Evina. Try again!"

Evina squeezed her eyes shut and focused. She squealed and was thrown against the wall by an unseen force. She crashed and slid to the floor. She opened her eyes in horror. She looked as if she'd seen a ghost. She held her hands up. They were shaking.

Raven wished she could hold her child.

"What happened?" Jax asked.

Evina turned to him slowly, a haunted look in her eyes. "I've never seen *anything* like this before. My power isn't helping."

"Mama!" Koa shouted so loudly and full of agony that Raven couldn't bear it.

She nuzzled Koa's neck. "Baby. Please wake up for mama. Please," she begged. "Fight him, Koa!"

Koa went still.

Raven sat up and looked at her daughter's face. Koa's eyes were wide open and terror-stricken. Unsure of what to do, they all watched her. Koa's face was white as snow. Her lips covered in blood. Her eyes were bloody as well. She'd been ripping at her eyelids with her nails, as she tried to awaken herself.

"Koa," Raven breathed.

Raven gasped as Koa shot into the air. She hit her head on the stone ceiling and fell back onto the bed in a crumpled ball.

Jax ran to her. He took her into his arms. "Koa? Are you all right?"

Koa turned to him with a look in her eyes that made sent shivers through Raven. She'd never seen such fear in a person's eyes. She could only imagine what horrors her daughter had faced in her demonic nightmare.

Koa looked at Jax as if she didn't know him. She stared at his face. She touched his cheeks and mouth. Koa's lips trembled and she fell into tears. She pressed her face into Jax's chest and wept. Then, she abruptly stopped crying and grabbed Jax's face.

Her mouth turned into a snarl.

"Change my mother back," Koa hissed. "Change her back now! I want that demon sent back to Hell!"

Jax's brows furrowed as he looked at Koa. She squeezed his jaw in with her hand. She looked lethal.

"Koa, I already told you. I cannot reverse the curse. Maybe the Alchemist can, but I'm fairly certain that this is permanent."

Raven put a paw on Koa's leg. "Koa, sweetheart. Let him go. It's not his fault."

Koa looked down at her mother. Her bangs were in her eyes, but she didn't care. Her face was full of torment. She released Jax and fell to her knees. Her head hung and she sat there in complete silence.

"What happened in your dream with Bund, Koa?" Alice asked.

Koa glanced at her from under her brows. In silence, she grabbed her Lyrinian sword. She wiped her mouth of blood and stared at the wall. For a moment, Raven wasn't sure if Koa was going to respond.

She simply stared at the wall with an intense look on her face. She sighed. "He showed me things."

Alice lifted a brow. "Like what?"

Koa narrowed her eyes at the angel. "He showed me how you're all going to die," she said and pushed past Alice to leave the room. She flew then, through the corridor.

Alice held onto the door frame and looked after Koa. "Where are you going?"

Koa's echo reached Raven's ears.

"To the Oracle."

CHAPTER 29

"Micka," Halston said. He dialed a few codes on the faceplate on the dashboard of his car. He ran his hand across the leather dashboard.

This was his favorite car. A Maybach Landaulet. He had it stocked with weaponry and all of the necessary electronic machinery that he needed to go from street to sky. He turned on the stealth mode and the car vanished from sight.

The car lifted into the air. Halston never flew on airplanes. He didn't trust… human error.

Micka's face came up. She smiled at him. He glanced at her image and went back to dialing the other agents he needed to send orders to.

Micka was pretty and unique. She had creamy almond-colored skin, high cheekbones, and full lips. Her soft brown hair was always wild and springy, and she had dark brown eyes that always seemed to hold a secret.

You'd never guess that she was an angel as well. Not an ancient angel like himself that had witnessed the beginning of life and the creation of the Earth, but one from Heaven nonetheless.

"You're all right," she breathed with relief. She covered her heard with her hands. "Thank God."

Halston smiled back at her. "Thank you, Micka. I didn't know you cared so much."

Micka raised a thin brow. "Oh, no sir. Don't let it go to your head. I just don't want to have to train a new boss."

Halston chuckled. "And I thought I was the one who does the training."

Micka leaned in closer to the camera. She lowered her voice. "That's what we women allow you men to think."

Halston chuckled again. He entered a tunnel and the surroundings darkened. It would be a long journey to the headquarters. Egypt. He would head to the airport. The others needed his guidance.

"I see," he said. "Or is the other way around?"

Micka shook her head. "No. It's pretty much just the way I said it." She folded her arms across her chest. "Now, what is it that I can do for you?"

Halston set his car for automatic flight and let the computer take him to his destination. He climbed into the back seat and lengthened the space between the front seat and the back seats. "Get Rohan to set up surveillance on Wryn Castle. I have a feeling that Greggan will soon contact his sires."

"If he hasn't already," Micka added. "Any news on Lexi or any of the other Wryn clan leaders?"

Halston shook his head. He feared that Greggan had Lexi, which meant that he had important intelligence on various VRS locations. He pulled out a case from under the seat. Once he opened it, he pulled out a small device and a case of glowing Netherworld pens.

"We have bigger things to worry about. Let's just focus on one thing at a time."

"Got it. Anything else?"

"Yes," Halston said. "I want you to be ready to go into the field."

Micka's face brightened. "Are you serious, sir?"

Halston clicked a glowing pen. "Yes. I think you're ready to be set loose again."

Micka's smile widened. She clasped her hands before her face and squealed with delight. "I won't let you down."

"I never thought you would." Halston sat back in the seat and started writing on the air. "Just promise me that you won't overdo it. Keep it clean. Keep it discreet. And above all, don't let Koa know that I sent you."

Micka winked. "Don't worry. I've got it."

Halston nodded. "All right. I need you to pick an agent and wipe out the Yeltin Colony. They've sided with Greggan, and I want them all dead."

Micka's smile faded. Her shoulders slumped. "Is it that bad, Halston? So bad that we have to kill innocent vampires?"

Halston raised a brow. He grimaced. "They aren't innocent. They're enemies, and I want them wiped out." Halston could not tell her what he'd learned. He now knew what Bund had planned. No one was safe. "And collect the souls."

Micka nodded. "I understand."

Halston looked down at his hands. They were only going to get dirtier. No one ever said fighting evil would be easy. He'd been around since the Earth's birth. He knew what needed to be done. That's why he was the boss.

He sighed. He needed to do all that he could before he met with Viktor. Halston didn't regret his night with Koa, but knew that Viktor would never forgive him. He needed leverage if he was going to keep his place as a general in the Netherworld Division. He needed a miracle to win back God's favor now.

His head throbbed. God saw all. His father knew what he had done, and there was no turning back now.

Halston rubbed his temples and tried to focus on the matters at hand. "Oh, and give me an update on Rohan's research of ways to bring the Alchemist into this world."

"Done," Micka said. "We're on it!"

Halston reached over to cut the connection. "Good luck."

"And good luck to you too, sir."

CHAPTER 30

Awkward silences weren't Koa's favorite way to pass the time. So, she cranked up the volume in Halston's jeep and pretended not to notice how amazed Jax was at the strange musical device.

They didn't speak a word to each other as they drove from the countryside where the church was located to the National Rail towards Brighton.

Rain poured onto Koa and Jax as they emerged from the station. It was night and they had arrived on the last train of the evening. Koa was glad that there wasn't a crowd. They nearly had the station to themselves.

The gusty winds reached them from the sea, and Koa zipped up her black hoodie. Jax stood there watching her as the rain made his short red hair turn slick and flat against his head. He didn't seem to mind. His face was serious, darkened by worry.

She'd heard his words while she was in her nightmare, and she was touched by them. But right now, there wasn't time to talk about such things.

Koa shuddered as she looked away from Jax. She was still shaken up by the horror of her nightmare with Bund. She couldn't shake the feeling that he was still with her. Her eyes darted around to each shadowy corner, searching for his gangly form hiding in the dark.

But more than any of the emotions she felt, rage surfaced above them all.

Koa pulled her hood over her head and started up the stone sidewalk that stretched up the steep hill. Jax followed her in silence.

The wind and rain was starting to annoy Koa.

What did you expect? Koa thought to herself. *This is England*.

They walked straight up for about half an hour and Koa's legs burned from the workout.

She nodded towards the row houses on the left. The last time Koa had seen the Oracle, her house had been in a heavily impoverished area. She noticed the neat gardens in front of the brightly-colored houses that Brighton was famous for, and the bikes left outside. This was a much safer area, a definite improvement from the Oracle's last home.

Koa saw the number 209 and nodded to a pastel green door. "That's it," she said to Jax.

"Following you," Jax said. "I may have shared prophecies with her in my sleep, but I've never actually seen the woman before."

Koa put her hands in the pockets of her hoodie and led the way up the narrow stairs. She glanced at the potted plant on the floor at the top and knocked twice.

Jax stood right behind her as they waited.

The rain picked up and beat on them as they huddled beneath the awning. A cold wind swept through and Koa's mouth parted when the Oracle's door creaked open. Koa reached for the door handle and paused when Jax put a hand on her shoulder.

She glanced over her shoulder and began to question him when she heard a loud growl come from inside the house. Jax's eyes widened as he looked past Koa and pulled her from before the door.

Koa gasped as a loud explosion sent them both crashing across the street. Everything went black and all sounds were muted as Koa opened her eyes to bright red flames. Jax was already on his feet and holding a hand out to help her up.

Koa groaned and tried to regain her senses. She took his hand and he pulled her up. Koa winced at a sharp pain in her head. She touched the back of her head and felt a sharp shard of wood. Her heart beat wildly as she yanked it out and stared down at the bloody shard.

Wobbly, she turned around as all sounds returned to her at full volume. She quickly regained her senses and drew her sword. It cried out and the rain hissed as it turned into steam at hitting the hot blade. A pack of wild reanimated Netherworld vamps raced from the flames of the Oracle's burning house and into the narrow street.

They didn't even pay any mind to Koa and ran around her. Koa frowned and lifted herself in the air for a better look at what was happening.

From high in the air, Koa could see the overturned cars that were parked on the street. Now they were smashed to bits. She swallowed, wondering what sort of bomb caused such a calamity and what those vamps were doing there.

Her questions were answered as the Oracle stepped from her burning house and over the rubble. Her spectacles were blacked out and her short, squat, body was engulfed in blue light. The Oracle's black and gray hair had come out of its bun and hung long and wild all over her face. Her mouth was twisted in rage as she walked to the middle of the street. She held her cane in one hand and an ancient book in the other.

Koa flew to her. "Are you all right," she shouted down. Her voice seemed too soft to hear over the loud storm.

The Oracle glanced at her and held her cane towards the pack of running beasts. She mouthed something and another explosion erupted from the end of her cane, sending calamity and flames towards the beasts. They tried to run. They slipped across the wet street as they tried to flee.

They were not quick enough. The flames squealed through the night air, down the black streets, and into their pack. Howls of agony filled Koa's ears as she watched them get burned to ash within seconds.

Mouth open in shock, Koa watched as the reanimated vamps were turned to nothing.

The night was quiet again.

The rain seemed to lessen, and the cold, chilling, wind subsided.

Koa shot a look back to the Oracle who stood there, absorbing all of the mess that she had just made. The red flames were carried away from the cars and homes and all directed to the Oracle. They seeped into her body as she went to one knee and held her head down. The cars were lifted into the air and put back in their parking spots.

The Oracle's hair flew wildly as she outstretched one arm and held herself steady with her cane with the other. Homes and broken windows were put back to normal. Jax stood across the street watching in stunned silence, until all was once again calm.

It was as if nothing had happened.

Koa covered her mouth with her cold hand.

"Get down here, child," the Oracle shouted at her. She turned to walk back into her newly formed house. "Come in for tea before you catch a cold."

CHAPTER 31

Koa sat down on the Oracle's sofa. She had a towel wrapped around her hair and another around her shoulders. She held a hot cup of honey tea in both hands and enjoyed how the warm cup felt against her palms. She watched the Oracle as she set her books back in place and allowed Jax to help her set some of her fallen furniture upright.

"Your neighbors," Koa asked. She took a sip of the hot tea. "Are they all right? Are they going to cause trouble for you?"

The Oracle scoffed. "What neighbors?"

Koa lifted a brow. "The other people who live on this road."

The Oracle paused from putting books away and looked over her shoulder at Koa. She smirked. "No one live here but me, Koa. Oracle smart lady. I buy entire street, girl."

She went back to humming a Chinese song as Koa slumped back against the sofa and drank more tea. Surprisingly, the Oracle's new home was drastically different from the filthy cat hoarder's nest she lived in the last time. This place was clean and neat, even if it did have an odd moldy smell to it.

Jax finished setting the sitting room back right and sat onto the sofa beside her.

"Now what?" Jax asked.

The Oracle picked up her cane and turned it to him. "I want to know why the prophet is here." She crossed the room and pointed the tip of her cane into Jax's chest.

Koa looked confused. She put a hand in between them. "What are you doing? You told us that I had to return there. Wasn't bringing Jax and the others back part of the plan?"

The Oracle never broke her glare from Jax. "I never say to bring him here. I don't care about the others. But *he*," she tapped the tip into Jax's chest as he just stared at her with a straight face. "He should not be *here*."

Koa came to her feet. She put both hands on her head. She shook her head. "I don't understand. What do you mean? I thought you and Halston had this all planned out!"

Jax and the Oracle held their stares. Koa had a feeling that they were doing more than just staring at one another. Koa sensed the tension. They were speaking and yet she could not hear the exchange for it was all in their minds. A prophet and an oracle. Koa folded her arms and watched them. She wanted to know what was being said.

"What is going on," Koa said as she dropped her arms. "I just want some answers. I'm getting so tired of all the secrets. Please, someone talk to me."

The Oracle stood and placed her cane's tip on the floor. She took Koa's hand in hers and Jax shot to his feet. Koa shrieked as a bolt of what could only be described as lightning shot into her body. Jax shoved the Oracle aside and caught Koa as she fell to the floor.

Koa shook. During that quick touch, Koa had heard something. A voice that wasn't the Oracles had shouted at her.

"Do not trust!"

Those words still echoed in Koa's head and were so loud that she felt dizzy. A sharp migraine made her wince as she tried to clear her vision. She squeezed her eyes shut and opened them again. When they opened, Jax was holding her and looking down at her.

The Oracle was gone.

CHAPTER 32

Outside waited a surprise.

Greggan.

Koa tensed as she stopped at the top of the stairs.

He stood there at the bottom, in a heavy fur coat, as if he was expecting a snow storm. His hands were folded before him.

Koa's cheeks reddened. She pulled out her sword and pointed the tip at him. "Have you come to surrender, Greggan?"

Greggan stroked his long red beard with a gloved hand. He ignored Koa's words and looked past her at Jax.

"My son," he said. His face was emotionless, but his eyes hid something as he looked upon Jax. "My one true heir. Why have you betrayed your family name for this little whore?"

Koa's eyes widened. She glanced back at Jax to see him looking down at the slick wet stairs. His jaw was clenched, but he would not speak up to Greggan.

"You coward," Koa hissed. She didn't know where the venom came from, but she would have expected him to at least speak up for himself if not for the girl he claimed to love.

Greggan shot a heated glare at Koa. There was actually fire behind his eyes.

Jax put a hand out to stop Koa from acting rashly. "Father, you don't belong here. None of us do. Why can't you return to the kingdoms you conquered and be content with what you have? The angels will not allow you to continue this way."

Koa glanced at Jax. He looked down once more as his voice lowered.

"I won't let you continue this way."

Koa was surprised to hear him finally speak up. Surprised, and proud. She gave Greggan a spiteful grin.

Greggan wasn't amused. His fiery gaze went back to Koa even as he spoke to his son. "If you choose to fight for the side of a half-blood whose fate is already sealed. There will be nothing I can do for you or your sister."

Jax nodded. "So be it."

Greggan's eye twitched. He pulled something out of his pocket. Koa gasped at the sight of a lock of short blonde hair.

She knew it by sight and scent.

Lindley's hair.

Her insides screamed.

"You bastard!" Koa shot down the stairs with a wild swing of her Lyrinian sword. She wanted to lop his head off. She thought she'd go mad at the thought of something happening to her pet. They were bonded. She was supposed to protect her.

Greggan roared and his arms sprouted red flames. He was quicker than she anticipated. He slapped her with a hand covered in flames. Koa winced at the pain and scrambled to her feet.

Memories of being tormented by flames haunted her, making her cover her head with her hands and scream. He'd tortured her for hours, on many occasions, in secret, for pleasure. Koa squeezed her eyes shut. Her own screams filled her ears. Even after the flames vanished from her cheek, she felt the exposed muscle sizzle.

"Stop this!" Jax shouted.

She was prepared to go back in for more, but Jax beat her to it. He darted down the stairs like a shadow and pressed his dagger to Greggan's throat. Koa was worried. Jax was so much slimmer than his stout father, but Koa had seen Jax in battle. What she hadn't seen was Greggan in battle.

Greggan's eyes were red with fire and hate.

Koa looked at Jax with narrowed eyes. She tasted her own blood. Not only had Greggan's flames eaten away at her flesh, but her jaw was broken. Even so, she could already feel it healing. At least none of her teeth had fallen out. Those always took the longest to regenerate.

She nodded from her place on the wet street. "Do it! Kill him!"

Greggan swirled out of Jax's grasp and backhanded his son across the face, just as he had Koa. He grabbed Jax by his hair and pulled his head up. With a knee, he pinned Jax to the wet sidewalk and pointed to Koa.

"You risk everything for her," Greggan growled. "What is she but an experiment? A toy to pass to that demon. Let her go, Jax. Let the demon have her and let's rule this human world together."

Koa saw the look on Jax's face. He was torn. Through the soft rain, she wasn't sure if it was just rain or if tears were streaming down his face. His expression was stoic, and he didn't speak a word. He let Greggan hold his head up, snatch his dagger, and hold it at his throat. If Greggan slit his throat, it would not be a fatal blow, but it would take a while to recover.

Koa's heart broke as she looked into Jax's eyes. He was ready to give up, and she couldn't help but feel that it was her fault.

She charged at Greggan. He let Jax go, came to his feet, and whistled. Koa frowned as a large cloaked figure seemed to step out of the shadows. She paused in her steps as she caught a glimpse of its face. It had patches over both eyes and translucent skin.

Her eyes widened in horror as the creature tossed a small body into the street.

Koa shouted in fury as it wrapped its cloak around Greggan and vanished.

"No!"

Horror struck Koa's heart. She stood before the naked body of a dead young woman. Blank blue eyes gazed at the dark night sky.

Lindley.

Koa stared down at the beautiful face of her pet. Her friend. Her hands balled into tight fists, and she started to shake. The anger was so violent that Koa feared she'd rip someone's head off. She wished Jax would step away. He had a hand on her shoulder, consolingly, but he had no idea how the power within her boiled. Her grief almost outweighed the rage. Almost.

Her jaw tightened she ripped Jax's hand off her shoulder and fell to her knees.

Jax caught her by the wrist. "Don't touch her, Koa!"

Koa cried out in sorrow as she looked down at Lindley's dead body. Her insides raged with a mixture of sadness and anger. Her eyes were swollen from the pouring of warm tears that gushed from her eyes.

She'd failed yet another pet. This time, she was too late to fix her mistake. She could not turn Lindley into a vampire like she did with Ian. Lindley was gone.

Koa wanted to hold Lindley and sob, but Jax's warning held her back. Having no way to release her anger she pounded the street with her hands so hard that they bled.

Koa paused. She sucked in a breath. Sparks flew from her fists. She gasped. The sparks sprung up her arms and from her chest. Blue light started to glow from Koa's chest, and outward. She jumped to her feet. She patted her chest and tried to put out the light that flickered around her.

She covered her mouth. Her heart was beating so fast and loudly that she could hear it pulsing in her ears. She tried to control her breathing.

"*What the hell was that*?" Koa whispered.

She glanced over at Jax who had stood and was now walking down the hill.

He hadn't seen a thing. She closed her eyes and sighed. Something felt strange inside of her. Something aside from the presence Bund had linked to her. Something new, and powerful, and wicked in a way that made her feel invincible.

Koa opened her eyes. She'd only ever seen something even remotely like that from one race of being.

Angels.

CHAPTER 33

Koa shook her head. Nonsense. There was no way she could have an angelic shield. Her very nature as a half-blood vampire was so anti-angel.

She looked to Jax, careful to not let her gaze go back to Lindley. She was spent. She had no more tears to cry. All she wanted was to kill Greggan and Bund.

"Jax," Koa called. He ignored her. She frowned. "Jax!" She knew he heard her and yet he continued to walk down the sidewalk towards Brighton Pier.

She bit her lip in frustration and ran after him. She clicked her sword into a baton and secured it on her belt. She pushed Jax in the back with both of her hands. He swirled around and caught her wrist.

"I know you heard me! You're just going to run," Koa shouted in his face.

"What Koa?" he shouted into her face. "What do you want? You want me to kill my father, is that it?"

Koa shook her head, appalled by the question. "Isn't that what we all want? Look at what he did to poor Lindley! She deserves to be avenged."

Jax pushed her away. Koa flew back at the force of his push and landed on her heels. She watched Jax continue walking and chewed her lip. The frustration almost sent her after him for more of a fight.

Too much had happened in one night. Her mind could barely wrap itself around it all. Koa restrained herself. She tried to put herself in Jax's shoes. She'd never even told Jax everything about her treatment from Greggan when she lived in the palace. How could he know the true extent of his father's evil?

Koa flew to him and landed beside him. She walked at his pace in silence. He didn't resist when she took his hand in hers and gave it a squeeze.

"I'm sorry," Jax said. He gave her a sidelong glance. "It's just hard for me. I've always been dutiful for the most part. The only time I disobeyed him was when it came to you."

Koa nodded. She chewed the inside of her cheek. She wanted to tell him so badly. "I know. Don't you think I deserve to be avenged? If not Lindley and the countless humans he's killed in the short time he's been here!"

Jax paused. His brows rose suspiciously. "What do you mean?"

Koa pursed her lips. She felt as if she'd explode. She'd never spoken of what was done to her in secret.

Jax pulled her into his chest. He smelled her wet hair. "I'm sorry."

Koa was silent, uncomfortable in his embrace.

"I just want to send him back to the Netherworld. I never wanted to kill him. He is still my father."

Koa was a bit taken aback by his words. Still, she nodded. She kept her thoughts to herself. Perhaps Jax didn't want to be the one to do it, but she surely wouldn't think twice at ending his miserable life.

Koa called Michael to take care of Lindley's body. He wore gloves and protective gear to pick her up and take her to the lab for examination. He was an odd looking fellow with a large bifocals and scraggly gray hair. He never even spoke a word. He just took the body in silence and left in his black van.

Koa hated what had happened to Lindley. She was supposed to protect her. Visions of Lindley's sad face kept flickering through her memory. She pushed them aside and tried to focus on the better times they'd had.

She cracked a ghost of a smile as she remembered the day she'd met Lindley. It had actually been at Ian's choosing ceremony. She'd caught a whiff of Lindley's sweet scent and went straight for her through the dancing crowd of humans and vampires. With one arm around Lindley's waist, Koa had kissed her and claimed her.

Koa shook her head. She didn't want to remember anything anymore.

She was tense as she held the steering wheel with both hands and navigated the narrow streets. They'd "borrowed" a car and were headed back to the Church.

Do not trust.

Those words continued to repeat themselves in Koa's head.

What did the Oracle mean? Koa wondered. She glanced sidelong at Jax. He looked out the window. He was so quiet and reserved. She did not remember him being that way before. It was almost as if something was bothering him as well.

Koa looked away and focused on the road. She'd almost forgotten that he had seen her kiss Halston. She figured that was why he was acting so solemn.

When they pulled up to the church, Jax got out of the car and slammed the door shut. He stood there completely still for a moment, and looked up at the bright moon. The rain had died down a bit, but it still sprinkled on Jax's face as he looked upwards. He closed his eyes and Koa saw his shoulders slump.

Koa thought that he might look back and say something to her, but he didn't. He stepped away from the car and walked up to the doors of the church without a word to her.

Koa sat there and leaned back into the driver's seat. Her stomach was unsettled. She felt so guilty. She watched him disappear into the darkness of the church and sighed. She wondered if she even needed to say anything. Perhaps it was easier to just share an unspoken knowledge that they would not be together again.

She perked up when she saw her mother run out of the church and across the meadow of poppies. She quickly got out of the car and ran to Raven. Raven leapt into her arms.

"What happened?" Raven blurted.

Koa stroked her wet fur and carried her towards the church. "Long story," Koa sighed.

"Tell me all of it."

Koa nodded. "Of course. Let's get inside and warm up."

"Are you hungry? How do you feel?"

Koa shrugged. "I'm okay. Still a little shaken up by that horrible nightmare, but I'll survive."

Koa hated lying to her mother. She felt awful. Her stomach churned and she was tense, afraid that Bund would pop out of the shadows at any moment. She knew that sometimes lying was necessary. She didn't want Raven to worry. Raven had enough on her mind. Koa felt a sharp pain in her throat. She still had to find a way to break her mother's curse.

Koa wanted to scream. There was just too much to do. She was only one girl. When she entered the church and walked down the stone stairway to Halston's den, she paused in the doorway.

Something flooded into her as she stood there and looked inside. There was Tristan, he was strapping weapons to himself and wearing human clothes to hide them. Evina was in a pair of jeans and shirt that was too small for her breasts, but her arms were folded across her chest, and her hair was long across her shoulders and reached her hips. She popped her bubble gum and nodded to Koa. She turned her back on Koa and revealed a smaller sword strapped to her back.

Koa raised a brow. Even Ian was up and looked ready for battle... in his own way. He waved at her and typed away on Halston's computer. "Tracking Spoons' navigation chip. Looks like he's in the St. Paul tube."

"Good," Alice said. "Spoons is the best demon tracker around. We'll have Bund soon." She cracked her knuckles and looked to Koa. "Ready, Hun?"

Koa's mouth opened but she was speechless. Her gaze went over to Jax. He stuffed his Netherworld daggers into his sleeves and avoided eye contact with her.

"Ready…" Koa's voice trailed. She looked back to Alice. "For what?"

Alice shook her head and chuckled. "Why, dear girl, we didn't put this team together to just sit around playing video games. It's time for battle. We're all ready to kill that demon. Now, tell me, *are you ready* to make him pay?" She gave Koa a serious look, with no trace of her former smile.

Koa nodded with wide eyes. Alice wanted to stop Bund as much as she did, maybe even more. Koa looked at all of them in awe. That's when she realized that this was not all on her shoulders alone. She had help. She had a team of Netherworld soldiers, and somehow, that gave her a little confidence.

A grin crept onto Koa's face. "Yeah," she said. She tapped her hilt with her black painted nail. "My sword hasn't tasted blood in a while."

CHAPTER 34

The Netherworld Division headquarters was underground in the Egyptian desert. Halston had traveled all morning and his patience was growing thin, but this was one instance when he was not the one calling the shots. He was going to a meeting where he would have to answer to his boss.

Viktor would certainly have a lecture planned out for Halston.

Halston was not looking forward to it. The governing body was composed of the purest of angels, completely without sin. They looked down on Halston for being one of their fallen brethren, but even they knew how hard he worked to redeem himself.

The hot desert sun beat down on Halston's head. He put his hat back on and waited. Sweat beaded on his forehead and he sighed.

Halston hated waiting. He was anxious. Koa was back in London, with Bund and Jax. He wanted to be there with her, not standing in the heat, waiting to explain himself.

Halston knew what he was doing. Now, he just had to convince the other angels to believe in him. He just hoped he would not be judged for his night with Koa. He'd given in to his bodies urges, but it was more than that. His heart reminded him of that fact every moment of the day.

Either way, Halston was a fallen angel, just with one more mistake on his record.

Viktor stood near the window with his back turned to Halston. The sun fell in a sliver on the tall angel's face. His white wings were closed and neatly strapped to his back. He almost looked human, but an angel like Viktor wasn't tainted with human sin, so his glow never dimmed.

Halston was lucky to still have his glow, even though he had lost his wings. He could call his glow whenever he wanted, and it got a little stronger each year, with each deed. Perhaps one day he would have enough good deeds stored up to get his wings back.

Halston waited.

Viktor didn't look at him, but he spoke, in that quiet monotone voice of his. "Do not support what God condemns. Vampirism and blood guilt."

Halston felt his blood turn cold. He had to use everything within him to not cry out in anguish and sorrow. It was a direct confrontation, one that Viktor knew would hit Halston's core.

Viktor looked back at him, finally. His eyes were a bright silver that made Halston want to hide from their light.

"Why is the half-blood still alive, Halston?"

Halston froze. He was speechless. This was not what he came there for.

Viktor folded his hands before him. The sun seemed to brighten behind the angel, as if God displayed his approval for the general of the angels.

Halston swallowed. "What do you mean?"

Viktor didn't blink. "Koa. The half-blood. Why haven't you killed her yet?"

Halston felt a stab of pain in his heart. Why would Viktor ask him that? He knew how he felt about Koa. Halston was certain that he knew. He couldn't even imagine such a thing as killing Koa.

"Bund. That is who I came here to discuss." Halston spoke quickly, hoping to take the focus off of Koa. "And Greggan, the vampire king. We need to stop them."

Viktor nodded. He seemed to reflect on Halston's words for a moment. "This is true. But if you kill the Half-blood, and her mother, they will lose their interest in the human world. If you seal the Gate, they will have no way to harm our humans any longer. If you did your job, the vampires would be extinct, and we could return home. Why have you disobeyed God again?"

All of the color drained from Halston's face. The shame overwhelmed him. He fell to his knees as the tears streamed down his face.

Halston swallowed a lump in his throat. He had to try. He had to speak his peace. "But the mother."

Viktor blinked. "The creature without a race."

Halston shook his head. "No, I don't think she is like the other nephilim. I think she's different."

"Does it matter?"

Halston nodded, eagerly. "Yes. I think it does. She can do things that none of the others can. She can banish people for good."

"Banish people?"

Halston nodded again. This was his chance. His only chance to save Koa and her mother.

"Yes. I am not sure how she does it, but she can make people disappear somehow. She only did it in times of desperation, but imagine if she used her power for us."

Viktor made a sour look. He shook his head. "Did you not hear me, Halston? Do not support what God condemns. She is an abomination, and that is all there is to it."

Halston took a step closer, his hands folded in prayer. "Please. You have to see the good in what she does. Maybe she is a sign."

"Sign?"

"Yes. Nature's way of righting what is wrong with the world."

"You sound like a human, Halston. Nature? Signs? Have you lost your faith in our Father?"

Halston's shoulders slumped. "Of course I haven't! But what if this is God's way of putting the world back in order? This woman can rid the world of all the evil nephilim."

Viktor looked down at him with those ethereal silver eyes and regarded him with pity. "I see that you have some sort of personal affection for these women. It worries me. Our brethren once had the same affections, and they forgot their purpose. They fornicated with human women, and gave birth to monsters."

Halston sighed. "You don't understand. It's not like that."

Viktor straightened his shoulders. He gave Halston a pointed look and folded his arms behind him. "Answer one question for me, brother. When God passes judgment and calls us home, do you want to join us… or do you want to be left behind with the other sinners of the Earth?"

Halston gasped a breath. The choice should have been easy. It was all he wanted since he saw the error in his ways.

The night he left Heaven to follow the traitor Satan, he knew what he'd done was wrong. For centuries, he'd tried to fix his error. Why couldn't he speak? Koa's face. Her sweet smile faced him and he felt his heart break into pieces.

Halston nodded. He shoved her face from his mind and looked back up at Viktor and answered the angel's question. "I want to go home."

CHAPTER 35

Koa was glad that the rain had finally stopped and that the sky was clear and star-filled. She held her mother tightly before they once again parted ways. She breathed in her scent and closed her eyes. "I love you, mama," Koa whispered.

She hated leaving her daughter, but she and Alice were to stay hidden while Koa and the others went to Lady Colleen's grand ball.

Raven spoke softly. "I love you more."

Koa pulled back and looked her mother in the eyes. "Not possible," Koa replied.

Raven snuggled her again and Koa put her down on the ground.

Alice gave Koa a hug. Koa was surprised by the angel's actions. She was even more surprised by how strong Alice was. She hugged her firmly and patted her back. She pulled away and held Koa out at arm's reach. Her gray eyes were serious, and stern. There wasn't a trace of humor on her face like Koa was used to seeing.

Koa shivered. The clouds above were rolling in behind Alice, and made the angel look almost gothic in the pale gray light.

"Listen, Koa," Alice began. "You're a smart girl. I know you will do the right thing." She shot a quick look at Evina and Jax. She leaned in closer to Koa.

"Keep an eye on them," Alice said.

Koa's eyes widened. She almost jumped at hearing Alice's voice in her head. It was a sensation that she was not used to. The look in Alice's eyes made her think twice about showing that something had happened. Instead, Koa kept her face free of any indicator that Alice had used her angelic skills on her.

Koa spoke back, timidly at first. "*I understand.*" She didn't ask if there was a reason why she shouldn't trust the vampire siblings. The answer was obvious. Greggan was their father. There was always the slight chance that their familial ties would be stronger than the mission.

"If you feel, at any point, that there is something amiss with the two of them, tell Tristan. He was created to kill vampires. He will protect you."

Koa was a little caught off guard that Alice thought that either of them would hurt her. She spoke aloud, so that everyone could hear. "Take care of my mother until I return, will you?"

Alice patted her shoulder gently. For a moment, she didn't say anything. She just looked into Koa's eyes, driving the severity of what she had warned further into Koa's mind.

"I always do," Alice winked with her usual cheerful grin. *"You take care of that young vamp of yours. He's a sweet young vamp."* she added and waved to Jax, Evina, Ian, and Tristan.

Koa watched Ian. He looked so out of place, even now as a vampire of a few weeks.

"Now be good, children." She pointed to her black belt that held her skinny jeans around her narrow waist. She tapped the leather with her pink manicured nail. "Don't make mama whip your shiny little butts if I find out you've been misbehaving," she said with a mock look of scolding at the three of them.

Koa laughed lightly.

"Is that a promise," Ian asked. He seemed to be trying to suppress a silly grin.

Alice pointed at him and narrowed her eyes. "You're asking for it." She gave Koa a look of amusement. "I didn't know he was so cheeky."

He laughed and she cracked another grin, shaking her head in humor.

Koa waved and blew a kiss to her mother. She watched Raven and Alice walk away into the town of Carlisle. The night was cold, but calm, and Koa felt that there was hope. Hopefully tomorrow night… she would kill herself a king.

CHAPTER 36

Halston waited outside the tube. Being back in England felt good to him. He frowned. A secret was eating him from the inside: a secret that he could tell no one, and yet his holy father knew.

Halston checked the time on his watch. The many dials helped him track the true time in the human world as well as the Netherworld.

It was an unusually sunny day with an occasional cloud cover. Train passengers flooded out the underground station in hordes. Everyone was in a hurry. No one paid him any mind as he held his paper up and pretended to be reading the day's news.

He gave a woman a smile as she paused to fix her stiletto.

He held a hand out. "Need a hand?"

She nodded, smiling, and held onto his arm while she secured her shoe's sling around her ankle. She stepped down and grinned at him.

She glanced up at the building across the street. Still smiling, she said, "He's good. I don't see him anywhere."

Halston grinned. He almost didn't recognize Micka. She had quite the gift for disguises. Normally she would wear her dark hair in its natural state, springy and full. She would dress very professionally and wear only comfortable, flat shoes in the office.

Today, she wore a snug-fitting black dress with small red roses. It was belted at her slim waist and flowed over her voluptuous lower half, landing right above her knees. The black stiletto heels were a nice touch. Her hair was straightened and lightened to a rich mahogany that went well with her chocolaty skin tone.

Halston was impressed with the makeover. She needed to infiltrate a vampire clan, and her new look was a perfect start. He flicked a piece of lint off her shoulder. "At least he's good at what he does."

"So," she asked, looking at him with those big brown eyes that he was sure turned many a fellow into melted butter. "When are the rest of us going to meet this Nickolai Frost? This legendary human that can cheat death." She suppressed a giggle and rolled her eyes. She scanned the buildings around, looking for a glint of light. "As if a human could really do such a thing."

Micka pulled her red sunglasses out of her large purse and put them on. They were too large for her slim face, but Halston figured that was the modern style. Bug-eyed shades. She applied red lipstick to them and pressed her lips together.

Halston shrugged. "Viktor trusts him, and so we must. We can use him. He has infiltrated the Colony."

A low buzz prompted her to check her phone. She raised a finger to Halston. "Pardon me." She scrolled up the glowing touch screen with her finger. "Rohan is still working on that project for you. He found what you're looking for." Her full lips grinned as she looked up at Halston. "He should be done by this evening."

Halston gave a nod and leaned against the side of the tube's entrance. "Good. I need to get the Alchemist into this world if this plan is going to work."

Micka raised a thick, perfectly arched, brow. "May I ask what the plan is exactly?"

Halston shook his head. His eyes hid a secret that he would not reveal to anyone.

Micka sighed. "Of course." She put her phone in her purse and stood straight. She folded her arms and looked ahead. "I want a raise after this."

Halston grinned. He lowered his voice and shielded his eyes from a fleeting ray of sunlight before the clouds hid it once again. "Oh come now, Micka. All you have to do is kill a few ancient vampires and store their souls in the hourglass for me."

Micka gave him a look. "I love how easy you make all of that sound. I know you're up to something fiendish. I can only imagine what you're going to use those vampire souls for. I wasn't born yesterday."

Halston chuckled. "Of course not. I was there when you were created, and I saw the qualities our father gave to you. I know you can do this without making a mess of things." He moved a lock of her soft hair behind her ear. "And I know you can be discreet."

Micka relaxed her shoulders and looked up at him from behind her completely blacked out sunglasses. She smirked. "That's the nicest thing you ever said to me."

Halston laughed heartily and folded his newspaper.

She nudged him in the side and started off. She glanced back as she hailed a taxi. "I still want that raise," she grinned.

CHAPTER 37

Koa always loved Cumbria. It was an English county full of rolling hills and natural green beauty. The people were friendly and much more relaxed and hospitable than Londoners. Here, people simply had more time for one another.

They went to the center city of Carlisle where they checked in to one of Lady Colleen's hotels to change and prepare for the ball.

Greggan would be there, Koa just knew it.

Lady Colleen insisted that they enjoy her hospitality and stay at her hotel and arrive in a two of her personal cars.

Koa showered and changed into a black gown. She frowned at her reflection, unsure of why she needed to dress so formally. She was glad that she was at least allowed to pick out her own gown from the assortment that Lady Colleen's designers had brought. It was floor-length, with a corseted top that cinched in her tiny waist and billowed out at her hips.

She liked the Victorian touch with the bustle and a high slit to her thigh. Now, for a place to keep her sword. She hid the sword, in its baton form, on her right thigh, opposite the exposing slit.

"Are we going to a theme party or something?" Koa asked. "Lady Colleen sure has an outdated taste for fashion. What is this, the 1800's?" She frowned at her image in the full length mirror. She looked like she was about to start singing opera. All she needed was a parasol.

Evina stepped beside her in a red dress. She gave Koa a little bump with her hip and pushed her way in front of her. She put her hands on her hips and smiled at her reflection.

"I mean, come on," Koa said as she fluffed her skirt. "It reminds me of my damn wedding gown!"

"Quit your complaining. It's work. Don't forget that, sweetheart."

Koa stepped back and watched the vampire princess. Koa had to admit that Evina was stunning. But when was she ever not stunning? She folded her arms across her chest as Evina turned from left to right, admiring her own image. She tousled her red tresses and covered the tattoos on the side of her scalp.

"Done checking yourself out?"

Evina looked over her shoulder. She smirked. "Almost," she said with a wink.

Koa shook her head but laughed a little as she pulled on her leather knee-high boots. Evina waved her hand at Koa with a horrified look on her face.

"No. Those won't do." Evina kicked her leg up and showed off her blood-red stiletto heels. "Wear something a little classier."

Koa made a face. "I really don't care. I can't kick someone's ass in stilettos. My boots are fine."

Evina shrugged. "Suit yourself. I can fight in anything."

Koa's face heated. That was an underhanded insult. She kicked the boots off and felt ridiculously short beside Evina without them. "Fine. I'll wear the stupid crystal shoes like a Cinderella reject."

Evina squeezed Koa's shoulder and smiled. "Good girl. I knew you'd see it my way." She hugged Koa to her and smiled in the mirror at their reflection. "Look at us. We're going to have all of the boys drooling."

"That just sounds gross," Koa grumbled as she opened the shoe box and gazed down at the shining pair of shoes. There was even a diamond-encrusted bow on the top of the shoe. "Why would you want a drooling man?" She pulled them out and slipped them on. Koa was short, but she hated heels. "Couldn't I at least wear a wedge?"

Evina laughed. "You're insufferable. Let's get a move on. I'm dying to meet this Lady Colleen." She pushed her corset in and adjusted her bosom. "I hope all of the anticipation is worth it." With one last wink at her reflection, Evina headed for the door. Dressed in elegant gowns, Evina and Koa left the room and stood before Jax and Tristan in the suite's sitting room.

Jax looked elegant, as was expected. Ian was adorable, as was expected. But…to see Tristan in a suit made Koa beam.

Evina clicked her tongue and folded her arms as she beheld the giant man. "Looking good, Mr. War-Breeder." She stepped closer to him as her heels clicked along the wooden floor. She smoothed his broad shoulders and sniffed his neck.

Tristan grinned at having Evina so close to him.

Evina looked up at him and purred. "You even smell nice."

Tristan straightened his tie. "Well, you know. Soap and water can go a long way."

Evina sniffed him again and closed her eyes in bliss. "I could get used to you this way."

"Snap out of it, Evina," Koa laughed. "You're getting too into character."

Evina glanced over her shoulder. "It is hard to tell when I'm genuine," she poked Tristan in the chest. "Or simply… tempting."

Tristan swallowed and shook his head. Evina laughed at his frown.

"Hey! Stop that!"

Koa couldn't suppress her laugh. The only one that remained serious was Jax. He watched them from his seat in the lounge. Calculating.

Koa sighed. She grabbed her clutch from the bar and headed to the door. "Let's get a move on. The party starts soon."

CHAPTER 38

Koa all but pressed her forehead to the window of the shiny white Rolls-Royce as she strained to get a look at the Colony. The thick fog shrouded the small island. Two more Rolls-Royce's followed behind with the others.

She couldn't handle the anticipation, so she rolled down her window and stuck her head out for a better look. Her hair flew around her face as she looked out towards the stone medieval castle.

Mist sprayed onto her face and she smelled sea water. Sea gulls flew above, calling to one another as they circled the bridge. Koa looked down as they crossed the bridge. Waves crashed against the stones and drowned out the light music that played inside the limo.

Butterflies fluttered in her stomach as she went over in her head what she would say to the Wryn's rival clan. The Netherworld Division rarely had to deal with these vampires. They kept to themselves and were secretive in their human blood dealings.

Koa had always wondered what set them apart from Lexi and the Wryn.

"Close that window, Koa," Evina said. "That air is messing up my hair."

Koa snorted. "That's just too bad," she teased with a smirk.

Evina shrugged and continued humming to herself. She smiled at her reflection in her hand mirror and twirled a lock of her red hair. She rubbed her teeth to make sure that her red lipstick hadn't stained them. Then, she clicked her pen to send a message to Jax.

Koa glanced at her as she wrote on the air. Netherworld dialect was beautiful, and Evina's flowing penmanship made the golden letters look even more ethereal as they clung to the air and faded with an unseen wind.

The smell of blood wafted into Koa's nostrils. She and Evina stepped out of the limo and onto the stone courtyard. Her mouth hung open as she looked up at the castle before her. She'd always thought that Wryn Castle was a stunning sight: dark and gothic. The Colony however, was a spectacle.

The castle was white like it came out of a fairy tale book. A drawbridge opened up to the courtyard. There were masts holding up flags of the vampire nation. Flags from various kingdoms in the Netherworld, represented in the human world. Koa looked up at the poles amazed by the lush detail of the different clan crests.

Lady Colleen's flag was raised the highest, equal to that of the United Kingdom flag at least. It was a black flag with a golden serpent hissing with its tongue out and coiled.

Koa marveled at the beautiful gowns the women were wearing. She realized that they were going to fit right in. Guests were already filling into the castle, with champagne glasses in their hands and decked out in their best jewels.

"All right," Evina said softly. "Remember what I told you. Sweet smile."

Koa nodded and smiled at the armed escort. They didn't look like the slick guards that protected Wryn Castle. These guys looked military. They had silver crossbows and silver breastplates like the guards in the Netherworld.

They looked Koa and Evina over. A very dashing looking vampire followed close behind them. He was slim and tall, with salt and pepper hair. He wore black-rimmed glasses and a green bow tie with his tailored black suit.

He gave them a bow and reached a hand out for Koa. Koa took his hand and did her best curtsy. She felt entirely foolish doing so, and nearly lost her balance, but the gentleman didn't seem to mind.

"Lovely to meet you, Queen Koa," he said and kissed the back of her hand.

When she looked up at him his green eyes caught her gaze. She shuddered when she looked into them.

He reached for Evina's hand and did the same. "And you as well, Princess Evina. I am Rezinger, and you two are absolutely smashing."

"Aww," Koa said with mock flattery. Something about him made her instantly dislike him. She couldn't help it. It always showed up on her face. She faked a smile. "Thank you."

"You're not too bad looking yourself," Evina said with a flirty grin. "Let's see," she said as she circled him with her seductive strut. "You were thirty-seven when you were sired. What were you before you became a vampire? Something…" She put her finger to her lips as she stood before him and thought.

Koa folded her hands before her and gave Rezinger a bored look. "She's always like this," Koa whispered.

Evina winked at her. She pressed her bosom to Rezinger's chest and sighed. He swallowed and tried to avoid looking down at her cleavage.

"Hmmm, what is that I sense? A man of law? No, no, a man of *politics.*"

Rezinger raised a well-shaped brow. "You're correct," he said and took a step back. He gave her a small smile. "I've always heard that true Netherworld vamps had amazing skills. Tell me, princess, what else can you do besides figure lowly New World vampires like me out?"

Evina laughed. She gave Koa a wink. "As if I'd tell you," she said. She took Koa's hand and nodded ahead. "Lead the way, Rezi."

Rezinger didn't show whether or not he was annoyed by having his name shortened. He kept that same smile on his face and turned to lead them from the courtyard to the castle.

CHAPTER 39

"When is Halston going to return?" Raven asked Alice.

She walked alongside the angel through a lovely courtyard in the center square. Raven kept her voice down as they passed by a pair of older women sitting on a bench in front of a fountain.

Alice shrugged. "He will show up just in time. Just like he always does. Lucky bastard."

Alice abruptly stopped talking. Raven froze. She could feel something. A strange sensation bubbled in her stomach, flooded her body, and rose up her throat with a gasp.

Danger.

She turned to run but Alice picked her up instead. "I knew it was too quiet!" She growled. "There are too many. We need to stay together."

They were being chased, but Raven could not position herself where she could see what was chasing them

Once they were out of human sight, Alice shot into the sky and landed on the roof of one of the buildings.

Alice's gray eyes scanned the scene below.

It was dark, but Raven could see something move from the alley to the right. Raven felt her body go cold. "Vamps, Alice. Two of them… and something else. I don't know that scent. He frightens me."

Alice nodded. Her face was serious. "Greggan sent his best. That's the second queen right there, Lera. And that creature you smell is a Scath. I've seen him before in the Netherworld. He's a creature from hell. His name is Trinity. I don't know who that other vamp is. It doesn't matter much." Her pink hair was blown into her eyes but she didn't reach to move it.

An arrow shot through the air. Raven tensed. It wasn't a normal arrow, but one that had an almost translucent chain trailing behind it. It stabbed right through Raven's chest.

Raven cried out in pain and Alice gasped. She quickly grabbed her and held her tight when Lera started pulling on the chain.

Raven winced. The pain was almost as bad as the transformation into a cat. She wished she could shed a tear for the agony she felt.

"Let her go, Alice!" Lera shouted. Alice screeched as Trinity vanished and reappeared behind her. He wrapped his arms around her neck and squeezed.

Alice refused to let Raven go. Raven felt herself growing weaker.

"Poison," she cried.

Alice kicked both of her feet up and slammed her boots into Trinity's chest. He didn't let go. Raven realized it at the same time that Alice did. She would have to let Raven go to break free from Trinity, and it did not look like she was quite ready to yield.

"Your angelic shield," Raven called.

Alice couldn't breathe. Trinity was suffocating her. She spoke to Raven inside her head. *"I can't. It would kill you too. I won't let go, Eunju."*

Raven felt herself fading. The pain didn't fade, it persisted. *"You have to. Do something quickly!"*

Raven saw tears in Alice's eyes as she started to fade. Raven clawed Alice's face. It was all that she could think to do. Alice refused to let go.

Raven squirmed out of Alice's tight embrace and jumped to the ground. As she leapt, Alice threw her arms out. The vamps froze. Raven's descent paused in mid-air.

Alice let out a guttural battle cry that seemed to make the city tremble. "No!" Alice shouted. Raven had to fight to turn her head to see Alice. Alice had broken free from Trinity's grip.

They had succeeded in making that angel truly angry.

Alice's gray eyes turned white and cloudy as she growled. Alice stepped off the side of the building and walked on air. Wind swept around her body as she lifted her arms. Trinity and the other vampire were lifted from the ground.

Lera ran. She seemed to be just out of Alice's range.

Raven breathed with relief. Her eyes widened when Alice activated her angelic glow. The vamps immediately began to burn. The power of the sun radiated from her small body.

Raven looked around. The light was so bright that she was sure the humans would see what was happening. She felt guilty to have Alice blow her cover just to save her. Her guilt was quickly replaced by dread when she felt her body get snatched by the translucent chain at the end of the arrow.

Lera grabbed her from the air, and ran like the wind.

CHAPTER 40

Koa tried to hide the fact that she was impressed with all of the décor and showmanship of this place. Evina was busy dancing with one of Lady Colleen's guests as Koa stood with a glass of wine. She drank down the Merlot like water and watched everyone.

She was almost reminded of the Netherworld. These vampires loved the old styles and traditions, unlike the Wryn clan that embraced modern ideals, styles, and society. Everyone at the ball was on their best behavior. It made Koa a little nervous. She was not the most tactful person.

She smiled as she watched Ian work the room. He was such a charming man, his vampire traits just brought his personality out even more. He told jokes and danced with girls. Although he was awkward, they loved him. Ian saw her from across the room and raised his champagne glass in the air.

Koa smiled and raised hers as well. "Cheers," she mouthed and they both drank.

Koa stood taller when she saw Jax approach her. She placed her empty champagne glass on the nearest server's platter.

She gave a slight nod to him and couldn't keep from smiling once he flashed his charming smile at her while ignoring the gorgeous women that tapped on his shoulder and tried to divert his attention.

Koa noticed how every woman in that room seemed to be watching the prince. They knew he was royalty, wealthy, and he was clearly one of the most attractive men at the ball.

Koa did like the attention, even if it was from looks of jealousy. She ran her fingers through her hair.

Jax took her hand. "Would you like to dance?" he asked.

Koa's cheeks reddened and she looked around at the guests. She shook her head. "I don't dance," she said with a giggle.

Jax gave her a gentle pull. "Come now. Don't be shy."

Koa sighed and let herself be pulled onto the dance floor. She never liked dancing, but she'd surely never danced in this style. Flowing movements and twirls like out of a classic movie or a ball room competition, Koa tried her best to keep up. She tripped over Jax's feet and he simply laughed.

Koa blew her bangs out of her eyes and laughed as well. She held onto his neck and gazed into his enchanting eyes. She wasn't afraid to look too deeply or to have him look back at her. Somehow she was confident. Even as she wondered what the clock around his iris meant.

Koa closed her eyes as he spun her around. She almost forgot where she was as she let the music take over. It drowned out the sounds of chatter and she felt as though she and Jax were floating on air.

It was lovely. Before she knew it, she was having fun. She opened her eyes and saw the clock in his eyes tick. She narrowed her eyes. "Your eyes," she said. "What is that clock? I don't remember it being there when we were younger in the Netherworld."

Jax stopped. He gave her an odd look as the color drained from his face. Koa tensed. She sensed that she had said something wrong. Her stomach sunk as she felt an odd wave of warning.

Jax dropped his hands from her waist, gave her one last look, turned and disappeared into the crowd.

Koa stood there in stunned silence. "What was that about?" she whispered. Before she could dwell on what had just occurred, Rezinger stepped beside her.

"You're a lovely dancer, Queen Koa," he said.

Koa closed her eyes and sighed. Her shoulders slumped. Her chance to go after Jax had passed. She opened her eyes and gave Rezinger a sidelong glance. "Please, do not call me that. I am not King Greggan's wife. What happened when I was a child was against my will. I am not a queen."

Rezinger nodded. "My apologies."

Koa turned to face him full on. Her face was serious. "But I am a princess. Princess Koa of Elyan, and I am tired of being stalled. You tell your mistress that I want to speak to her now."

Rezinger's smile faded but he nodded with a bow. "As you wish." He then turned to execute her wishes.

Koa followed behind him. She waved for Evina to come along. The red-haired temptress stopped playing with the group of men that she had entranced.

Rezinger paused and looked back. He raised a brow. "I'm going to relay your message."

Koa grinned. "Great. I'm coming to relay it myself." She waved him forward. "Go on. Continue."

He frowned, adjusted his bow tie, and continued through the ball room. Whispers tickled Koa's ears as she followed. Everyone watched them, wondering what was happening. Evina met her and kept pace as they finally made it through the crowd at to the great hall.

"Where are we off to?" Evina asked.

"I'm tired of waiting. We're going to talk to Lady Colleen."

Evina clasped her hands. "Excellent. Those gents were getting boring."

Koa shook her head. "You're like a kid, did you know that?"

Evina laughed. "So what? I've been stuck in the Netherworld since I was born. Who can blame me for wanting to have a little fun? New World vamps are so gullible. I can tempt them with my eyes closed, and my hands tied behind my back."

"With your boobs spilling out your dress, it doesn't take magic to tempt a man," Koa scoffed.

"Hey now, you little tramp. Watch your mouth," Evina warned, with a devilish grin. "You're just jealous. I would be too, if I had the body of a little boy."

Koa jabbed her in the ribs. "Bitch."

They shared a laugh and it felt like old times, but Koa was reminded of the severity of the situation when Rezinger stopped at the end of the hall, pulled a hidden lever and the floor moved beneath them.

Evina clutched Koa's arm as the three of them were taken down by elevator. The walls were of shining stone and it became dark the deeper they went.

Koa watched Rezinger as he turned on a light on the floor. Bright light shot up and illuminated their tiny enclosed means of transportation.

"You could have warned us," Evina said as she held onto Koa for balance. She glared at Rezinger.

Rezinger spoke under his breath as they continued to descend.

"What was that?" Evina demanded.

He flashed a charming smile, which had stopped working on Koa hours ago. "Nothing, princess. I'm just a little curious to how Lady Colleen will react to being awakened."

Koa made a face. She pointed to herself and Evina. "Do we look like we care? You'd think she'd be a little less rude with us as her guests. It's not like we're ordinary New World vamps."

Rezinger nodded. "Oh yes. Of course. You're special," he said. "I must remember that."

Koa pursed her lips. "Now I know why I don't like you. Condescending prick." She folded her arms and turned to Evina.

Evina smiled. "Calm down, sister. He just doesn't know any better," she said.

They came to a stop and Rezinger stepped back as one of the walls opened up to a cavern. A circular device, held stationary by iron brackets, stood in the center of the cavern. Behind it were bars that blocked the way to the next room.

"What is this?" Koa asked as she stepped out of the elevator.

"Oh, Koa. Doesn't it look familiar?" Evina said as she approached it with eyes of wonder.

Koa thought. It did look vaguely remember. "Refresh my memory for me," she said. "It's not as if I'm well rested. My mind's a little fuzzy."

"It's a portal," Rezinger said.

"A very ancient one," Evina added. "I haven't seen one of these since I was a child." She looked at Rezinger. "How did you get one?"

Rezinger shrugged. "Lady Colleen brought it with her when she left the Netherworld, I suppose."

Evina and Koa shared a look. "Lady Colleen is a Netherworld vamp?"

Rezinger made a face. "I thought you knew?"

Koa noticed a look of smug joy in his eyes. He took great pleasure in surprising them.

Evina sucked in a breath. She gripped Koa's hand and turned her to face her. Her tattoos moved and Koa felt a jolt of power surge into her body. Within seconds, she and Evina shared important information without Rezinger's knowledge.

"Koa. I know where I've heard that name now. Colleen is the sister of King Cidden of the western dominance of Jiran. She is one of the sentries sent out to explore the New World when my father found a way to escape centuries ago. She's one of the original vampires that spread our line to make the vampires here! She is not a weak vamp.

"We'd better be careful with this one. Trust me. Those western vamps are not to be trifled with. Father tried to conquer them once. He obviously lost. King Cidden is ruthless, even moreso than my father, but he isn't as power-hungry. But anyway, when the angels found out how the Netherworld vamps were getting free, they sought those sentries out and sent them back or killed them. Colleen is the only one they did not find! How did Halston not know this?"

Koa swallowed hard to keep her dinner down as Evina released her from the bond of her temptress powers. She tried to keep a straight face as Rezinger looked them over.

"Are you all right?" he asked.

Koa nodded. She took a breath and steadied herself. "Fine. What are you waiting for? Activate the portal."

CHAPTER 41

"Tell me again," Bund said. He crouched low to the ground, just beyond the black gates of Wryn Castle, as Greggan stood beside him. "What you'll give me if I kill the Halston."

Greggan watched the moon. The clouds shrouded it, but it was still a majestic sight. He looked down at Bund. "Everything. The Netherworld will be yours for the taking. You'll have my armies and the forces you need to take the entire civilization of nephilim. Just leave the human world to me."

Bund grinned. His sharp teeth flashed in the night. "That all sounds peachy keen and all, but I want the half-blood too."

Greggan tightened his jaw. "What will you do to her?"

Bund chuckled. The sound was unlike a human or vampire laugh. It sent chills through the vampire king. "That's my business."

"You'd better start producing results then," Greggan said as he stood before the massive black structure that stood of the edge of a cliff that overlooked the sea. Wryn Castle. He had cleaned it out and made it into a home. If only he could keep Bund from targeting vampires. He didn't let Bund know, but he had noticed how vampires whom he'd invited to the castle from the surrounding colonies were disappearing. It didn't make sense to Greggan. Why would a demon want a vampire? He could not think of what purpose they would serve him.

Greggan prepared to head to Lady Colleen's grand ball. He closed his fur coat and held onto a shiny new cane. He had special transportation prepared and he was ready to arrive in style and fashionably late. It was his chance to end this little resistance the Netherworld Division was putting up.

Bund came to his feet. Black wings stretched open and he hovered in the air. "You don't trust me?" He flew closer to Greggan's face. A low snarl made Greggan tense.

Greggan looked away as Bund's eyes turned into a pool of black. Black veins coursed through his pale, almost translucent, face. Greggan held his ground as the demon circled him, sniffing his trench coat.

"Of course I trust you, Bund. But in order for this arrangement to work, we must be mutually beneficial to one another."

Bund chuckled again. He landed in a crouch and looked up at Greggan with those sinister eyes. "I thought setting you free… and letting you live was beneficial enough."

Something in Bund's voice alarmed Greggan. The demon had threatened him before, but this time something was different. Was it the change in speech? Perhaps it was the entirely different accent. Bund had rarely spoken in such a way that made Greggan truly fear him. Now, his body went cold. He put a hand on the hilt of his sword.

Greggan made a clicking sound with his tongue. Bund rose to his full height and stood taller than Greggan. He snatched Greggan's sword from its scabbard and held the blade diagonally across the vampire's throat.

"Yes," Greggan swallowed, uncomfortable. He eyed the blade. "I only meant that…"

Bund shook his head. He spoke softly, calmly. "Shh," he whispered. He leaned in closer to Greggan's face. Black eyes gazed into the vampire king's. "You only meant that you thought I was a fool."

Greggan shook his head. He held his hands up in surrender. "No. That's not it at all. Listen."

"You all think you're so smart. So clever." Bund grimaced. His eyes narrowed into a glare. "But I've fooled you, Greggan. I've fooled you all."

Greggan took a step back and Bund took one step forward. He grabbed the back of Greggan's head and pressed the blade to his throat. Black fire burned behind the demon's eyes. "But I have seen Heaven and Hell. I have been around since before you were even a seed in your mother's womb. Did you really think that I'd be around the world that long and not have the power to outsmart a lowly vampire like yourself."

Greggan was speechless.

Bund removed the sword. He grinned. "I didn't think so." He raised a brow. "Thought you were the clever one?"

Greggan's lips parted. He started to speak but Bund raised a finger.

Greggan closed his mouth.

Bund's grin widened. "Good boy." He lowered his wings and lowered the sword to his waist.

Greggan stood completely still. He imagined summoning help, but he was unsure if he was faster than Bund. He swallowed, and glanced at his sword in the demon's hands.

"Greggan," Bund called.

Greggan looked up. Their eyes met.

Bund tilted his head. "Didn't anyone tell you that I could read your thoughts?"

Greggan paled and before he could blink, his head was separated from his shoulders and he was staring at the moon, waiting for his body to reanimate. He would rise again. His body would reform into another creature, one that was more primal, but stronger. Greggan could have another shot, but with the demon hovering over his body, waiting to kill him again… he didn't want to.

CHAPTER 42

Koa waited with Evina as Rezinger approached the portal. He opened the control panel and dialed a series of numbers. The portal ignited with the sound of bells. The globe-like ball in the center started to spin as the gimbals twisted around it.

Rezinger came to them and held out an enclosed fist. "Only one of you can go in. I only have the one earth stone." He looked from Evina to Koa. "Which of you will it be?"

Koa stepped forward. She held her hand out and Rezinger placed the earth stone in her hand. Koa looked down at the flat black rock. In the center of it was a green Netherworld symbol. The language of the angels and the heavens.

It was cool in the palm of her hand and she felt oddly at peace as she held it.

"Don't forget what's at stake, Koa," Evina said.

Koa turned to her and nodded. "Never," she replied.

"I'll wait out here with Princess Evina," Rezinger said. "Once you get inside you'll want to take the hallway on the right. Don't go left or you'll get lost. Then, you just follow that hallway and take a right at each end. Got it?"

"Got it. Never turn left. Only right."

He patted Koa on the shoulder. A smug grin came to his lips. "Good luck."

Koa raised a brow and looked down at his hand on her shoulder. She shrugged it off. "Don't ever touch me again," she said and flew backwards to the portal. "And how about grabbing a few more of those earth stones for my friends."

Rezinger nodded. "As you wish, Princess Koa."

Evina gave Koa one last nod and mouthed a word.

Careful.

Koa closed her eyes and allowed the portal to suck her body into the spinning golden globe. Colors flashed before her and she felt her body get squeezed, pulled, and spat out onto the other side of the gate.

Koa shivered and crouched on all fours as she waited for the sensation to pass. Her vision slowly cleared and she came to her feet. She saw Evina and Rezinger on the other side. Rezinger went to collect more earth stones while Evina pressed her back to the stone wall and waited.

"I made it," Koa shouted over to Evina.

Evina didn't look over. She drew something on the air with her pen.

"Evina," she called. Koa's brows furrowed.

Nothing. Not even a glance.

"Rezinger?"

Still, neither of them looked at her. Koa's shoulders slumped as she realized that they could neither see nor hear her. She sighed and turned to the opening of a narrow hall. She walked inside and found two halls. She stared down the hall on the left and saw light at the end. She glanced over her shoulder to the other hall, the right one, and saw a thick fog and darkness.

She shook her head. "Just perfect. Of course I need to take the creepy hall," she said under her breath. She tapped her left thigh and made sure that her sword was still secure in its strap. Then she took a breath and set out for the right hall as Rezinger had advised.

Stepping into the fog was like entering an icebox. The chill in the air was almost unbearable, especially for someone who barely had on any clothes. Koa rubbed her arms and frowned as she looked around.

The walls were very close and were made of stone. The intense smell of dirt and coal clung to the air as she continued down the hall. At the end of it, she once again glanced left. Her eyes widened as she saw a black figure walking away from her. It appeared to be a man, but it was completely burnt until blackened and carried a long pole.

Koa gasped inwardly and quickly ran into the right hall, away from whatever that was. Her heart quickened as she hurried down the hall and to the end. She didn't even bother to look to the left, she simply ran into the right hall and was greeted by a door.

The door was at least nine feet tall, yet slim. There was a small hole cut in the shape of the earth stone. Koa was already tired of being alone in that labyrinth of hallways, so she placed the stone in the hole and pushed it open without a second thought.

Her squeal echoed throughout the entire labyrinth as snakes hissed at her from the other side of the door. Koa reached under her skirt and grabbed her sword. She flew to the ceiling to get away from the hundreds of snakes that filled the newest hallway and clicked the button to release the sword from its baton state.

The power of the Lyrinian blade was ignited. It shot into Koa's palm and filled her body with red hot rage. She calmed herself and flew down the hall and away from the snakes.

"Who are you?"

Koa paused in the air. The voice sounded faint, distant. She looked around and saw no one. Koa frowned. "Where are you?"

"I asked the question first, child. Who are you?"

Koa swallowed. "Princess Koa of Elyan."

The hissing faded and the snakes vanished. A woman came from around the corner with her bow and arrow pointed right at Koa in the air. She dressed in Netherworld style and had her black hair pulled into a braided bun. Behind her was a black wolf.

Koa held a hand up. "I was told to come here by Halston. I'm not an enemy."

The woman eyes flickered a glow as she shot an arrow at Koa's sword, knocking it from her hand. Koa followed her sword downward and landed on her feet beside it on the floor.

She looked up from under her bangs. "Nice shot."

The woman relaxed, but only slightly.

"Lady Colleen, I take it," Koa said as she picked up her sword and clicked it back into a baton.

Lady Colleen nodded and lowered her bow. She looked Koa up and down. "The mysterious half-blood finally comes to pay a relative a visit."

Koa raised a brow. "Relative?"

Lady Colleen turned and motioned for Koa to follow her. "Didn't Alsand ever tell you about your pretty Aunt Colleen?"

CHAPTER 43

Koa followed Lady Colleen through her underground labyrinth. She was amazed by all that she saw down there. It was almost as if she was in the Netherworld again. Everything was decorated in the same lavish style.

Once they left the drab, dark tunnels, they stepped into Lady Colleen's private quarters. Colorful drapes of gold and royal blue hung from columns making the entire room look like one giant canopy bed. Vampires sat quietly on the floor reading, drinking wine, and lounging about on the plush cushions laid out.

As Koa walked behind her aunt she noticed that even Lady Colleen was dressed in ancient Netherworld fashion. Everyone down there was. Koa wasn't opposed to the Victorian and Roman mixture of dress. She kind of liked it better than the modern style above.

Colleen's corseted top made her waist look tiny and the bustled skirt was wrapped in layers almost like a geisha. It was a rich royal blue and made her black hair stand out. Her bony exposed shoulders were pale as a sheet of paper. Still, her skin glistened as if it had been brushed with jewels.

Koa thought to herself how amazing her mother and father's genes were. Everyone was so beautiful. She noticed someone staring at her as she walked by. An older gentleman. Koa raised a brow. He definitely stood out in the midst of such artificial youth.

Koa sniffed the air. He was human. His hair was pure white without a trace of any other color. It was almost as if his hair had always been that color. He bowed to her as she walked by while everyone else ignored her.

Koa nodded her head and couldn't take her eyes off of him. She realized that he wasn't as old as his hair made him appear. He only had small wrinkles at the corners of his small, deep-set eyes. He watched her from his low bow. He secured his thin glasses on his nose as he stood back up to his full height, which wasn't much taller than Koa.

"That's Nickolai Frost," Colleen said with a wave of her hand.

Koa stopped walking. She looked at Colleen. "*The* Nickolai Frost?"

"Yes," she answered. She held her arms out and motioned for Nickolai to come forward. "Let me introduce you to one another, even though he is quite aware of who you are."

Koa swallowed and looked at the older man with even more curiosity. He reached out for her hand.

"Lovely to meet you, princess." His dark eyes were unsettling.

Koa shook his hand. For a moment she couldn't speak. She simply stared into his eyes. She wasn't sure what she was expecting. She'd heard stories about the mysterious human that seemed to be the real Julian Grey. He never aged beyond that of a man of his forties and had been around for much longer than a normal human should live.

"Likewise," Koa said.

He was not a normal human.

Nickolai turned his attention to Lady Colleen. "I'll go and feed the beasts." He gave Koa a look. "You two young ladies can take care of yourselves while I'm gone, right?"

Colleen laughed. "Of course." She tapped her bow with a long finger nail.

Nickolai nodded. He winked at Koa. "I'm sure we'll see each other again soon, princess," he said and started off.

As he walked away, Colleen leaned closer to Koa. "He likes to think of himself as my bodyguard," she whispered.

"I heard that," Nickolai called over his shoulder before continuing away.

Colleen smiled and put her hands on her bony hips. She shook her head. "I won't deny it. He is quite handy to have around." She sighed. Her wolf came and sat beside her at attention. He eyed Koa.

Koa felt a strange sensation flood her body. There was something about the way the wolf looked at her that made her feel incredibly uncomfortable. His eyes were too intelligent, and the way he looked at her was not the way an animal looked at a human.

It hit Koa. She knew the real reason Halston had sent her there.

She took one startled step back. Her eyes looked from the wolf to Colleen. "Who is that?"

Colleen's smile widened. She nodded in approval. "You are a clever girl. Halston is always right."

Koa looked back at the wolf. "Speak."

The wolf gave Koa a look and looked to his master.

Colleen petted the wolf's head. "This is Oren," Colleen smoothed the white fur on his head. "Go on, darling, speak. She is a friend."

Oren gave Koa a look. His voice was otherworldly. "Hello," he said simply.

Koa felt her heart pound. Her cheeks flushed with anxiety. She stepped closer to them both and fell to her knees before Oren. "Who is he? How did this happen? Was he cursed as well?"

Colleen sighed. "Come this way, darling. We can talk somewhere more private. Come," she held a thin hand out. "Please, off your knees in that lovely dress."

Koa took her hand. She was growing impatient. She nodded quickly and followed behind Oren and Colleen to the back of the room that was sectioned off by a half wall and clear of all visitors.

Colleen poured Koa a drink from her bar and nodded for her to sit down on one of the chaise lounges in the corner. Koa drank her wine down and flopped onto the golden chaise. She tapped her toes and bounced her knee as she waited for Colleen to leisurely lay across the chaise. She looked perfect, as if she was about to have her portrait painted.

Oren rested on his stomach beside the chaise and watched Koa as he laid his head on his front paws.

CHAPTER 44

"Oh good," Bund said. He stood from his seat behind the large executive desk. He clapped his skinny hands as Lera carried a gray cage into the room.

Inside was a black cat with ethereal green eyes that held the secrets to Koa's true lineage.

Bund grinned. "You did it. Fine job, young lady. Fine job indeed."

Lera stopped walking abruptly. She raised a thin black brow as her eyes scanned the room. She frowned up at Bund. "Where is King Greggan? Why are *you* here?"

"Dead," Bund shouted with glee. "The king is dead! The king is dead!" Bund chanted like an excited child. He slammed his fist on the desk before him and grinned a toothy grin. "*Finally,* I can stop listening to his annoying voice! And yes, I don't have to watch him stroke that stupid red beard of his anymore!"

Bund's chuckle filled the study.

Raven searched for a way to get out of her cage. She was useless against Bund in her present form. She needed to run and hide. She knew he only had one plan for her, and that was to kill her.

Bund stepped from around the desk.

Raven was surprised to see him dressed so formally. Her fur stood on end. He was planning on going to the ball, not Greggan.

He folded his hands behind him. "And you, dear lass, can call me master. No, better yet, call me daddy!"

Lera fell to her knees. She dropped the cage with Raven in it. Raven braced herself for the impact as the cage hit the floor and rolled a few feet away. Raven crashed into the steel bars. She watched the latch though. It was almost loose.

Lera cried out. "No!"

Bund laughed and threw up his fist. "Yes!" Bund cheered.

Lera covered her face with her hands and wept. Her cries were almost heart-wrenching, but Raven was glad that Greggan was dead. One less villain to worry about.

Bund grimaced down at Lera as she sobbed like a woman who had lost the man she loved.

"Seriously?"

Lera wailed and pulled a dagger from its sheath. She positioned it above her heart and glared at Bund with teary eyes. "You bastard. I will never call you master."

Lera stabbed herself in the heart and sucked in a breath of pain.

Bund rolled his eyes. "Jesus Christ," he mumbled. "Loyalty is such a stupid thing." He watched Lera writhe on the floor. "You idiot," he shouted in disgust at her dying body.

She died a painful death and all was quiet. For a moment.

Bund sighed and spoke to Raven. "You see that nonsense? What a waste."

"Loyalty is not stupid. No one will ever be loyal to you. It's a beautiful thing, and you know nothing of beauty, you monster," Raven said from her cage.

Bund shook his head and ignored her. He had seen Netherworld vamps transform many times. He'd seen at least a thousand Netherworld wars. As he watched Lera's body start to mutate, he sat back down and raised a brow.

"Oh yes," he said. "This is good. I can use this." He clapped and cheered. "Come on, old girl. Let's give these pesky agents something to really cry about!" She continued to mutate and transform. Her body began to reanimate itself and she let out a feral cry that was half woman and half beast.

Bund laughed then as Lera stood on all fours, howling like a wolf. He held his stomach and laughed like a maniac. He snapped his fingers and sent a few souls her way. He stood watched the souls enter her body. "Yes!" he cried.

Lera's body became bigger and bigger. She cried out in pain as the souls entered her body. She went from standing on four legs to two once again. She screamed, not knowing what was happening, and Bund continued his assault. He sent more and more souls across the room. When all went quiet, Bund clasped his hands before him.

He had a grin plastered to his face. "Beautiful. My own creation," he breathed in wonder.

Before him was no longer a vampire queen, nor a reanimated woman, before him was the first vampire to make a third transformation.

Lera looked down at her body. Naked and in the shape of a woman once again, there was much that was different about her. She marveled at her new body and looked across the room at her new master.

"What have you done to me?" she asked. Her eyes were red, her skin was smooth, but black as ash. Her hair was the same bone-straight black that she was born with, but now, she was the most powerful vampire to ever exist.

Bund grinned and leaned back against the desk. "Good," he said softly. His eyes were glazed over as if he was in deep thought, or daydreaming. He watched Koa, drinking and socializing as if it was just another day. He couldn't wait to surprise her with his plan. He breathed in deeply and looked over at the empty space between the bookcase and the window in the corner.

He nodded. "You can come out now, Trinity."

Trinity materialized out of the air and stepped out of the darkness. He silently awaited instruction.

Bund clasped his hands and looked at his team. They may have been outnumbered, but they were bringing the power of Hell to the party.

CHAPTER 45

Koa sat and drank from her flute of champagne. The alcohol barely had an effect on her. She was glad. She needed to be alert when Greggan showed up. Lady Colleen stroked Oren's fur as she lounged across her chaise in her calm, regal pose.

She was so elegant. Koa envied her that.

"So, we're family," Koa asked. Small talk wasn't her strong suit, but she was anxious about Greggan's anticipated arrival.

Lady Colleen nodded. "Indeed. We are of the same royal blood line. One of the most powerful in all of the Netherworld and this world. We come from the first vampire created by the fallen angels, dear girl." She rested her head on the arm of her chaise and looked up at the high ceiling. "There was a time when our line were like gods. Before the first war, and the exodus of our people to their prison."

Koa pursed her lips. "It's better than being exterminated," Koa said.

Lady Colleen lolled her head to the side and gave Koa a cool look from across the room.

Koa didn't look away, even though she wanted to.

"The words of a child. One that's been fed the same nonsense the Netherworld Division likes to brainwash its agents with."

Koa frowned. "Nonsense? It's the truth. Would you prefer another war?"

Lady Colleen sat up. Her grin was unsettling. "Perhaps," she said as she stood. "I think it's time I check on my guests upstairs. You'll be all right down here, won't you?"

Koa nodded despite her annoyance. She wanted to continue their conversation.

Koa's watch buzzed. She glanced at Ian as he came into the large den with Evina, Rezinger, Tristan, and Jax. Koa held the champagne in her mouth. Her heart nearly stopped. She saw the looks on their faces and she knew something was wrong.

She set the glass down and clicked her watch. Her eyes never left the faces of her team. A familiar voice spoke softly, calmly.

"They took her," Alice said.

Koa heard the words, she knew their meaning, but somehow she could not react. She could not move, or think, or even remember to breathe. A strange sensation filled her belly and she recognized it. It was odd, like a pain, but stronger. Like love but more intense.

Koa balled her fingers into a tight fist. She bit hard into her lip, so hard that she tasted her own salty blood. Her heart beat too quickly for her to even begin to calm down. She fumed and shook with rage. Tears stung her eyes and she suppressed the urge to scream at the top of her lungs. She narrowed her eyes and looked at her hands.

"Koa," Ian called softly. "I'm sorry but we'll get her back."

Koa shot a glare at him. "You know nothing, Ian. Nothing at all. They are going to kill her," Koa was surprised to hear her voice crack.

Something shot her in the back. She gasped. The shock and the pain left her stunned into silence.

She reached around to touch what had been shot into her back.

Koa's face paled.

It was a stake.

Ian quickly pulled it out and she fell to her knees.

The room went into chaos then.

An eruption of shouts and cries filled the room. Koa looked up to see Nicolai Frost and a team of Netherworld agents, angels and humans, flood the room like a small army. To her surprise and dismay, they were shooting at everyone in the room.

Everyone.

Koa didn't break her gaze from Nicolai's as she pulled her baton from her garter belt. She swung the sheath off the sword and let it extend into its full length.

Nicolai pointed and gave commands to the agents and ran into the battle.

Koa sucked in a breath, fighting through the pain in her back. She glanced to her side.

Evina was already fighting.

At least Koa knew who was on her side now. Betrayal stung almost as much as the grief and worry for her mother.

Evina tossed her sword into the air and it never came back down. Instead, it swirled above her head, as her tattoos seemed to dance along her skin. She closed her eyes and knelt in the center of the room. A temptress at work was a wonderful sight to behold.

Koa was glad that she was with Evina. Every male vampire within range of Evina's temptation fought for her, killing without care for their own lives. They yelled like wild men and threw their bodies at the agents to protect her.

Koa held her sword in front of her and waited. She was more than ready. They had no idea of the wrath that they'd unleashed. Koa no longer cared what happened to her, or about rules, or about the Netherworld Division at all. As far as she was concerned, they'd betrayed her. Her old comrades were now her enemies.

Tristan walked over to her. Koa looked up at him with pleading eyes. "What is happening?"

Tristan looked down at her with an alarming look. He pitied her, but he did not move to help.

Koa shook her head as realization filled her body. Tears stung her eyes. "No, Tristan," Koa whispered. "Not you too."

Tristan looked away. His metal gauntlets were glowing. "You have to understand something. My people were created to kill vampires. I have my orders to wipe out this clan. But, I promise, I won't lay a hand on you, Koa."

Koa felt a tear drop. She'd been betrayed. No one told her what the plan really was. The Oracle was right.

"Do not trust," Koa whispered in sorrow.

Tristan shook her head. "I'm sorry," he turned away for her.

The heartbreak was overwhelming. She was on her own now. On her own with a handful of vampires.

Koa choked back tears. The pain fed her fury. She came to her feet and growled in frustration. One by one, Koa sliced through the agents with a fury never seen from her before. She'd never felt so betrayed in her life. Not even Halston had revealed to her the true plan.

They sent her and her mother out there like cattle, decoys, just to draw out Greggan. Koa shouted when someone ripped her dress. She shot over to the agent like lightning, kicked him in the chest with both of her legs, and landed on top of his body. She leaned down with rage in her eyes and twisted his neck until she head a satisfying snap.

Her eyes searched for Jax and Evina.

Koa feared for their lives as Tristan entered the battle. Her eyes widened as big as saucers as she beheld his power.

The large War-Breeder held up both arms, increased the glow of the metal gauntlets on his wrists, and slammed his fists into the floor.

The sound was deafening as the ground cracked and a force field of red light ignited from around him, and rippled outwards in a circle. Every vampire within the range of his power cried out and burst into flames. The agents within range were immune to Tristan's power. They were relieved that he ended their battles with the vampires.

Tristan glanced at her with eyes of black. He was not her friend anymore. He was a horrific monster that made her fear for her life.

She lost it.

Koa cried out as a shot of pain filled her belly.

Bund.

Her lips trembled as he cackled inside her head. She forced it out of her mind. She would not yield.

The pain within persisted, but she didn't have time to pay it any attention. She would fight it. She would fight Bund's hold on her.

An agent, one that she didn't recognize, took a shot at her with a crossbow. Koa clenched her teeth. She stabbed with expert precision, knocking their heads clean off and smashing their skulls in. The Lyrinian sword squealed with glee. It tasted blood, human blood, and went from black to red.

The power their souls gave the sword swarmed inside of Koa's body. Drunk on blood lust, Koa felt woozy, as if she was floating on clouds the entire battle. Koa barely realized that everyone had stopped fighting after a while. She was so overcome with pain and euphoria that she barely realized that she was floating and glowing.

Koa looked down at her body and her brows furrowed. The glow was almost like Halston's, but different. Sparks flew around her, crackling along the air and hitting the ground, transforming into steam.

Koa cried out and crumpled to the floor. The glow went out. Her eyes burned with tears, but they would not come. Instead, that strange feeling filled her. She realized what it was far too late.

Koa reached out for Ian as he ran to her. He was covered in blood. She was sorry that she missed seeing him in action. She squeezed his shoulder. The look of agony and fear in her eyes made his face pale even whiter than it was.

Koa clutched him and fell to her knees.

"Koa!" Jax called. "What's happening?" He rushed to help her up.

Ian tried to steady her. She fell to the ground once Ian was shot with something that was way too quick for her eyes.

Koa sucked in a breath as she fell to her knees. Bedlam filled the room.

Screams. Shouts. Cries of anguish, sadness, and pain. Koa fell onto her back, nearly paralyzed. Jax searched the room with his eyes to see what had happened.

Blood filled Koa's eyes as she looked up at Jax while he held her head in his lap.

"What's happening?" Jax shouted again.

She reached for Ian's hand as he gasped for air and looked down at his bloodied shirt. A thin stake protruded from his chest.

She only had time to speak one word. "Bund!"

Koa's eyes fluttered closed. And the world went red.

CHAPTER 46

Halston waited in the back of the hired car. He was dressed in his finest suit, shoes, tie, and cuff links. His blonde hair was perfect. He was prepared for this night. This was the night that would change it all.

This was the night when he could finally return home

He felt heavy-hearted. He thought he would feel excited. Instead, as the car pulled up to the Colony, he felt only dread. He did not want to do what he set out for. When the car stopped, he saw that the guards were not at their posts.

He sighed. "It has begun," he said under his breath. He took out his infinity gun and stepped out of the car. He looked up at the sky and really took it all in. The moon was so bright on this night. There were no clouds. There was no rain. All he heard was the buzzing of nature. Then, he heard the bone-chilling screams.

Halston slammed the car door shut, set his face in determination, and shot the first vampire that came running out of the doors. She was young and beautiful, and covered in blood already. Halston shot his infinity gun and ended her screams and pleads for help.

He watched her fall, and stepped over her body to enter the castle. He walked through the castle like that for what seemed an eternity. Grim-faced as he killed every vampire in sight, without prejudice, without mercy.

Halston checked his watch. Greggan should be making his grand entrance soon. He crunched on broken glass and slid across the room a few feet in the spilled blood. The bodies were piled up as his infinity gun made its rounds through every black heart in the ballroom.

The smell of blood was so strong. Halston was tired of dealing with it. He was ready for this era of blood fiends to end.

The scream of the infinity bullet filled his ears. Once every vampire was dead, it returned to its resting place in the barrel of his gun. He stood there for a moment, listening to the sound of peaceful silence. There were no gurgles, cries, or second transformations. When the infinity gun did its work, there was no second chance. There was nothing but death.

Halston closed his eyes and spread his arms as his angelic shield ignited. The power of the sun emitted from his body and turned all of the gore and vampire remains into ash.

"Jesus Christ," Halston heard a voice call from behind. His eyes opened and he froze.

It was not the voice he was waiting for.

Halston turned around and watched in confusion as Bund entered the room. Bund looked different. He wasn't haggard, or disheveled. He'd actually dressed up for the occasion. The demon actually looked decent.

Halston knew then, that he had been tricked. Bund had finally given up his convenient disguise of ignorant bliss. Halston's jaw tightened. He'd always known Bund's true self would come back eventually.

Bund gave Halston a look of almost-genuine surprise. "You sure know how to ruin a party, Halston." He covered his mouth in mock sadness. "I mean… my god. We need to get you to counseling, brother."

Halston balled up his fist. "Where is Greggan?"

Bund's eyes widened. He sucked in a deep breath as if he was about to give a long speech, instead he shrugged. "Dead."

Halston looked down at the ashy floor.

"Next question," Bund said.

Halston glared at him. "What are you doing?"

Bund cracked a grin. "Beating you, brother."

Halston darted across the room towards him and shoved him to the floor.

Bund slid on his back and laughed the entire time. "Whee!" He shouted gleefully. "Come on, brother, let's play!"

Halston's breaths sped up. He ran his hand through his hair. What was happening?

"Stop calling me brother! We are not brothers anymore, and never will be again." Halston pointed his infinity gun at Bund as he came back to his feet.

Bund's smile faded as he looked at the gun. He gave Halston an awed look. "This is it? Your only weapon? Pitiful."

Halston began to speak but Bund raised a hand to silence him. He looked off into the distance and started to hover off the ground.

"Sorry, Halston, dear boy. But I've been collecting souls for centuries. You might as well turn around and walk away. You will never be as strong as me." He laughed at the look on Halston's face. "This was fun though. Truly priceless, but you see, I have business to tend to," he grinned at Halston and the world seemed to go still for them both. "I have a half-blood to torture and her soul to eat."

Halston's eyes widened and Bund flew away, through the wall, and to his only love.

Halston was frozen for a moment. He didn't know where to go, or what to do. Bund had his Koa, and he was defenseless against him. He looked at his infinity gun and said a prayer. There was only one thing he could do.

Halston felt a tear trail down his face.

He would not be returning home on this night.

CHAPTER 47

Halston raced through the castle, searching. He found his way to the lower levels and ignored the persistent calls his watch was giving him.

Micka's face came up as a hologram. "Halston! Where are you? I have the hourglass!"

Halston paused. "Where are you?"

Micka's image looked around. "I don't know. Still near the entrance."

Halston closed his eyes in annoyance. "Bloody useless," he said under his breath. He changed direction and flew back the way he had come.

"Maybe if you would have told me what this was for, I would be more useful to you!" Micka fumed. Her image vanished for a second.

Halston almost stopped flying to call her back but he didn't have the time. Her image popped back up after only a moment. Her face was even angrier. "Pardon me," she said. "I took out the guards."

Halston didn't reply. He needed that hourglass. His head pounded. Sweat beaded on his forehead and dripped from his face.

He hated changing plans at the last second.

When Halston reached Micka, he held his hand out and she dropped the hourglass in his hands. She tapped her feet as she looked him up and down. She on the other hand, still looked immaculate in her green ball gown.

"Looks like I'm a little late," she said and folded her arms.

She nodded to the hourglass as Halston simply stood there staring at it.

"Dear Father," Halston whispered.

Micka unfolded her arms. She put a hand on Halston's shoulder and leaned over to get a look at his face. "What's wrong, Halston?"

She stumbled backwards when he opened the hourglass from the bottom and poured the contents into his mouth. Hundreds of vampire souls flooded Halston's body.

Micka crawled backwards, away from him, in horror. She looked at him as if she looked upon a ghost. Her lips trembled. Tears filled her eyes. "Halston, no," she cried.

Halston's face twisted in despair and he fell to his knees.

Micka came to her feet. She shook her head and tears flung off her cheeks. "I can't watch this. You're on your own now," she said and shot into the sky.

Halston truly did feel alone at that moment. He buried his face in his hands.

CHAPTER 48

Halston let the light shed from his body as he made it to the den. He walked there, fighting the pain, as the transformation began.

He stood in the archway and saw Koa's body hanging by its feet, against the far wall.

Bund was there. Jax and Evina were chained to one another and screamed from the inside of the fire pit.

Tristan was held immobile by the hellion named Trinity, the only creature strong enough to keep his dear friend prisoner.

There was no turning back now, even if Halston wanted to. Seeing Koa thrash in pain. He did not want to. He wanted to kill Bund and save Koa.

Halston's hair, once blonde, became darker, until it was black as night. Pain no longer existed, for his rage and sorrow took over completely. He was tormented by the fact that he was giving up his last chance for redemption, his last chance to go home. It made him fall to his knees.

Halston's heart was broken, and so he let it turn cold and black. The blackness and the evil, seeped through his skin. His veins turned black and covered his face and he clenched his jaw as the black flames of hell consumed him and completed the transformation. He balled up his fists and closed his bright blue eyes.

The black flames licked and danced wildly around his body, cleansing him of all purity. They claimed his goodwill and power, and replaced it with something darker. The power of evil burned itself into his skin. It raced through his blood and etched itself onto his bones.

Halston opened his eyes and revealed a pool of black. When he stood, all sounds returned at full force, and he was no longer an angel.

Bund turned from Koa as Halston entered the large den.

Halston stepped over bodies. He kicked some aside.

Bund frowned. "What happened to you?" Realization hit Bund and it showed all over his skinny face. His jaw fell.

Bund started to stutter. "G-g-good move, brother. I didn't know you actually had it in you." His face became nonchalant. "How many did you have anyway? Souls, that is?"

Halston was the one to grin now, cruelly, evilly. "At least a hundred."

Bund nodded. "Nice. I'm impressed."

Halston's grin widened. "At least a hundred *vampire* souls." He raised a brow.

Bund swallowed. His face couldn't have gone any whiter.

"Those are the most powerful, right?"

Bund removed the dagger from Koa's belly, licked it clean, and stabbed it back in.

"Well, now. That's right. You know what, Halston? We are brothers again," Bund said with his arms outstretched. "We're no longer enemies. We are brothers in darkness, you and I."

Halston closed his eyes at the truth in Bund's words.

He had completed the transformation. It was final.

Halston was a demon.

What happened next was a sight to behold.

Halston ripped his infinity gun from its holster and black flames covered the once-silver steel that had become black. The infinity bullet growled. Halston's eyes fell on Bund and all of his repressed hate filled his gaze until Bund stepped back.

"Now, tell me where Koa's mother is," Halston ordered calmly. He'd never felt so powerful in his entire existence.

"With Lera." Bund held his arms out. "Wait until you see her. My creation. You'll be so proud. Come, now, brother," Bund called.

Halston raised a brow. "I have no brothers, or sisters, or any family." He stepped forward and Bund held his hands up in surrender. There was something sinister in Halston's voice. Something unearthly that Bund had never heard come from the good and pure Halston.

Halston glanced over at Koa and felt a strange sensation flood his body. There she was, completely ignorant to what had happened because of her. Blissfully unaware, as always. A selfish little girl had stolen his heart. That feeling that filled his body didn't last long, for the rage returned and ignited his once-angelic shield. No longer golden and pure, his shield had become gray, with red sparks flying around his body.

Bund hurried to ignite his own, but it sputtered and fizzled the moment Halston raised his hand and bared his teeth. He sucked the power right out of Bund's shield with one flick of his wrist. He let Bund's shield merge with his own and grinned evilly at the sensation of true power.

"You see, Bund, I've wasted so much time trying to find a way to end your pitiful life in way worthy of a pure angel," Halston's grin widened. "When all of this time all I had to do was become the enemy and rip your head off."

Bund held his hands up. He stepped back, prepared to make a run for the exit. He knew that he was no match for Halston. He knew that he had unleashed death itself. It took a lot to make an angel choose the dark side. Bund started to sweat. Halston chuckled at seeing this.

"Yes," he hissed. "Fear. You should be afraid of me." He shot the infinity gun and watched the bullet escape the front end of the gun. Something had changed.

Something Halston had only anticipated. His brows widened with approval as the bullet took another form. It reached out two skinny black hands and shoved its body out of the gun. Like a tiny black fairy, the bullet flew before Halston's face.

Halston grinned. His creation had true life now. Its small face was that of a monster from one's dreams. Tiny red eyes, two holes for nostrils in the center of its ashen face, and sharp teeth.

Halston whispered to it. "Kill them all."

This new creation snickered. "Yes! Yes!" It closed its eyes, grinned, and shot off at the speed of… a bullet.

Halston watched it leave the room and go after all of Bund's minions. He didn't need to audibly specify whom he wanted killed, because the bullet was in tune to Halston's very thoughts. It knew what Halston meant, and Halston knew that it was his most reliable weapon.

It started with Trinity, shouting through his brain. Tristan fell free, but didn't move. He didn't know what to think of Halston.

Halston saw the look of doubt on Tristan's face. He didn't blame him. To his surprise, Tristan stepped to him and stood ready.

"What have you gotten yourself into this time?" Tristan asked.

Halston gave him a look. He smiled. He was pleased. "My friend. My only true friend," Halston said to Tristan. Then, he shot off and tackled Bund with the power of Hell.

And Hell fought back, but it was not enough. Bund tried. He did. But he was not strong enough to compete with Halston.

Halston's black shield sparked, and he grabbed the demon by his neck, crushed it in his fist, and watched Bund's face morph into that of a Shadow's. He lost his physical body. It burned off like clay until there was nothing but the blackness underneath.

Bund was nothing more than a tightly knit cloud of smoke, voiceless, and helpless. Tristan held out a hand. He opened a vial, and Halston sent Bund's soul into it. He stoppered the vial and handed it to Tristan.

With a snap of his fingers, he stopped the flames that tore away at Jax and Evina. They had both passed out from the pain, and looked to be disfigured piles of mush.

Halston looked down at them in disgust. He wasn't sure if he wanted to keep them.

"They did everything they could to protect Koa," Tristan offered, as if he could tell what Halston was thinking.

Halston's shoulders slumped. He nodded. "Good. I can use them. Let them lie there and regenerate."

Tristan nodded and watched as Halston's gaze went to Koa.

"I did what I could to keep the agents off of her, but it was a challenge to do two things at once. I killed as many vampires as I could. The mission was thwarted when the demon arrived."

Halston nodded. He understood the difficulty of their mission, even he had gone against what he had planned to do.

He watched Koa. She was no longer held in the grips of Bund's binding spell. He felt a peace within him. She would awaken, and she would hug him, and thank him for saving her life. This Halston was certain of.

A smile came to his face. He was free. He could do whatever he wanted. Koa could be his and they could hide from God's gaze for an eternity.

Halston loosened her feet and pulled her to the ground. He spoke softly, "Koa," he called.

Her eyes opened, she took one look at him, and frowned.

Halston cried out.

Koa took the dagger out of her belly and stabbed Halston in the chest with it. "Die, you demon! Die! You have no control over me!" She cried out as the dagger was filled with all of the power that fought to be released.

Halston tried to speak. His mouth hung open and his face twisted in pain. Why did she stab him? Why did it hurt so much? Halston feared for his life then. He realized that Koa did not recognize him.

She grinned cruelly as her power wedged the dagger deeper, sucking the life from him. Her eyes were glazed over. She wasn't even fully awake yet. She was still waking from Bund's torment of her soul.

Halston had no choice. He grew weaker with each passing second. He grabbed her face in her hands and felt the tears trail down his cheeks. With a cry, he twisted her neck, and pushed her body far across the room.

He looked back once, certain that she would awaken, and vanished before she regained consciousness and went after him again.

CHAPTER 49

Koa woke up to the sound of Jax's voice. She sat up quickly. She was shaking. She was so cold and drained.

He held her steady and pulled her into a hug. "Darling, you're all right."

Koa swallowed. Her throat was dry, and her voice came out weakly.

She looked up at Jax with hope in her eyes. "Did I kill him, Jax? Did I kill Bund? Are we safe?"

The look on Jax's face perplexed Koa. He opened his mouth and started to speak, but no words came out.

Koa sat up on her elbows. She put a shaking hand on his, as if she could calm him.

"What is it? I was certain that I killed him," Koa said. "Was it a dream?"

Jax gave her a look that sent chills into her already tortured soul. The look in his dark blue-eyed gaze worried her.

"What is it?"

Evina stepped up. She was naked. So was Jax. Koa couldn't remember what had happened.

"No, Koa. You didn't kill Bund. Halston transformed into a demon to save you. He killed Bund. And then you nearly killed him."

Koa's hand shot to her mouth. Tears welled. She shook her head as she looked from Evina to Jax. "I don't understand!"

They went silent. Koa shot to her feet. The pain nearly made her fall back down, but she was determined. Nothing would stop her.

Evina wiped tears from her eyes. "I've never seen someone do what you did, Koa." She shook her head as she looked Koa up and down. "What are you?"

"Where did he go?" Koa asked in between sobs. Her heart broke more and more with each moment that she was without Halston. She had to find him. "Where is Halston?" She wailed.

Jax and Evina shook their heads.

"He left," Jax answered. "You did something that frightened him into fleeing. Tristan left as well."

"I'll find him!"

"Wait!" Jax called.

Koa ignored him. Koa flew from the room. She screamed in anguish and sorrow as she flew through the labyrinth. How could she do that to Halston?

She vowed to find him. She had to. Halston gave up Heaven for her, and she would not rest until she was in his arms again.

Viktor stood at the edge of the bridge and watched as Koa flew from the castle. He looked up and followed her with his silver eyes. Such a rage filled his entire body that it was difficult to keep his composure and remain grounded. He wanted to go after her himself and end the rebellion of the children his disobedient brothers and sisters created.

So much rested on his shoulders alone. Halston had betrayed him, just as he had expected. All because of that disgusting half-blood. Viktor knew that he only had himself to blame. He knew he shouldn't have trusted Halston to follow through.

Halston could never make the hard choices. He was the weaker angel. Too soft and easily manipulated.

Not like Viktor.

No promises of love, power, or riches could persuade him to deny God's will.

Viktor was never tricked into leaving Heaven to follow the traitor Satan to the human world. No. Viktor was strict in his resolve, and he would do what was necessary to bring the Earth from the threat of Hell.

Viktor squeezed his eyes shut and breathed in the cool night air. He folded his wings and calmed himself. He could not go after Koa.

Not yet.

"What are you waiting for, Master?" Nicolai asked. He pointed to Koa's flying body. "She's getting away!"

Viktor turned to walk back to the black car.

"Patience," he said calmly.

Nicolai ran his hands through his white hair in frustration. "At least let me take a shot at her."

Viktor shot a glare at Nicolai that made him stumble backwards. A wind swept through and Viktor glanced at the full moon.

"Listen to me carefully," Viktor said in his monotone voice that never changed. His silver eyes were unsettling, and Nicolai had been his assistant for hundreds of years, and still wasn't used to them. "I want you to tell Micka to come to headquarters."

"May I ask why," Nicolai asked.

Viktor paused. He waited for the driver to open his door, and got inside. He held a hand for the driver to hold the door open for a moment longer and looked out at Nicolai. "Tell her this. She is now in charge of Halston's division. A promotion they call it. I want to brief her on her next mission."

Nicolai nodded. "Done." He slipped his hands into his jacket pocket. "Mind sharing her mission, Master? You know I won't tell anyone."

Viktor looked past Nicolai at the castle. "Follow the half-blood, Koa Ryeo-won to the demon, Halston, and kill them both."

A grin came to Nicolai's face. "Good plan, Master. I like it."

Viktor nodded and gave Nicolai a pointed look, one that shone his silver gaze over the pale man's face. "We will wipe all nephilim from the Earth. And you," he looked away, balling up his fists. "*You*, my friend, can kill that abomination. Find and kill Koa's mother."

Nicolai's eyes glowed for a moment. "With pleasure."

Academia of the Beast

K. N. Lee

Chapter 1

Ava lay there with her eyes wide open. Screams. Yells of terror. Her ears ached with the sounds of chaos, and she knew she should run or hide. Instead, she was frozen, in bed waiting for whatever was out there to come and get her.

She whimpered. Her eyes stared up at the thin white sheet that she had pulled up over her head.

Get up!

Get up, Ava!

Ava shook her head. "No," she whispered. "I'm afraid."

The voice inside her head was silent. She wondered if it was gone. Maybe it finally gave up on her.

Get the hell up, Ava!

Ava jumped at the sudden yelling inside her head. She sucked in a breath, pulled the covers down and sighed.

"Oh, all right," Ava grumbled. "No need to shout."

Slowly, she sat up in the small hospital cot. She listened. The screams grew louder, and her fear rose at an alarming rate. She was too afraid to move any further, but her hands started to shake.

She needed to calm down.

No you don't! Harness that fear, Ava. I think you're going to need it!

Ava hoped she didn't. She didn't like what happened when she was too afraid, angry, sad…too much emotion was not good for Ava.

She held her breath. It was as though her muscles were frozen, her chest rose and fell with short, anxious, breaths.

She heard loud footsteps running down the hallway. She shirked to the corner of the bed and pressed her back against the cold stone wall. She was perplexed by the darkness all around her in the empty infirmary. The usual medical equipment lights were out, so Ava figured that the power was down.

Being alone was something she hadn't experienced since she'd been sent to that boarding school months earlier. She never thought she'd feel this way, but now she wished she had someone there with her.

I'm here with you, the voice whispered.

"You don't count," Ava whispered back.

The double doors burst open. Ava wished that she could make herself really small and hide.

She was only slightly relieved when she saw the schools nurses, along with Mr. Grant, noisily entered the room. With them came a flood of light from Nurse Catherine's large flashlight. Within their arms they carried a hysterically screaming girl.

Ava felt ill. The girl's blood dripped steadily along the freshly washed floor. Ava covered her mouth and nose. The smell made her stomach twist painfully.

Don't tell me blood scares you too!

Ava frowned. "*Shh.*"

Pathetic.

The nurses immediately started working on the girl's wounds, simultaneously yelling at each other and trying to figure out what happened to her.

Ava gasped when she realized that the girl was one of her only close friends, Marisol. She suddenly felt courage enough to leave the safety of the bed and venture closer to the busy, huddled group.

"Marisol! Marisol, try to calm down honey, tell us what happened!" Nurse Catherine was trying her hardest to get Marisol to use legible words. Marisol's wretched screams drowned out everything they said.

"GET ME OUT OF HERE!"

Those sudden, coherent, words sent a shiver up Ava's entire body. She was sure that everyone else felt the same.

Then, Marisol wept. She chocked on her sobs. "Please, please. It's still out there, I just know it. *Please,*" she pleaded, her voice was like that of a small child's.

There was the briefest moment of silence as they processed what she had just said.

"What's still out there?" Mr. Grant asked the question they were all wondering.

Ava was too afraid to even guess.

You know what's here. They found you.

Ava's face twisted with worry. She felt like she might vomit. She shook her head, willing it to not be true. *Please, no,* she thought. *Please, God.*

Oh stop sniveling, Ava. I thought I taught you better.

Ava felt tears sting her eyes. She ignored the voice. All she could think of was what had finally found her. No one was safe.

"The thing that attacked us! Where's Logan? Where's my boyfriend?" Marisol tried to sit up. She cried out as the pain pulled her back down. She was soaked in blood and tears. She was weakened as the adrenaline from the attack wore off.

Ava betrayed her stealthy approach when she was finally close enough to see the mangled mess of Marisol's right arm. Her hand flew to her mouth, stifling her own scream.

Crap, the voice said. *That thing tried to make a meal of her.*

Overcome with shock, Ava absently backed into the medical cart. Stainless steel utensils crashed to the linoleum floor. Everyone turned to her.

"Get her out of here!" Mr. Grant, her favorite teacher, pointed towards the doors, then returned his attention to Marisol.

Ava couldn't stop staring at Marisol's chewed arm. The blood was everywhere. Her face was pale, flushed from the trauma. Ava had always been squeamish around blood. Their eyes met as Marisol weakly rolled her head to the other side. They were nearly lifeless, as the usual vitality of her beautiful blues faded. With a twitch, Marisol tried to reach out to her.

"Ava," she mouthed.

Ava gulped.

"Run."

Ava's face blanched. She turned to her sister. Ella's body floated beside her, wearing the same dress she had died in. Pale as a ghost, with hollow eyes, she looked back at Ava.

She's right, Ella said. *You better run.*

Academia of the Beast

Coming Winter 2014

Biography

Amateur artist, traveling enthusiast, and wannabe rock star, K.N. Lee is an American author who resides in North Carolina. She enjoys writing fantasy, horror, and twisted short stories. She also writes poetry and does a great deal of promoting other authors on her websites. When she is not cooking traditional Asian meals for her friends, she travels the world and practices foreign languages.

Her works include, The Chronicles of Koa: Netherworld, Dark Prophet, Wicked Webs, Empty Your Heart, and the paranormal collection of short stories, Thicker Than Blood. She lives with her two dog, Raven.

Note from the author:

"I hope you enjoyed this novel. If so, I'd appreciate a quick review on the product page of Amazon and Barnes & Noble." –K.N. Lee

www.Kn-Lee.com

www.WriteLikeAWizard.com

www.Facebook.com/knycolelee

27742831R00148

Made in the USA
Charleston, SC
20 March 2014